Dead In Your Shoes

KARA ROTH

Published by Inicio Press
https://www.iniciopress.com/

Dead in Your Shoes

ISBN: 978-1-998315-08-6
978-1-998315-07-9

For my beautiful mother and sister. Mary Ann and Heather, try not to have too much fun until I get there.

Dead In Your Shoes

CHAPTER 1

Desperate For Rain

Defense attorney Mervin Boutté sat on the uncomfortable wooden bench at the end of the second floor of the New Orleans Municipal Courthouse. The ball of his white buck shoe was pressed so firmly against the marble floor that his whole leg vibrated with nervous energy. Despite the improvements to the old courthouse, the current air conditioning system in no way competed with the humidity that hung in the air. Sweat dripped down poor Mervin's back, and his glasses began to fog. He removed the thick-framed spectacles and gently wiped his tie on the lenses to remove the humidity-induced condensation. Mervin turned his attention to the large window to his right and viewed the passing cars on Perdido Street, which glinted shards of sunlight right back at him. He took a haggard breath and cast his glance across the hallway to an elderly woman knitting black and gold yarn on the opposite bench. He needed a distraction.

"Weatherman said it might rain today," Mervin said loudly enough in the hope that the woman would pick up on the fact he was trying to make conversation.

Knitting needles still in hand, the older woman looked out the window, cleared her throat, and flatly stated, "Naw, it ain't gonna rain today."

A bit relieved that she had responded and curious about her certainty, Mervin shrugged. "Don't know. That's just what they said on Channel 4."

The woman kept at her needlework without looking up. "Channel 4 wrong. It ain't gonna rain today. The trees ain't singing for their supper yet."

Mervin paused for a moment, mildly concerned that he had just initiated a conversation with a crazy person. Knitting yarn in July isn't exactly a ringing endorsement of sanity. He was too intrigued not to ask, though. "The trees aren't singing for their supper?"

The woman laid her needles in her lap and looked again out the window. "Weatherman is always wrong because he don't listen to the trees." Mervin followed her eyes through the window to the sparse lining of trees that wrapped around the courthouse parking lot.

"What do the trees say?" Mervin was oddly interested in what the response might be.

"Oh, they don't *say* nothin'. They sing."

"My apologies. What do they sing, Ms…?"

"Doris. My name is Doris, with a D." Old Doris sympathetically decided to allow the quiet tranquility of her only source of air-conditioning to be disturbed to converse with the nervous man. She sighed, still staring out the window. "Well, when it get real good and hot like this, the trees, they start gettin' antsy." Mervin was strangely captivated. "Ya see, they get all antsy from being so hot and real thirsty. They know they gotta sing. So, they call on their friend, the wind."

"The wind?" Mervin asked.

"Yes, the wind. Now hush, don't interrupt me." Mervin put up an apologetic hand and placed it back on his vibrating knee.

"The wind knows how to help out his good ole friends, his friends being the trees, of course." Mervin nodded as he shifted his weight. "So, the wind starts blowin' away. Blowin' so hard it makes his friends, the trees, start swayin' back and forth. Wind is just a ticklin' their bark, rockin' their limbs, rustlin' through their leaves. That rustlin' makes the prettiest sound you dun' eva heard." Doris leaned her head back against the cool courthouse wall and gave a contented smile. "Mmmm, so pretty. That's how trees sing."

"But why do the trees need to sing, Ms. Doris?" Merv asked, genuinely interested at this point.

"The trees are singing to the sky. They thirsty and awful desperate, desperate for water. They singing for rain. They singing for their supper."

Merv's mouth slightly gaped open. He looked back out the window and noticed the trees were stagnant. Not a single leaf stirred. The only movement among them was a stray, panting dog lounging in their shade.

"Now you, on the other hand"—Doris pointed a knitting needle at Merv and gave a raspy laugh through the teeth she had left—"you look like you gonna be eatin' good tonight."

He rubbed a hand over his belly with a smile. "And why do you say that, Ms. Doris?"

"The way you rustlin' round over there means you 'bout to sing one hell of a song," she cackled.

Merv gave an acknowledging chuckle. "Let's just say I hope to go to bed on a full stomach tonight."

Doris smiled understandingly as she pointed the needle at him again. "Well, the other thing you should know about trees is—"

Just as Merv's new friend began to speak, the corner of his eye spotted District Attorney Marissa Morgan stepping casually from the interior staircase onto the second floor of the courthouse. As she did, Marissa Morgan turned to her right to enter the large hallway that led to a conference room she had commandeered as an unofficial office.

"Excuse me, Ms. Doris. It has been a pleasure." Merv jumped up, adjusting his waistband before heading straight down the hallway. She curiously watched him hustle, pretty well for a man his size, directly toward the district attorney.

Old Doris pursed her lips, almost sad the nervous man didn't get to hear the last part. She said it aloud anyway. "The other thing you should know 'bout trees is, if the wind blows 'em too hard…they snap."

After stepping onto the second floor, Marissa Morgan unintentionally and unfortunately caught eyes with the oncoming Mervin Boutté. Without hesitation, she promptly turned in the opposite direction and confidently marched toward the other end of the hallway. Despite being thirty years her senior and a good hundred pounds heavier, Merv managed to catch up to her surprisingly quickly.

"Marissa," Merv panted.

"I do believe you mean District Attorney Morgan," Marissa Morgan crisply stated without looking at him, keeping her eyes straight ahead. Her dark, shiny hair remained motionless despite the impressive speed of her high-heeled steps.

"I need a minute," he pleaded between huffs.

"I'm not doing this with you, Mervin. It's an open-and-shut murder one. The family wants the death penalty. And unfortunately for your client, it's my duty to pursue that."

"Oh, come on, Mari—" Merv quickly corrected himself. "District Attorney Morgan. It was a crime of passion, at best. Any jury will be able to see that."

"Ha. You call that a crime of passion?" The district attorney refused to meet his glance and continued at her pace, but Merv could practically feel her sharp eyes rolling in annoyance.

"What if I told you my client has information about a suspicious death?" Poor Merv and the overworked inner-thigh threads of his seersucker suit were trying their very best to keep up with her.

"Oh please, some jailhouse rumor that your client probably conjured up is not going to take the death penalty off the table. And by the way," Marissa Morgan scowled, "the only thing worse than your desperation is your perspiration." She waved her hand as if swatting a mosquito. "Goodbye, Mervin."

The dismissive wave caused Mervin Boutté to stop momentarily, giving the district attorney two good strides in front of him. After a quick straightening of his light blue tie, Merv's mind flashed back to old Doris, and he bolstered his courage. *Time to sing for my supper*. "What if the suspicious death is in regards to a one Mrs. Juniper Wells?"

At this, the district attorney abruptly stopped dead in her tracks. Had she heard him right? She had, indeed. After a long, silent pause, she smoothly crossed her arms and slowly began to tap the toe of her black high heel on the marble floor. Without turning back, Marissa Morgan calmly stated, "I'm listening."

CHAPTER 2

Desperate Not To Be Alone

Nine Years Earlier

"You're coming," Kay called out over the sleek white kitchen bar as she poured two glasses of her cousin's favorite wine.

"Like hell I am," Celeste practically sang back. Celeste, Kay's cousin, was lounging under her cashmere throw and casually filing her nails on the long black leather couch in the living area. Kay and Celeste were in their upscale French Quarter condo in the heart of New Orleans. It was a pretty swanky place for a couple of gals in their late twenties without the faintest idea of the real world.

Kay breezed into the room with bare feet in a black and white chevron print dress and handed a glass of wine to her cousin. Despite their shared contempt for one another, they instinctively clinked their glasses together and, in unison, absentmindedly muttered, "Cheers," before taking a sip.

Kay swallowed hard and pulled her head back with a sour face. "Ugh, I don't know how you drink this."

"That's because you're uncouth, darling," Celeste apathetically stated as she took another sip and admired her nailwork.

Unoffended, Kay rolled her eyes and slid onto the matching black leather chair across from Celeste. Kay and Celeste were cousins by blood, and by blood only, in both of their minds. Kay's father and Celeste's mother were brother and sister, similarly, by blood only.

"Why are you doing your nails? You never do your own nails," Kay asked as she took another sip, resulting in another sour face.

"My girl is out of town this week, and I don't trust anyone

else with cuticle scissors." The mere thought made Celeste cringe.

Kay tossed her hair over her shoulder and flopped a hand over her heart. "Heaven forbid," she gasped in an exaggerated southern drawl.

Celeste was a year older than Kay. Celeste's parents bought the lavish three-bedroom condo for their daughter to live in her freshman year at the University of New Orleans. Unfortunately, due to their daughter's wickedly snobbish personality, she was unable to find anyone to actually live in it with her. The next year, when Kay was due to start her freshman year at UNO, her father asked her to move into the condo with her cousin. "Do your old dad a favor, Kay. Aunt Colleen doesn't want her living alone. We're all here in Baton Rouge, and we worry about you girls being in New Orleans. I know how Celeste can be, but I think it would be for the best." Of course, like any good southern girl would, Kay listened to Daddy despite the love-hate relationship with her frigid cousin.

Almost a decade later, they were still loving and hating each other in that same condo. It hadn't been so terrible after all. Their social paths didn't particularly cross that much in college, and now, Kay traveled quite a lot for work, so they rarely saw much of each other.

"And what is this thing you want me to go to again?" Celeste sighed, now bored with her nails; she allowed her cousin a limited amount of attention.

"So, remember how I got stuck on that flight back from Denver on Tuesday?" Celeste tilted her head and looked vacantly at her cousin, signaling she had no clue what Kay was talking about, nor did she care.

Kay tried to stay agreeable out of necessity. "Well, I was flying back from Denver on Tuesday for work. After we boarded the plane, the pilot came on and said there was some sort of mechanical issue and we would be delayed for takeoff. We ended up sitting on the plane for an hour before we even got off the ground." Celeste responded to her cousin's explanation with an impatient "get on with it" wrist roll gesture.

"Anyway, I was sitting next to this guy. Probably early thirties, very handsome, nice, funny. I like funny."

"That is because you admire qualities in others that you

do not possess."

"I am funny."

"You saying that you're funny might be the funniest thing I've ever heard." Celeste gave her jab an amused smirk. "Now get to the point, cow."

"He's from here. His name is Wes Allen. We talked the entire flight, and I, well, really enjoyed his company. Apparently, the feeling must have been mutual because he invited me to some anniversary party he's having tonight. And..." she took a deep breath. "I would really rather not go alone. So, would you please come with me?" Kay gritted the last sentence through her teeth. It pained her to ask her cousin for this favor, but she was desperate. None of her other friends were available, and she was unfortunately out of options.

"Are you done speaking?" Celeste looked Kay right in the eyes.

"Yes."

"Good."

"So, are you coming?"

Celeste intentionally dragged out a long exhale and leaned her head back onto the arm of the couch. She stared up at the black and gold embossed chandelier that hung above them. What Celeste lacked in all-around general likability, she more than made up for in the looks department. Slim, but with curves in all the right places, 5 foot 7 (without heels), tan skin, an angelic face framed with a perfect blonde bob, and big blue eyes.

Her beautiful cousin stared at the chandelier for so long that a confused Kay eventually craned her neck to look up to see if she was missing something. She finally repeated, "So, are you coming?" To which Celeste quickly replied, "Nope," as she sat up and reached for a magazine from the coffee table.

"Fine," Kay huffed as she stood to leave the room.

"Where is this party anyway? Probably at some trash bar surrounded by junkyard dogs and barbwire fences."

Kay, sensing the slightest possibility of an ounce of sympathy from her cousin, picked up for her phone from the coffee table. "I don't know. He sent me the address. It's at his friend's house. Matthew Wells."

Celeste's perfect eyebrows raised slightly, and she leaned forward. "Did you say, *Matthew Wells*?"

"Yes, I think that's it. Why? Do you know him?"

"Bless it. You really are bottom barrel. Matthew Wells? The Wells family is one of the wealthiest families in New Orleans. Do you not read the paper?" Celeste began flipping through the very magazine that she had retrieved from the coffee table. She scraped her newly filed talons across the pages, finally stopping and holding the magazine up. Kay squinted at the glossy page. It was a man holding a puppy at the opening of a local animal shelter.

"Celeste, that's not the paper. That's a social magazine."

"It's on paper, isn't it?" Celeste snidely volleyed back.

If Kay knew one thing about her dear cousin, it was that she thoroughly enjoyed being around people just as pretentious as she was. Her aunt had admittedly done very well for herself when she married Celeste's father. He was the senior partner of a very prestigious law firm that had multiple practices all over the Gulf Coast. Money was definitely not a problem for Celeste, and she loved being around people who shared that same lack of a problem.

Celeste twirled a strand of her blonde hair around her finger as this new information filtered through her brain. Finally relenting, she sighed, "Fine. I suddenly feel charitable. I will accompany you."

One side of Kay's mouth curled upwards. "Well, thank you. I really app—"

"But only if"—Celeste threw up a cautionary palm—"you change that atrocious outfit."

"What are you talking about?" Kay stood and put her hands on her hips in a flirty pose to lighten the mood. She threw on the extra southern drawl again, "I think it's rather becoming."

Unimpressed, Celeste rose from the couch and tossed the cashmere throw down while turning to go to her bedroom. "Well, I am *becoming* rather nauseated at the sight of it," she snubbed over her shoulder. She glanced back at Kay before making her way down the hallway. "Change it. You look like a God damn MC Escher painting."

Kay knew better than to tell her cousin how much she really liked the man from the plane. They had talked for hours, peppering their conversation with the occasional too-loud bout of laughter. Their chatting didn't feel forced like most mid-air small talk. It just felt natural and good. By the end of the flight, they were both quite sure the surrounding passengers were annoyed with their never-ending banter, but for some reason, with this guy, Kay had thrown airplane etiquette to the wind.

"The Uber is going to be here in five minutes. You ready?" An hour later, Kay called down the hallway from the entrance of her bedroom to Celeste's closed bedroom door. She walked toward the kitchen in nude heels, which echoed from the high ceilings with each step. She stopped short as she walked past the large gold mirror hanging in the hallway, giving herself a final once-over.

Kay was, in fact, a pretty little thing. Petite, 5 foot 7 (in 4-inch heels), long dark auburn hair with fair skin, full lips, and big blue eyes (probably the only thing she had in common with her cousin). She pressed both hands down the front of her fitted blush-colored dress, a bit nervous but quite impressed with the reflection. *Not bad. Not bad at all.*

"Don't rush me, troll," Celeste called back. She closed the door to her bedroom behind her so quickly that it caused a gust of air to momentarily puff her dress as if she were a modern-day Marilyn Monroe. Celeste always closed the door to her bedroom, always. Kay turned to her cousin and took her in.

"What?" Celeste defensively asked as she noticed Kay's eyes locked on her. She stood with her head cocked in a sheer white razorback dress that allowed her blonde hair to graze her collarbone and slim shoulders.

"Nothing. You just look…you look very nice."

"Ugh. Jealous much," she scoffed as she flipped her hand and strode past Kay. "I guess that dress is *somewhat* of an improvement, though."

Taken aback that she had just received a compliment, albeit a backhanded one, Kay turned again toward the mirror and gave herself a flattered nod of approval.

"I'm waiting!" Celeste's shriek summoned from the front door.

CHAPTER 3

Desperate To See You Again

Wes Allen stood next to his best friend, Matthew Wells. They were in the center hall of Matthew's rather large home on Esplanade Avenue, located right off the Mississippi River on the cusp of the French Quarter. An eclectic group of seventy-five or so well-dressed guests sipped various cocktails, making small talk under the cathedral-like ceilings lined with elaborate crown molding. Waiters with white button-down shirts and skinny black ties swirled across the original brick flooring of the fifty-foot-deep hall, bearing silver trays of appetizers and champagne.

"Not a bad turnout." Matthew shrugged his big shoulders and took a swig of his bourbon as he eyed the room.

"Yeah, I think so. Appreciate the hospitality, man," Wes thanked as he snapped out of whatever he was thinking about and scanned the center hall.

"What's up with you? You've been looking around like you're trying to cross the border with blow smuggled up your ass." Matthew tossed that thought around for a moment before leaning closer to his friend. "Wouldn't happen to have any, would you?" Unfortunately, his usual party favor provider had been a little low on inventory lately.

Wes chuckled. "Nah, man. I'm just keeping an eye out for that girl I invited."

"What girl?" Matthew furrowed his brow.

"The girl I met on the plane." Wes continued his scan of the hall.

"Oh right, the flight chick. She hot?"

Wes hesitated and then slowly nodded with an ever so slight, amused expression. "She's alright."

Matthew put one of his big bear-claw hands on his friend's left shoulder and gave him a good shake. "Look at that face. My boy is all smitten and shit." Matthew whooped and smacked Wes on the back a little too hard. "Alright then, I'll have to check her out." He surveyed the room with disappointment. "Especially because the talent in here tonight definitely ain't worth going to the show for."

Matthew was a big guy, hence the big bear-claw hands. Large frame, tall, sandy hair, brown eyes, and chiseled features. Being in his early thirties, he was very good-looking, but years of partying gave him a Ken-doll-that-was-accidentally-left-outside-for-a-couple-of-days-type look. That being said, luring in "talent" had never been an issue for Matthew Wells.

"That's because, with all the girls in here, the show would just be a rerun for you." Wes patted the back of his hand on Matthew's chest and took a sip of his beer. "She's bringing her cousin, though. Maybe she'll be decent."

"Who is?" Matthew looked confused after being distracted by a passing possible rerun.

Wes sighed as he swirled his beer and side-eyed his friend. "Flight chick. The girl. Kay."

"Oh no." Matthew shook his head hard. Now, it was Wes's turn to be confused.

"What?"

"When girls bring their *cousin* to a party, it's always some desperate heifer begging for a night out because she's usually stuck at home googling people from high school or doing feng shui or some dumb shit like that."

"What are you talking about?" Wes laughed.

"I don't know. I'm pretty sure that's what they do." Matthew kicked back his whiskey. "Doesn't matter because I'm not heifer-sitting for you tonight, bro." He shook his head again and finished off his drink. "And I'll tell you another thing—" He pointed a finger at his friend from the same hand that was holding his now empty glass.

Wes put a halting palm up to the forewarning finger. "Well, she just walked in, so how about you hang onto that whiskey wisdom for a bit."

Matthew turned toward the large, arched glass double front

doors to see Kay and Celeste casually walking through the entrance. He put his bear claw on Wes's shoulder once again. "Well, well, well, you do not disappoint my friend." He admired the new party guests approvingly. "Which one's flight chick?"

Wes proudly smirked and raised his beer. "The blonde's all yours."

The chandelier lights glistened on Celeste's dewy skin as she spoke through a fake smile like a ventriloquist. "Do you see him?" Reciprocating her cousin's communication tactic, Kay replied, "I don't think so."

Celeste quietly growled through her perfect teeth, "Going to kill you. Head to the bar." They slyly weaved with the jazz music through various small groups of laughing and chatting party guests in search of social sanctuary.

Just as they were steps away from the tall, white linen-covered table standing in front of a ceiling-high wine rack, Wes walked toward them with a sweet smile. "Kay, you made it. I was beginning to think you were stuck on another tarmac." *Stupid. That was stupid.* He kicked himself but kept smiling.

Relieved at the sight of him and thankful that he was just as handsome as she remembered, Kay couldn't help but mirror Wes's sweet smile right back at him. He was, in fact, just how she remembered: average height with a muscular build, hazel eyes with bright flecks of green, brushed-back wavy brown hair, and a nice smile with dimples to boot.

"Well, thank you so much for the invitation, Mr. Allen," Kay jested. Her schoolgirl nerves suddenly got the better of her so she deflected his attention. "Wes, this is my cousin Celeste." She cast an introductory hand toward her cousin.

"Nice to meet you, Celeste. Thanks so much for coming." His friendly welcome was met with an icy smile and nod.

"You'll have to excuse my friend's manners. Please don't hold it against him. I'm sure he was simply awestruck to be in the presence of such beauty." Long gone was frat boy Matthew. He had been transformed into dashing southern gentleman Matthew. He confidently stepped forward, balancing a silver tray with four filled champagne glasses and flashing a Rhett Butler grin.

Kay was slightly amused by this juvenile entrance, while Celeste's expression suddenly went from cold to coy.

"Sorry, man. Kay, Celeste, this is my good friend Matthew. He let me use this old shack of his for the party tonight."

"You have such a lovely home, Matthew. Thank you for having us," Kay greeted politely.

"Hmmm." Celeste intentionally and noticeably examined the walls of the center hall as she grazed a glass of champagne from the tray and raised it to her lips. Wes handed a glass to Kay and took one for himself as they exchanged entertained yet apologetic glances for their counterparts. Matthew plucked the remaining glass and handed the tray to a passing waiter.

"Well, don't you sound like a purring tiger? Do you like it?" Matthew tilted his champagne glass toward the wall Celeste was still viewing.

"I think *like* would be a bit of an overstatement." She smoothly slid her eyes back to Matthew with an alluring smirk.

Please don't be a bitch. Please don't be a bitch, Kay pleaded inside her head. Thankfully, however, Matthew seemed intrigued. The pair locked eyes as he responded, "And why do you say that, my dear feline?" Kay breathed a sigh of relief, realizing Matthew was more interested in Celeste's appearance than her ill-mannered commentary.

As if sensing Kay's understandable uncomfortableness, Wes put a calming hand on the small of her back and whispered in her ear, "Well, this is a stunning sight."

"Like the viewing room at an asylum," she whispered back, still keeping her eyes on Celeste as if to will her to behave.

Wes gently rubbed his hand up and down Kay's back and quietly said, "I meant you."

"Oh," Kay mouthed as she blushed and shyly raised her hand to the side of her neck.

"I work in interior design. One of the main objectives is to ensure that the room is a reflection of the person. You didn't decorate this place yourself, did you?" Celeste asked almost rhetorically. To her credit, the room had clearly been decorated by someone with a somewhat dated aesthetic.

"Very perceptive, Celeste. I did not. Perhaps you could give me a fresh perspective. Are you taking on any new clients?"

"Not at the moment." Kay decided to let her cousin's lie slide for the sake of conversation. She knew Celeste hadn't worked in over a year. Why work when your trust fund checks have that many zeros? "Unfortunately, I have had to become very selective. You can't be too careful who you work with these days."

"Especially if they use cuticle scissors, right Celeste?" Kay couldn't help but chime in.

"Buuut, seeing as you are in such obvious need, I might be able to make an exception in your case, Mr. Wells." Kay's body tightened at Celeste's offer. Wes had only introduced his friend as Matthew, not Matthew Wells. Thankfully, the reference to his last name appeared to go unnoticed.

"I would consider it an honor if you could squeeze me in." Matthew let his suggestive response hang in the air with a devilish grin. At that very moment, his pants began to vibrate. "Excuse me." He pulled his cell phone from his pocket and glanced down to see that it was an incoming call. JUNIPER WELLS lit up the screen. Matthew quickly declined the call and returned the phone to his pocket.

"Well, it is a big place." Wes looked up at the sky-high vaulted ceiling. "Maybe you should give her a tour, Matthew. So she can see what she's in for." Wes took a sip of his champagne, trying to encourage his friend to allow himself some alone time with Kay.

"I think that's—" A more than agreeable Matthew attempted to respond as his pants began to vibrate again.

"Do you need to get that?" Celeste offered cordially, trying to hide her displeasure at the second interruption.

Matthew glanced down at his phone. JUNIPER WELLS lit up the screen again. "I apologize. Yes, I better take this. I won't be long, though." He turned his sights directly on Celeste. "I'll be right back. Don't you move."

"No promises." She gave him a flirtatious pout of the lips, followed by a quick wink. "We tigers like to prowl."

Yuck. You trite little trollop. Kay cringed at her cousin's overt display. But as Kay cringed, Matthew appeared to melt.

Almost breathless, he turned to Wes and practically pronounced to the group, shaking that same drink finger at Celeste, "Like her. I like this one. Don't let her out of your sight." Wishing he had x-ray vision, Matthew scanned Celeste from heels to hair one more time before turning away and heading across the room, phone in hand.

As if on cue, a man approached Wes. "Hey, I've been looking all over for you." He was very nice looking with a tall, slim build and glasses that framed sloped green eyes.

"Well, I've been right here entertaining these lovely ladies," Wes responded in a way that he hoped the man would understand as he leaned his head toward Kay and Celeste. Taking one look at Wes's companions, Danny did understand.

"Ah, that makes perfect sense, and, might I say, I can't blame you. Hello ladies. Allow me to introduce myself. I'm Daniel Boutté." He extended a considerate hand to Kay and shook hers before doing the same to Celeste.

"Kay, Celeste, this is my partner, Danny."

Kay immediately flushed. *Partner? Oh no, no, no. Anniversary party. Had she read this all wrong?* The corners of Celeste's mouth wickedly curled up as she read the coloring of Kay's face and thoughts.

"Really?" Celeste kept up the wicked expression, enjoying seeing her cousin squirm. "How long have you two been together?"

"Five long years," Danny replied proudly as he straightened his spectacles. "That's why we threw this little celebratory soiree together."

Kay felt as though she were shrinking. *He just used the word soiree.* Of course, Celeste decided to dig the knife in a little deeper. "Well, I think that is just wonderful. The two of you make a beautiful couple."

Champagne suddenly sprayed from Wes's lips, creating a mist that saturated Celeste's entire left arm. "Ahhh!" she yelped in disgust as Wes doubled over, grasping his knees and going into a rather decent coughing fit. Danny quickly handed Celeste his drink napkin, which she snatched and began dabbing her arm as she scoffed, "Ugh! Never in my entire."

"He's sorry. You're sorry, right, Wes? Say you're sorry." Danny mumbled the last plea as Kay tried to suppress her amusement at the unfolding scene.

"Yes," he managed through more coughing. "I am so sorry, Celeste." Wes tried to regain his composure as a few more coughs huffed out.

"You better be glad this is good champagne," she snarled as she wiped the remaining champagne shower from her arm.

"You just caught me off guard. We have an architecture firm. Danny and I, we're not…I mean, we're just business partners."

Hallelujah! Kay mentally celebrated.

"Well, you could have fooled me," Celeste snapped, offended and truthfully, a bit disappointed.

Danny, seeing a double win by saving his friend from getting his eyes clawed out and having the opportunity to speak to the beautiful Celeste alone, jutted his elbow out and offered, "Celeste, might I escort you to the bar? We can freshen your drink and get you some more napkins."

Celeste cooled slightly. "Yes, please, before I am accosted again." Straightening her frame, she hooked her arm through Danny's and flicked her blonde hair at Wes. She tried to appear calm as she allowed Danny to walk her to the bar. The offer was one she didn't care to accept, but to still be standing in the same spot when Matthew returned was not in her best interests. *Shouldn't appear too eager. I already showed too much of my hand with that stupid tiger quip.*

"So." A slightly embarrassed Wes turned to Kay and let out one last cough into his cuff. "Alone at last."

"And you're not gay," Kay excitedly said a bit too loudly, causing a neighboring group of party guests to cast a judgmental glance in her direction.

"No, definitely not gay," he chuckled. "I really am sorry about spitting champagne all over your cousin, though."

"Oh, don't worry about it." Kay dismissively waved. "Her body is so used to absorbing alcohol, her skin probably just soaked it right up." She peered over Wes's shoulder to see Danny and Celeste at the bar in what appeared to be polite conversation.

"Well, this isn't really what I had in mind for our first date." Wes watched her closely to gauge her response.

"Oh, we're on a date, are we?" She batted her eyelashes and donned a fake expression of surprise. "I thought we were both just co-handlers at the asylum."

"Funny." Wes played along. "I like funny."

"Yeah, it's funny you say that." Kay started to relax.

"Ok, so then let me take you to dinner this week to make up for it. I can't promise there won't be any crazies at the restaurant, though. This is NOLA, after all." He flashed his dimples, sending an immediate weakness to Kay's knees.

"I think that would be"—she looked down at her heels and back up at the dimples—"that would be lovely."

Thirty minutes passed. Unfortunately, the phone call with Juniper ended up taking much longer than expected. "Stupid bitch." An exasperated Matthew slammed the heavy door to his study and stalked down the hallway toward the party. He stopped at the entrance to the center hall and surveyed the room. Taking a moment to slow his breathing and calm himself, he thought, *Now where did she go?* His eyes jolted to a halt as he recognized two people standing closely at the bar in conversation. *Is that...? Is that Boutté trying to pet my tiger?*

Danny jogged from the bar back to Wes. "Hey man, I have to cut out."

"Already, why?"

"That's why I was looking for you. Fischer called and had some last-minute revisions to the plans. I promised him I'd have it squared away by morning."

"F-ing Fischer." Wes dragged his hand down his face in frustration. "Alright, you need help?"

Danny shook his head. "I got it. But I do need a favor from you, Kay."

"Oh, of course." She gave a small curtsy and looked at him with polite curiosity. "How may I be of service, Mr. Boutté?"

"Could you give Wes Celeste's number so he can send it

to me?"

Trying to mask her surprise, she smiled and replied, "Absolutely. No problem."

"Great. Thanks so much. Gotta run. Nice meeting you, Kay." Danny started toward the front doors, but after a few steps, he stopped and turned around as if having remembered something. With Kay's back to him, he caught Wes's attention and mouthed, "Is that the flight chick?" Wes tried not to be obvious and smirked with a small nod. Happy for his friend, Danny mouthed a complimentary, "Nice," with a thumbs up before heading back toward the exit.

"Well, Wes, it looks like we might have another inmate on our hands." An almost dazed Kay leaned her head on Wes's shoulder.

"Indeed, we might." He wrapped his arm around her and pulled her close as they muffled a laugh at their newfound private joke.

Celeste strategically arched her back as she downed her fourth glass of champagne at the bar. *Where the hell is that oaf? He better not have been snatched up by some skank.* Just as she was beginning to question her tactics, Matthew slid in next to her and propped an elbow on the bar. "Now, I thought I told you not to move." He flashed a naughty grin.

"Matthew, thank goodness you're here. I feel a bit lightheaded. Too many bubbles, I suppose. Is there anywhere I can get some fresh air?"

"Oh, of course. Come this way." Matthew looked genuinely concerned, mainly because he feared Celeste might vomit on his floor, but concerned, nonetheless. He took her hand and gestured toward the back of the center hall.

"I am so sorry. I guess I'm just not accustomed to having more than one glass." She gave herself a deserved mental round of applause as they headed for the back doors.

Matthew pushed open the tall glass double doors that led to the rear courtyard. The air was heavy, but a welcomed breeze from the Mississippi River eased the evening heat. Celeste stepped through the doors to see a large sparkling pool surrounded by cushion-covered wrought iron pool chairs.

The pool area was enclosed by an elaborate mix of palm trees, blooming azalea, and hibiscus plants dotted with twinkling landscape lighting. She stopped as she crossed the threshold, still holding Matthew's leading hand, and took a deep breath.

"Are you alright?" Matthew's eyes were wide with worry.

"I really do apologize. I guess I just needed air." She laid her hand on her abdomen and took another deep breath. "Yes, much better."

"Here, sit." Matthew gestured to the closest pool chair.

"Actually"—Celeste suddenly formulated a more tempting idea—"would you mind if I dipped my feet in the pool? It might help cool me off a bit."

"Please do." Matthew grinned with a bit of relief. He pulled off his blazer and laid it on the pool's edge. "Here you go, my dear feline."

Celeste slid her hand down her leg and seductively peeled off the straps of her wedged heels. "I can't sit on your jacket. I'll ruin it."

"I insist." He took her hand again and guided her to his jacket. Daintily sitting down, she slowly lowered her legs into the water.

"My goodness. Heavenly," she cooed, gently scissor-kicking her legs, creating small bubbles.

"Well, I'm glad you like it. You should come back sometime so you can take full advantage," Matthew suggested invitingly as he pulled one of the chairs close enough to give him a small glimpse down his beautiful guest's dress.

Take advantage? Why, me? Never, Celeste mused to herself.

"Have dinner with me next Saturday night," Matthew more so commanded than asked.

"Oh dear, I'm sorry, but my dance card is all full for that night. Your friend Daniel already invited me to spend Saturday evening with him."

Matthew inhaled sharply and clenched his jaw, attempting to hide his jealous surprise. "I see." Being turned down was new territory for him, especially for another guy, even more especially if that other guy was a wimp like Boutté. "Good for him. Another time then."

"I'll see if I can *squeeze* you in sometime, though." She

gave him another quick wink, and Matthew grinned back at her, admiring the suggestive reference to earlier. With that, Celeste suddenly recognized this was the best time to make her exit. "But I am feeling much better and really must be going. Do you have a towel?"

Still in the same spot, Kay and Wes were gazing at each other with sparkly eyes and shy smiles, conversing in low tones about anything and everything. *Those dimples are going to be the death of me*, Kay thought. Just as Wes was about to ask if they could go someplace quieter to talk, Celeste marched up to the couple.

"Excuse me, Carl." Celeste knew full well this was not Wes's name, but after the champagne debacle, she decided a little ego backhand was warranted. "Kay, we have to go."

"Why, what's wrong?" Kay looked around her cousin for signs of yet another inmate.

"I don't feel well. I need to go home."

"You're fine. What are you talking about?" She was sensing one of Celeste's temper tantrums.

"We are going," Celeste calmly yet sternly stated as she looked directly into her cousin's matching blue eyes.

Kay turned her head to Wes with an apologetic expression. "It's fine." He was disappointed but understood. "Let me get you ladies a cab."

A few minutes later, Wes held the cab door open as Celeste shifted to the far side of the backseat. Kay stood facing him with only the cab door separating them.

"I'll call you," he said with a smile.

"Looking forward to it." Kay rose on her toes, leaned over the cab door, and presented Wes with a kiss on the cheek. "Ohhhh," he playfully hooted and placed a hand over the welcomed lipstick mark.

"Doors were made for closing!" Celeste's voice shrilled from inside the cab. Kay rolled her eyes and lowered herself into the backseat as a very contented Wes closed the cab door.

As soon as the cab pulled away from the curb, Kay spun to her cousin and screeched, "What the hell was that, Celeste?"

"Oh my. Careful darling, your class is showing." Celeste looked up at the rearview mirror to see excited cabdriver eyes. The thought of having two beautiful women cat fight in the back of his cab would be quite an appreciated change from drunk tourists on the verge, and sometimes not just on the verge, of vomiting.

"I was saving you from yourself. You were practically giving away the goods. Desperate is not a good look." Celeste pretended to sound heartfelt, as if the quick exit was intended for her cousin's benefit.

"Okay, well…" Kay noted that a little reservation might win her a few extra desirability points. "What happened with Matthew and with Danny? I couldn't even keep up with what you were trying to pull in there."

"Oh, Kay." Celeste gave a patronizing sigh. "What does a dog do when he sees another dog chewing on a bone that he thinks is his?"

"He tries to take it," Kay immediately responded without thinking about the randomness of the question. "Wait, what the hell are you talking about?"

"Exactly. Not only does he try to take it, but he also desires it even more than he previously had because another dog has it. There may be many other bones lying on the ground of equal or perhaps even better worth, but in the dog's mind, he thinks that is his bone, and now he wants it even more." The cabdriver silently nodded in agreement from the front seat.

Kay rocked her head from side to side, thinking over what Celeste had just said. She caught on to the analogy her cousin was trying to make. It did make a bit of sense, in a manipulative way. "So, Matthew is the dog?"

"Correct."

"And Danny is the other dog?"

"Correct."

"And you are the bone."

"Correct."

"And what am I?"

"Just an inconsequential bitch."

"So, you are going out with Danny so Matthew will want you more."

"Brava." Celeste sarcastically clapped her hands.

Kay took this in and mustered a certain level of respect for her cousin's maniacal yet somewhat insightful methodology. After a moment of silence, she turned to Celeste, who was admiring her reflection in the cab window. "Did Danny say his last name was Boutté?"

"Yes. I believe so," Celeste replied while smoothing down her hair.

"Nothing comes to mind when you hear the name Boutté?"

"No, nothing comes to mind, Kay." Celeste threw an exasperated hand in the air.

"BOUTTÉ." Kay annunciated the name slowly.

Celeste's blue eyes floated upward as if she were trying to see her own brain. "Oh. Disgusting. I can't believe that someone who looks as old as you do can be so immature." She folded her arms across her chest and went back to her reflection.

After another quiet moment, Kay said, "Well, thank you for coming tonight. I really do appreciate it. That dress is very flattering on you, by the way. Very boutté-ful."

"Ugh, you are crass," an offended Celeste spat and looked back out the window. Despite her best attempt, though, a snort of laughter managed to escape her pretty lips before she could muffle it.

Kay crossed her legs and looked out her own window, pleased with herself. "Told you I was funny."

CHAPTER 4

Desperate To Get What You Want

The next morning, still wearing his clothes from the night before, sans jacket and shoes, Wes shuffled out of one of the guest bedrooms at Matthew's home. Being in such a good mood after seeing Kay, he'd had one too many celebratory cocktails and decided it was best to spend the night. Assuming Matthew wasn't awake yet, he made his way toward the kitchen for some much needed water. As he entered the center hall, he surveyed the room and felt a bit guilty about the state of the house. Empty glasses were everywhere, with plates of half-eaten appetizers resting on the now splattered, white linen-covered cocktail tables brought in for the party. Wes knew the maid would take care of it but decided he could at least pile up a few plates before leaving.

Suddenly, a loud cough came from somewhere. Due to the size of the house, he couldn't quite tell exactly where that somewhere was. Wes could tell it was Matthew, though; he knew his best friend's hangover howl when he heard it. He hadn't been able to find him anywhere in the last few hours of the party. *Where is he?*

"Matthew," Wes called out.

"Out here." A raspy roar echoed from the rear of the house.

Wes turned to see the back doors to the courtyard were open, and he made his way to join his friend. He raised a hand to block the morning sun as his lethargic steps carried him into the cool, inviting patio area. Matthew was in the pool with his big arms hanging over the side, cigarette in one hand, beer in the other. Wes looked around to see Matthew's blazer neatly lying by the pool's edge next to a crumpled pile of his clothes from last night. He trudged toward the pool and slumped onto a chair already beside Matthew's blazer. Pressing his palm to his forehead, Wes naively tried to push his headache away.

"Did you know Boutté is going out with my tiger?" Matthew took the last drag of his cigarette and dropped it into the empty beer bottle.

"What?" a fatigued Wes asked. Then, his dehydrated brain made the connection. "Oh yeah, I didn't know what the deal with that was. He asked me and Kay to get him Celeste's number last night." Matthew sloppily leaned his head to the side in confusion at Wes's response.

"Flight chick. Kay is flight chick."

"Right. Right." Matthew pushed his large frame back from the pool edge. Wes noticed he was swimming in nothing but his underwear. Something his friend had an odd tendency of doing when he'd had one too many and then another ten more after that. However, this morning, Matthew looked like it might have been another twenty more.

"You good?"

"Fine." Matthew submerged into the center of the pool to cool off before quickly popping up. He eased back through the water. "Just shit with Juniper and now this Celeste girl. My head just ain't right."

It came as no shock that Matthew seemed a little extra unglued because of Juniper's usual antics, but it was admittedly a bit surprising that he had even remembered Celeste's name. Matthew lifted his beer to take a swig shortly before noticing it was empty and contained his cigarette butt. "Grab me another one, will ya?" He pointed to the refrigerator built into the impressive stainless steel outdoor kitchen. "And one for yourself."

Wes wasn't really up for a morning beverage, but it was pretty obvious his friend could use some company. He begrudgingly hoisted himself up and pulled two beers from the fridge, which was normally stocked but had now been depleted to only six lonely bottles. "Maybe it'll help with my headache." He twisted his mouth and the tops off the beer bottles before handing one to Matthew and lowering himself back onto the chair.

"A little hair of the dog always does, brother." Matthew

raised his bottle with a well-lubricated grin and took a big gulp. Wes fought back nausea as he followed suit and squinted up at the morning sky.

"Look, I get the stuff with Juniper, but who cares about the other one?" He leaned back and continued looking at the clouds, trying to relax his friend.

"I don't know, man. Something about her." He shook his head and followed his confession with another distracted gulp. "You know she left me here?" Matthew rubbed his hand over his head to brush away the excess water from his sandy hair.

"You live here, Matt." Wes held the cold beer to his forehead and closed his eyes. "Of course she left you here."

"No. I mean here, here. Out here by the pool. I ask her out. She tells me she's going out with Boutté and then just bolts."

Wes lurched up from his reclined position and looked Matthew right in his glassy red eyes. "Are you saying you've been out here all night?"

The next few weeks were a bit of a whimsical blur. Kay's travel schedule was going to be light for a short while, so she and Wes got together as much as possible. It turns out she didn't need any extra points in the desirability category because Wes was most definitely enamored of her, and she with him. They talked through dinners, movie credits, and late-night pillow talk. Kay and Wes's relationship was off to quite the blissful start.

Celeste's social calendar had also been very busy. She was seeing Danny regularly. Dates that sadly always left Celeste nauseated with boredom; however, if she had regurgitated the contents of their awkward dinners, kind Danny would have considered it a privilege to mop it up. He was very taken with the enchanting Celeste. Daydreaming about the possibility of her actually allowing a goodnight kiss after one of their evenings together had become part of his daily routine. Daydreams that had yet to become a reality, much to Danny's dismay.

Matthew, who had also obtained the well-sought-after

number from Wes, called Celeste three times in those weeks. Each conversation followed the same pattern. Several minutes of witty banter mixed with sexual innuendoes, followed by Matthew asking her to dinner and Celeste unfortunately having to decline due to a prior engagement.

On this particular Sunday, Danny, Matthew, and Wes stood beside their individual tees with clubs in hand at the New Orleans Country Club driving range. Thankfully, the morning clouds delayed their sunburns as they practiced their swings before beginning another one of their frequent rounds of golf.

"So, how are things, Danno?" Matthew swung, resulting in a less-than-impressive distance for the golf ball.

"Good. Same old, same old." Danny straightened his stance and focused on his posture, overthinking the golf lesson he had earlier in the week.

"Really? Wes here tells me you've been going out with his new piece's cousin. What was her name again?" Matthew leaned his heavy body onto the hand resting on his driver, pressing it into the grass.

Wes pulled back and took a distracted swing. After watching the ball fall, he looked up at Matthew. His left-handed stroke allowed him to face his friend and put square eyes on him. *Don't get weird, Matt.* He knew Matthew was intentionally avoiding meeting his glance for this very reason.

Danny swung and cursed under his breath at the outcome. "Yeah, Celeste. I got to tell you"—a big grin spread across his face as he put another ball on the tee—"she is something else."

"Hmm." Matthew sucked his teeth. "So, you bang her yet?" He listened intently in the same position, which was now causing the neck of his club to bend. Wes cut him a look but decided to keep swinging. He knew he shouldn't interfere unless it went from swinging clubs to swinging fists, but that was a situation he hoped to avoid.

"Nope." Danny focused on his posture again. "Haven't even got close. Working on it, though. I think she's a proper, southern bell type." He swung and shanked the ball hard to his left.

"Damn, boy!" Wes exclaimed as the ball skated past his ankle.

Danny laughed aloud at himself. "It's the wind! Can't you see the wind is picking up? It's throwing off my game."

At this, Matthew's competitive nature decided to kick in; he hauled back and whacked his driver into the ball so hard that it sounded like a crack of thunder. The ball went flying straight, all the way to the far end of the range and landed just past the 300-yard marker. "Huh. Would you look at that?" He rubbed his jawline, pleased with his accomplishment. "At least somebody's banging something around here."

Celeste stood with crossed arms and rested her shoulder against Kay's bedroom doorframe. She inspected her cousin, who was concentrating on her vanity mirror and carefully applying makeup without noticing her presence.

"What are you doing?" Celeste asked, intentionally abrupt.

"Ah!" Kay jumped and dropped her eyeliner pencil. "Don't do that! I could have blinded myself!" She tried to smudge away the accidental eyeliner streaks from her cheekbone.

Celeste slithered toward Kay's bed and sat on it. "I would have been doing you a favor, darling." She used her palm to smooth the wrinkles of the comforter. "That way, you wouldn't have to see that hideous reflection of yours."

"Nice." Kay rolled her eyes as she removed the clip holding her hair back and impatiently asked, "What do you want, Celeste?"

"Can't a girl just check in on her cousin? I haven't seen much of you lately."

Kay rose and walked to her closet. She knew her cousin was up to something. "We never see much of each other, Celeste. Cut the act. What do you want?"

"I simply just want to know where you're going," she said as she shrugged in an attempt to seem disinterested as Kay pulled a navy blue dress from her closet and laid it on the bed.

"No," Celeste said sternly. She pointed to the other dresses hanging in the closet. "Put that back. The green one will do."

Kay pursed her lips. "If I wear the green one, will you just tell me what you want?"

"Yes." Celeste gave a nod of agreement.

"Fine." Kay snatched the green dress and tossed it on the

bed. "Now, what?"

"I just want to know where you're going."

"I have to fly back to Denver tonight, so I am having a late lunch with Wes before I go. He just finished golf with his friends, and I am meeting him at the club."

"Oh." Celeste perked up. "In that case, go back to the blue dress."

Kay let out a low, frustrated growl. "Is that all?"

"Who is he playing with?"

"I don't know." Kay threw her hands up. "I think it's Matthew and Danny. Can I get dressed now?"

"Yes. Yes, you may. Thank you. You've been quite helpful." Celeste knew that her new "relationship" with Danny would most likely be a topic of discussion during a long round of golf. Celeste also knew that it meant it was time to give a probably very jealous Matthew a call. She rose from the bed and escorted herself to the bedroom door. Quickly turning back and peeping her head into the room, she added, "Just don't wear those gray heels with that dress. They make your feet look like boudin."

"Out!" Kay slammed the door just as Celeste strolled away to formulate a plan.

Fifteen minutes later, Celeste pretended to relax on the leather couch as she waited for the front door to close behind Kay in her blue dress and white heels. Just as it did, she slid off the couch and smoothly walked to the door, looking through the peephole to ensure the coast was clear. Celeste flipped the deadbolt lock and obtained her phone from the kitchen bar. Eager with anticipation, she slinked back into her spot, covering her legs with her cashmere throw.

"What do you want me to say, Juniper?" Matthew yelled into the phone as he walked through his front doors and dropped his golf bag to the floor. He winced and pulled the phone away from his face to keep the ensuing screaming from bursting his eardrum. Just as he did, Matthew's phone lit up with an incoming call. TIGER flashed across the screen. He quickly put the phone back to his ear, risking a lifelong hearing disability, and yelled over the white noise on the other end,

"I have to go, Juniper!" More screaming came through the phone. "I'm hanging up now. Goodbyyye." Matthew ended the call and accepted the very welcomed incoming one.

"Well, hello, Celeste. I have to say that I am pleasantly surprised to hear from you."

"Yes. I am so sorry that I haven't been able to find a time for us to get into each other's…I mean, get onto each other's schedules." She pretended to make the misstatement as she thought, *Here poochy pooch.*

Matthew plopped down onto a couch in his lounge and began to remove his golf shoes. "I hope this means you've been able to find some time for me to take you out."

"As a matter of fact, yes. I have a client that unfortunately can't make it to a dinner meeting that was planned for this evening."

"Really? I can't believe someone would be foolish enough to cancel a chance to meet with you."

Celeste shifted uncomfortably. She hadn't thought that far ahead in her story. "Yes. Skydiving accident. Very tragic, indeed." She cringed at the ridiculousness of her own words.

"Oh…I'm so sorry to hear that." Matthew paused, not quite sure how to respond. "Well, I would hate for you to be alone, especially under such circumstances. I do have to fly out early to Vegas tomorrow morning, but you could join me at my place. I can have some dinner brought in, and I assure you the pool is just as, how did you say it, *heavenly* as you remember."

Celeste counted in her head for suspense purposes: *1, 2, 3, 4, 5*. "That sounds charming. I'll be by around eight." She hung up the phone without giving Matthew a chance to say another word.

Kay was drained as she pulled her luggage into the condo at eleven p.m. on Wednesday night. Her return flight had been delayed yet again. She wanted to call Wes to laugh about it, but all she could think about was her bed. Stumbling as she took off her heels, she made her way to her bedroom. The condo was dark. The only light guiding her was the glow from the streetlights on Ursulines Avenue peeping through the curtains. Assuming Celeste was already asleep, she tiptoed, heels in hand, to her room so as not to wake the dragon.

She woke up around seven the next morning. On days after Kay traveled, her boss was good enough to let her work from home. She climbed out of bed and stretched her arms to the ceiling with a well-deserved yawn. As her bare feet padded out of the room, she suddenly stopped. *What was that?* Kay waited for a moment, and then the sound came again. It sounded like a dull, inconsistent thumping or banging noise. The noise was coming from Celeste's room. Kay tensed. *She's never up this early.* She looked up and down the hallway but saw nothing out of place. *Something doesn't feel right.* Stealthily picking up a vase from the hallway table, she cautiously crept to Celeste's bedroom door.

"Celeste?" Kay whispered and gently knocked.

"Yes?" Celeste's voice rang out from inside of the room.

"Is everything alright?" Kay was clenching the vase, nervously wondering what was happening on the other side of the bedroom door. After a long pause, there was more thumping. "Celeste?"

"Oh, yes, I forgot about you. You can come in." Kay gripped the vase behind her back and opened the door an inch at a time, ready to pounce on a potential attacker.

In the room, Celeste was humming and obliviously trotting from her bed to her closet. Lying on the bed was a large suitcase filled to the brim with clothes. Kay breathed a sigh of relief with a slump of her shoulders as she let her arms relax by her sides.

"Is that my vase?"

"Yes. Yes, it is," Kay admitted defensively and set the vase on the nearby dresser. "You scared me to death. I thought you were being attacked by some psychopath in here."

Celeste halted her trotting and glared at the open bedroom door. Kay knew what the look meant. She gave her cousin a nagged look and slung her hand onto the knob, closing the door. "What are you doing?"

"Packing." A distracted Celeste pushed both hands down onto the clothes in the suitcase.

"I can see that. Where are you going?"

"Well, actually, I just got back, but I'm leaving again."

Celeste didn't look up as she pressed down the lid of the luggage, trying to force the contents to fit.

"Okay." Kay put her hand over her eyes with annoyance and fatigue. "Let's just go in order then, shall we? Where are you getting back from?"

"Getting married," Celeste stated plainly, focusing on the luggage case she was desperately trying to zip closed.

Oh my God. She's lost it. Kay froze. She glanced back at the vase, wondering if there really was a psychopath in the room. "Okaaay," Kay responded carefully to Celeste, who was still struggling with the zipper. "So, you got married?"

"Yes." Celeste uncharacteristically grunted as she finally managed to pull the zipper all the way around the bag. "Ha, got it." She hauled the bag off the bed and onto its roller wheels. She marched toward the bedroom door, swung it open, and whisked out of the room, rolling the heavy bag behind her. Kay, slightly dizzy from the potential insanity, followed her.

"Wait! So, you married Danny? How? When?"

Celeste suspended her march halfway down the hall and turned around. She testily looked at the bedroom door that Kay had yet again left open. Without taking her eyes off her possibly deranged cousin, Kay reached her arm back and closed the door.

"So, you and Danny got married?"

"Don't be ridiculous. Of course not." Celeste spun around and headed toward the kitchen. "I married Matthew," she casually announced back to Kay.

Kay thought she was going to faint with shock. "What?" She sprinted to the kitchen. "Celeste, seriously. What are you talking about?"

"Look, I don't have time for this. Matthew and I are leaving for Cabo in two hours," she replied dismissively as she scrolled through her cell phone.

"Why are you going to Cabo?"

"For our honeymoon, of course. Please try to keep up."

"But how could you be married to Matthew? I saw you Sunday. Today is Thursday." Kay was starting to go back to her original assumption that Celeste really should be an inmate at the asylum.

"Oh, ye of little faith." She tauntingly held her cell phone up to her cousin's face. Kay's blue eyes bulged as she took in the image. It was most definitely a picture of Celeste and Matthew standing in front of what appeared to be a gaudy white chapel.

Celeste sighed and recounted the chain of events, counting them off on her well-manicured fingers. "Matthew and I flew to Vegas Monday morning. We got married Tuesday. We flew back yesterday. I've been at his house since then. I came back this morning to pack for our honeymoon, which I must leave for right now." She twirled around and skipped as she strutted out the front door with her luggage and not so much as a backward glance.

Kay stood stunned in the kitchen, gawking at the front door. She looked around the now silent room as if searching for answers and then back at the front door in bewilderment. "What the fuck just happened?"

CHAPTER 5

Desperate To Be Like Juniper

Two weeks later, Wes pulled his black Tahoe to the curb outside of Danny's condo on Canal Street. He grabbed his phone from the cupholder and texted his friend to let him know. After replacing the phone, he used that same hand to lay on Kay's left thigh. She looked beautiful. Kay was wearing a rose-colored one-shoulder cocktail dress that Wes wanted to pull down the second he saw her.

"You ready?" He smiled as he gave her thigh a gentle squeeze.

"I guess so. This certainly should be interesting."

In most places, running off to Vegas and getting married was considered romantic and whimsical. Two people who were so in love they simply couldn't wait one second longer to be married. Down on the bayou, however, people just thought one thing…pregnant. The tale of Celeste's marriage to *the* Matthew Wells had become quite the salacious story, traded in country club steam rooms and Junior League meeting gossip circles. A tale that was told repeatedly and promptly followed by appalled gasps in reaction to the uncivilized nature of the couple's blasphemous union.

To subdue the wagging tongues of New Orleans society, Matthew's mother arranged for the marriage to be blessed by Father McDavid at Saint Louis Cathedral. A reception to celebrate the occasion was to be held at her estate that afternoon, following the private blessing.

"Thanks for the ride, guys." Danny opened the rear passenger door to Wes's car and hopped in.

"No problem." Wes preferred his hand where it was but moved it from Kay's leg to the steering wheel and pulled back onto Canal. He had obviously asked Kay to be his date to the reception and asked Danny to ride with them, knowing his partner probably wouldn't want to show up alone given the circumstances.

"Hi, Danny." Kay turned back to welcome him. "Wow, looking sharp."

"Oh, I bet you say that to all the girls," Danny mused sarcastically and tightened the knot of his tie as he settled into the seat behind Wes.

"No. I mean it. You really do look handsome." Danny did look handsome. Kay had been so taken with Wes she never really thought to take a good look at Danny. He was, in fact, a pretty decent-looking guy.

"Uh-oh. Watch out, Wes. I might have to pull a Matthew on you," Danny wistfully jested to his friend from the backseat. Wes and Kay exchanged a quick, knowing glance. Danny understandably hadn't taken the sudden upheaval of his romantic plans very well. The past two weeks had been a little rough for him.

"Challenge accepted, buddy," Wes jested back to alleviate the awkwardness.

"So, Danny." Recognizing a subject change might be best, Kay asked, "Have you ever been to Matthew's mom's house? Wes tells me it's quite a place."

"Oh yeah, tons of times. I must say, it is definitely on another level."

"Well, I'm sure we'll have a good time. Is Matthew's mom nice? I've never met her."

Her innocence caused Kay's car mates to suddenly begin giggling like teenage girls. "You haven't told her?" Danny slapped the back of Wes's seat.

"What?" Kay looked back and forth between the two chuckling men with a curious smile. "Told me what?"

"Just *beware the fan.*" Wes tried to hold in his amusement at the thought.

"What? What fan?" She was now excitedly confused.

"You'll shee." The words slid from Danny's mouth as he wiped laughing tears from his green eyes.

"Y'all really aren't going to tell me?" Kay was tickled that they were both now red in the face. "And Danny, have you been drinking already, mister?"

Poor Danny slurred between remaining chuckles, "Perr-rhaps."

Matthew's mother's house was not a house. It was, in every sense of the word, a mansion. Wes drove down the long driveway lined with moss-covered oak trees that hung so low they hid what lay before them. As he curved into the drive that circled a pool-sized spouting stone fountain, Kay's jaw dropped. The mansion was practically the length of a football field. Located on the outskirts of the city, it was a gigantic white structure with black hurricane shutters built in an exquisite antebellum architectural style, featuring massive wrap-around porches, sloping exterior staircases, large windows, and columns that would have made ancient Greece green with envy.

Two large white staircases bowed outward from the ground and met at the entrance to an enormous front porch leading to elaborate front doors made of solid oak. An astonished Kay whispered in childlike awe as she stared out the window at the stunning palace, "It's like Twelve Oaks."

"Good afternoon, ma'am." An attractive young man in his early twenties with light red hair opened Kay's door and extended his hand to help her from the vehicle.

"Gauge!" Wes stepped out of the car and rounded the front to shake the young man's hand.

Danny slightly stumbled out of the backseat and toward the valet before patting him on the back. "The old broad hasn't got rid of you yet?"

The handsome valet politely smiled as he straightened the black bowtie that wrapped under the collar of his crisp white shirt. "No, sir, not yet. Guess she knows a good thing when she sees it."

"Right you are, my man." Wes handed him the keys and flicked his chin upward to the house. "How is it in there?"

"Ummm." The young man squinted his green eyes in response.

Danny nodded with a laugh. "Understood."

"Well, in that case, let the mayhem begin." Wes laced

Kay's arm through his, and they headed up one of the exterior staircases to enter the mystical estate.

Walking through the mansion's massive front doors was like walking into a wind tunnel. Kay brushed back the hair that had blown across her eyes to see nothing short of a scene from *Gatsby*. The magnificent entrance hall was peppered with mingling, sharply dressed guests and presented a grand, sweeping, curved marble staircase that stretched upward toward a majestic balcony introducing the second of many floors.

Kay looked around in amazement. To her right was a drawing room lined with white linen-covered buffet tables. A small string quartet was quietly playing next to a grand piano in the corner of the room. To her left was a parlor room with heavy, cream-colored curtains and deep oversized chairs and couches. Small yet ornate side tables punctuated every wall of each room with vintage, iron-based oscillating fans; each was identical with black enamel paint and brass blades. There were dozens of them humming, blowing drink napkins, and cooling guests. Kay made a mental note not to let her hair or hand get too close to the spiraling blades. Despite her concern for locks and limb, she thought the display was absolutely ethereal.

"Well, I guess Matthew's mom wanted to make sure we didn't all die of heatstroke. I'll make sure to *beware* them," Kay whispered over the hum into Wes's ear, impressed with herself for decoding the source of Danny and Wes's car ride laughter.

Wes found her naiveness endearing. "No. It's always like this. These aren't the fans I was talking about." He laid his hand on her lower back as they stopped in the entrance hall under a towering chandelier.

"I'm going to hit the bar. You guys need anything?" Danny asked as he straightened his glasses, his eyes nervously flashing across the drawing room.

"In a minute. I just want to find Celeste and get the hellos out of the way." After she said that, Kay felt a bit bad, realizing poor Danny was probably desperate to retreat to the bar so he wouldn't have to make an awkward hello himself.

"I'll need one soon. Meet you there." Wes raised his brow

and cast a glance at the bar. Danny weakly smiled and turned to drown his sorrows.

"This place is amazing." Kay couldn't stop herself from arching her eyes upward. As she did, her eyes caught on the shadow of a person's back that was slightly peeking from the edge of the wall framing the upstairs balcony. There seemed to be some type of rapid movement and then a woman's yelp, which went almost unheard as it filtered down to the entrance hall.

The shadow suddenly came into full view as a woman. Rubbing the back of her hand, the woman rushed across the balcony corridor and immediately down the staircase toward the drawing room. Her jet-black hair was coiled in a low bun, and matched her equally jet-black dress. She darted to the pianist beside the string band and leaned to his ear as if directing an instruction.

"Who's that?" Kay kept her eyes on the woman.

"Who's who?" Wes looked around. Just as he tracked Kay's line of sight to the woman, the pianist started to play.

"Not sure. I don't recognize her." He laid his palm on Kay's bare shoulder. "Look, there's Celeste and Matthew. Do you want to—"

Kay cut him off by putting a biding hand on his chest. "Is that…?" She paused and listened closer to the piano music. "Is that the Funeral March?"

He tilted his head toward the drawing room to listen more intently. "Oh no." Wes's dimples suddenly went flat.

"No? It's not? Are you sure? I could swear that's the Funeral March." Kay tried to concentrate on the piano piece that had now initiated a hush in conversation among all the guests.

"It is. It is the Funeral March. Why am I not surprised?" Wes cast despairing eyes upward to the balcony. Kay followed his lead and raised her gaze as well.

Slowly gliding across the balcony aisle was the silhouette of a woman in a floor-length black dress. The silhouette approached the top of the staircase and turned to face the hypnotized eyes of the guests looking up at her. The woman staring down at the entrance hall was stunning. She looked like she was made of diamonds as the light of the chandelier sparkled on her black beaded gown. Pausing to allow the morbid music to echo through and encompass the entire hall, she elegantly flipped open a black lace hand fan as if it were an extension of her own hand. The woman gently waved the fan toward her face as she slowly descended the grand staircase, almost cascading in stride with the rhythm of the piano. As she reached the final step, the young valet was there to take her hand. He escorted the beautiful creature to the parlor as the surrounding oscillating fans waved her dress.

"Who…?" A mesmerized Kay was nearly breathless.

Wes whispered, "That's Matthew's mother. That's Juniper Wells."

Kay couldn't look away. "Dear God. She's fabulous."

The melancholy tune faded as the guests eagerly returned to their hushed gossip and polite buffet table grazing. The tables presented quite the spread, with everything from artistically sliced fruits to crispy, soft-shell crab. Tall floral displays, centered at each of them, brimmed with exotic flowers. Each arrangement was accented with, of course, juniper blossoms.

"Hey, man! You made it." A beaming Matthew approached in a black suit that stretched across his broad shoulders. His new bride was on his arm.

"Wouldn't miss it, brother." Wes shook his friend's hand. "Congratulations, Celeste. Matthew is a very lucky man."

"Thank you, Carl." She gave Wes a patronizing smile as her new husband looked a bit thrown by her response.

"Are those my shoes?" Kay's attention went straight to her cousin's feet.

Celeste looked gorgeous. Her blonde hair was waved and pulled back, exposing her recently sun-kissed shoulders. The fitted white lace cocktail dress that she wore was perfectly tailored and was accented with an absolutely beautiful pair of ocean blue stilettos.

Celeste squinted at Kay condescendingly. "Matthew darling, would you please look around?" She laid her hand on his forearm.

"Look around for what?"

"For poor Kay's mind." Celeste raised an eyebrow at her cousin. "Because she has clearly lost it." Both the men smirked at the verbal slap and eyed each other uncomfortably. "I wouldn't be caught dead in anything of yours, my dear," Celeste sneered.

Kay looked her cousin up and down. "Hmm, well, I guess that does make perfect sense. Wouldn't want the attire to be prettier than the corpse, now would we." Wes cleared his throat as a signal to let the matter go. At this, Kay reined in her cattiness and decided to save the argument for a later date, given the occasion. "Well, on any account, you look lovely. Congratulations, cousin."

"Excuse me, Mr. Wells." An older gentleman appeared and tapped Matthew on the shoulder. His oversized suit matched the oversized camera that was hanging around his neck. "Mrs. Wells—" Suddenly recognizing there was now more than one Mrs. Wells, he clarified, "Mrs. Juniper Wells requested that we get a few shots of the newlyweds out on the grounds."

"Oh, I—" Matthew began to decline, but Celeste cut him off. Any excuse to have her photograph taken and hopefully splashed onto one, if not many, of the glossy pages in the social magazines was more than welcomed.

"That would be perfect. Right, darling?" Celeste raised a pair of big blue doe eyes to her new husband.

"Absolutely," Matthew conceded without hesitation to please his angelic bride.

"Wonderful. Right this way." The photographer extended a polite directing arm and led the newlyweds to the front doors.

As soon as Matthew and Celeste were out of earshot, Kay looked at Wes in disbelief and tattled, "That bitch stole my shoes." She resentfully watched her heels walk out the door on Celeste's feet. "Guess she took something borrowed and something blue a little too seriously." Her eyes quickly floated around the room, hoping she hadn't just cursed the bride a little too loudly. As she did, she noticed they were being watched. Juniper Wells was curiously peering at them from the parlor.

Juniper Wells was lounging in her large, oversized cream-colored chair, fanning herself. She was not pleased with this sham of a marriage. A vile temptress had lured her son into a ridiculous union that was beyond reproach.

"Camille," she called over her shoulder to the woman with the black bun and black dress. The curvy woman appeared to be in her mid-forties with high cheekbones and sharp, dark eyes.

She took three strong steps forward and stopped at Juniper's side. "We've talked about this, Mrs. Wells. My name is EL-O-DIE." She articulated the syllables slowly and loudly as if trying to translate a foreign language to Juniper.

Juniper was expressionless as she fanned herself. "Yes, yes, and I am quite sure you spell it in some ridiculous manner with far too many letters." She cocked her head and narrowed her eyes at Elodie. "I don't like it. Your name is CA-MILLE," she reprimanded in an equally slow, annunciated, yet much louder tone.

Elodie was the third caretaker assigned to Juniper this year. The others only made it about a month before running for the hills. Mrs. Wells was not, one might say, the easiest to be an "assistant" to. She always referred to them as her assistants because she would rather crawl naked over broken glass than admit she actually needed a caretaker.

"Are you even an American citizen, Camille?"

Elodie sighed with aggravation. "Yes, ma'am. I'm from Chalmette."

"Ah," Juniper gasped as she threw herself back into the chair and began feverishly fanning herself. "Even worse."

Elodie sucked her teeth at the dramatic display and put her hands on her hips. "You done?"

"You've upset me terribly, Camille. Go." In one fluid motion, Juniper snapped the fan shut, cracked it onto Elodie's hand, and snapped it back open into fanning position without batting a false eyelash. The strike cracked across Elodie's knuckles with a *FWAPA* sound.

"Ouch! Stop doing that," Elodie hissed.

"Go!"

"Go where?"

"Get me those people." Juniper waved her hand to the opposite side of the room.

"What people?"

"Those two. Right there." Juniper pointed her fan squarely at Wes and Kay standing in the entrance hall. With a huff, Elodie walked over to the couple. She turned back to Juniper and pointed a questioning finger at the couple's backs.

"Yes, them!"

"Excuse me." Wes and Kay turned around to see a somewhat agitated-looking woman trying to appear pleasant. "Mrs. Wells would like to see you." Elodie glanced back to Juniper to direct their attention.

"Oh...of course. Thank you." Wes took Kay's hand, and they followed Elodie into the parlor where Juniper was seated.

"Camille. Get me another fan. I believe this one is broken."

"Wonder how that could of happened," Elodie muttered, rubbing her hand, walking away after delivering the couple.

Kay and Wes stood in front of Juniper as if awaiting execution. "Well, sit," Juniper ordered, and the two scrambled to sit on the couch to her left. "No. One on each side." She pointed her fan to the couch on her right. Like obedient children, Wes went to the right, and Kay sat to Juniper's left.

Kay sat and crossed her ankles, slightly frightened but also slightly excited to be in such close proximity to the striking creature. Juniper was tall and lean. A diamond comb cinched her blonde hair, which was perfectly woven into an exquisite quaff. Her dewy skin gave absolutely no indication of her seventy years. Delicate features emphasized her round brown eyes that outsparkled even her own beaded gown. Kay was quite sure that Juniper had made some plastic surgeon a very rich man, and if she had, it was worth every penny.

"Thank you so much for having us, Mrs. Wells. This is a wonderful party. Matthew seems very happy," Wes opened appreciatively. Juniper slid her head in his direction and eyed him with contempt at the insinuation that this marriage should make anyone happy, let alone her only son.

"Your face annoys me. I don't like it." *FWAPA!*

Wes grabbed his throbbing hand as Kay threw hers over her mouth in shock. She hit him hard enough to draw blood. *Beware the fan,* she recalled.

Juniper turned her sights on Kay and studied her. "And

who are you?"

"My name is Kay. I am Celeste's cousin. Thank you so much for having us to your home. It's—" Juniper put up a halting hand.

"So"—Juniper eerily stared Kay in the eyes—"you are the whore's cousin?"

Like a deer in headlights, Kay stared back into Juniper's eyes, nodding her head and almost hypnotically repeating, "I am the whore's cousin." As the words escaped her lips, Kay gave a slight gasp of embarrassment, not knowing if she, herself, was allowed to use such unpolished language in the beautiful creature's presence.

Recognizing Kay's rattled composure at the affirmation, Juniper gave a wicked smirk. "Fear not, child." She cooled and gave Kay one more hair-to-heel survey. "There is no shame in speaking the truth in my presence. A spade should be called a spade, and a whore should be called a whore."

Celeste strode back in through the front doors. She wanted to freshen up before continuing what had now turned into quite a lengthy photoshoot at her own request. She stopped in the center of the entrance hall and looked into the parlor. *Now why is that bitch talking to that bitch?* She attempted to appear pleasant as she drifted toward her new mother-in-law with a fake smile plastered across her perfect face. "Mrs. Wells, thank you so much for the photographer." Juniper looked up and received Celeste as if she were a complete stranger. Feeling awkward, Celeste stammered, "I hope my cousin here isn't bothering you. She can be quite ill-mannered."

"I'm sorry. I can't understand you." Juniper gave Celeste a bewildered look.

Celeste flushed and spoke a little louder. "Thank you for the photographer, Mrs. Wells."

"I still can't...oh, yes, of course, that's why." Juniper began to gently fan herself and nonchalantly scanned the room. "I can't understand a word you are saying because I don't speak slut."

Don't laugh. Don't laugh, Kay begged herself as she tightly pressed her lips together. She looked across to Wes, who was trying to do the same with bulging, hazel eyes. He shook his head at her as if trying to signal he wasn't sure he'd be able to hold it in.

"I see. Well, in that case, I guess I will be getting back to *my husband* then." An insulted Celeste turned on Kay's blue heels and marched back to the front doors.

Juniper watched her new daughter-in-law storm out of the mansion. "That harlot has bewitched my son. Some desperate trash voodoo magic has blinded him. It's atrocious. He would probably drink her bathwater with a ladle if he could."

"Well, I certainly hope not," Kay said plainly. "He would probably die of dysentery shortly after."

Juniper released a controlled snicker and looked at Kay with an equally controlled, small yet respectful smile. "Speaking of dysentery, my dear, your hair is the color of bloody fecal matter. You should dye it blonde. I don't like it."

"Oh." Kay put her palm on the crown of her head.

"However, you are a very pretty girl, and I find your obvious equal disdain for that slithering snake amusing." She tapped her finger to her lips pensively. "The enemy of my enemy is my friend." Juniper squinted her eyes in thought and fanned herself. "So, forgiving your, whatever that is"—she waved her fan at Kay's hair disapprovingly—"I like you." Juniper gave a conclusionary nod as if she had just made an official decision.

"Well, thank you, ma'am. That is very…kind of you. I like you very much as well."

"You may get me my drink." Juniper flipped her hand in the direction of the drawing room and went back to nonchalantly scanning the room.

Kay rose to fulfill the order. "Yes, ma'am. What would you—" *FWAPA!*

"I said go, child!"

Kay jumped. "Yes, ma'am." She grasped her injured hand and scurried through the entrance hall toward the drawing room.

"Wes." Juniper was intently watching her recent victim dodge fellow party guests in her hurry.

"Yes, Mrs. Wells?" He leaned forward.

Juniper allowed herself an amused smirk and pointed her fan directly at Kay's back. "Don't fuck it up."

Kay whisked through the entrance hall and into the drawing room, which was no small feat given the size of the mansion. She weaved through guests and dashed up to the large, oak, marble-topped bar. Danny was leaning against it.

"Hey," Kay smiled at Danny, slightly out of breath.

"Well, hello, Kay."

Drunk, definitely drunk, she sympathetically thought.

"This is my friend, Logan." Danny cast his hand to an attractive young man in his early twenties with light red hair and sensitive green eyes behind the bar cleaning a glass. Kay was pretty sure this was the Gauge that valeted Wes's car earlier, but she let the mental blip slide, given Danny's current condition.

Geez, Juniper keeps this kid busy.

"This is Kay, Wes's girlfriend," Danny slurred to Logan. Kay immediately blushed. It was the first time anyone had referred to her as "Wes's girlfriend."

"Well, Mr. Wes is a very lucky man. What can I get for you, Ms. Kay?" Logan greeted warmly.

"Umm. Actually, I'm not really sure." Kay bit her lower lip. "I was just speaking with Juniper, and well…" She rubbed her hand, still dazed from the whole experience.

"Did she hit you?" Danny asked excitedly.

"Well, yes. There was some kind of centripetal force movement that she did with her fan. It felt like a snake bit me." Kay laughed awkwardly; considering that she had just been assaulted, she somehow found it slightly amusing.

"That's a great sign!" Danny put both hands on Kay's shoulders in an almost congratulatory way. "She only hits people she likes!"

"It's true, ma'am," Logan politely affirmed and smiled as he rubbed his own hand. "It's a 'you only hurt the ones you love' kind of thing."

"Well, I guess that is nice of her," a now confused yet flattered Kay said. "She told me to get her a drink, but the fan hit me before I could find out what that drink should be."

"Ah. Say no more, Ms. Kay. She has her own drink. It's called the Juniper. I'll fix one up for you right now."

"Oh great." She was relieved that she wouldn't disappoint. "Well, I guess make it two then."

Logan's face suddenly got serious. "Did she ask you to get her two drinks?"

"No, but when in Rome, I guess." She raised her impressed eyes and injured hand to the high ceiling.

Logan gave Danny a worried, knowing look. "Oh no. For your own safety, Kay, you can't have one," Danny warned with concern. "Only Juniper can drink Junipers. I tried to do that once because I thought it would be…well, polite. She 'didn't like it.'" He lifted his right hand in front of Kay's face and tried to extend his index finger. "It still doesn't work right after that."

"I see." Kay watched Danny's green eyes, still very much focused on his finger, trying to will it to straighten. "I guess just a Juniper and a glass of white wine for me, please. I should probably get something for Wes, but I don't have enough hands."

"Let me get these ready for you, and I can have something brought over for Mr. Wes," Logan happily offered.

"That would be great, Looogan." She said his name a little slowly, unsure if it was, in fact, his name. He smiled and nodded at her as he got to work on the cocktails.

Within minutes, Kay hurried back to the parlor with the two drinks. As she approached, she saw Wes in conversation with Juniper as Elodie was handing her another fan. After the fan exchange, Elodie stood a few feet behind the queen's seat, waiting for another imminent request.

"Here you go, Mrs. Wells." The feeling of fear and simultaneous amazement of being in Juniper's presence returned to Kay as she handed her the glass.

Juniper took the drink without raising her eyes and took a long sip. "Delicious," she cooed, seeming rejuvenated. "Logan must have made it." She looked up at Kay and ordered, "Well, sit, child!"

"Yes, ma'am." She darted back to her original spot. Wes watched Kay sit and couldn't help but grin. He didn't enjoy seeing her slightly on edge, but the way she was handling

Juniper made him almost a bit proud.

Just as Kay sat, a young man in his early twenties with light red hair casually walked up to Wes and handed him a glass of wine. "Ms. Kay requested this for you, sir."

"Oh. Thank you, Gauge." Wes gave him a friendly smile.

Kay felt embarrassed again. "I'm so sorry," she apologized to the young man. "I called you Logan earlier at the bar. Your name is Gauge, right?"

"Dear child!" Juniper flashed Kay an insulted look. "Wes here was just telling me you were an intelligent woman. Can you not tell the difference between two handsome young gentlemen? This is Gauge. Logan is at the bar."

A relaxed Gauge walked to Juniper's side, chuckling. "Please don't be too hard on her, Ms. Juniper." He looked at Kay with understanding eyes. "It happens all the time, Ms. Kay. I am Gauge, and Logan is my twin brother. We've worked for the beautiful Ms. Juniper here for five years now."

An uncharacteristic motherly expression spread across Juniper's face when Gauge spoke, displaying the cause of her defensive nature and genuine care for the two young men. "Oh, Gauge, stop. You flatter me." Juniper sucked in her cheeks and fanned herself rather quickly. "Do go on, though," she encouraged.

He chuckled again. "Ms. Juniper has been very good to Logan and me over the years."

"Well deserved, my dear. Well deserved," Juniper practically boasted. She knew the twins were kindhearted boys, and having them around made her almost feel kinder herself.

"Ms. Juniper, while I'm here…" She perked up and gave her undivided attention to Gauge. "I'm going to man the bar for a bit while Logan takes Edward out for a quick walk if that's alright with you."

"That would be perfect. Please tell Logan to bring him around back and that I love him dearly."

"Logan or Edward?" Gauge joked without fear.

"Both." An amused Juniper fanned herself.

"Will do, and I'll have another drink brought over to you."

As Gauge walked toward the drawing room, Juniper beckoned over her shoulder, "Camille!"

"Yes, ma'am." Elodie quickly came to her side.

"Make a note to put Gauge and Logan in my will. I've been meaning to do it for years."

Elodie pursed her lips, wanting to remind Juniper that she was indeed her caretaker, not her secretary, but decided better otherwise. "Yes, ma'am."

Logan pulled Wes's Tahoe around the curved drive, leaving the driver's door open. "My lady." Wes opened the front passenger door for Kay to slide into.

"Well, thank you, Mr. Allen."

Logan ran around the side of the car to help Danny into the backseat. Poor Danny's equilibrium was a little off. "You got it. There you go." Logan gently hoisted him into the car.

Wes turned to Logan after he closed the car door and patted him on the shoulder. "Thanks, man. Good luck in there." He slid a twenty into the young man's hand as he shook it.

"Thanks so much, Mr. Wes. Good seeing you. Drive safe." Logan gave an appreciative smile before he hustled back up one of the outdoor staircases.

By the time they reached the end of the long driveway, Danny was already snoring with his head leaning against the window. Kay turned back and looked at him sympathetically. "Poor guy."

"Yeah." Wes sucked his teeth. "He's not normally like this. He was just really into Celeste, and the whole thing kind of caught him off guard. Well…" He quirked his mouth. "I guess it caught all of us off guard." Wes lifted his chin and looked in the rearview mirror to see his comatose friend's open mouth fogging up its resting place on the back window.

Kay felt a little guilty knowing that this had been Celeste's plan all along, given her whole dog-and-bone analogy the night of the party. However, in her defense, she had underestimated her cousin's powers of persuasion and had not seen things going quite this according to script. "He'll be alright. I think Matthew actually did him a favor," she confessed. Danny let out a loud snort and readjusted himself in his seat without regaining consciousness.

"Those boys seemed nice." Kay decided to change the subject as she pulled off her gold heels.

"Oh, Gauge and Logan? Yeah, they're really nice kids. I think Gauge is about to go for his MBA, and Logan is about to start law school. After Edward died, Juniper really needed the extra help and company," Wes said absentmindedly as he turned the car onto the main road. Kay tilted her head in thought as if trying to remember something.

"Edward?" she asked.

"Yep, Edward was Matthew's dad. He died suddenly a while back."

She was still confused. "Didn't one of those boys say they were taking Edward for a walk?"

"Oh yeah," Wes laughed. "Edward is also the dog. After Matthew's dad died, Juniper bought one of those dogs… What are they called? They're silver…" Wes wracked his brain for a moment. "Weimaraner," he pronounced a little too loudly, causing Danny to stir again. "Apparently, Matthew and Edward, human Edward, always wanted one, but Juniper would never let them have one. So, after he died…I guess she, you know."

"Awww. So she named the dog Edward," Kay said in a slightly creeped-out but understanding way. "Ok, so, the fans?" She curled her legs up on the seat as if she were a little girl asking to be told a bedtime story. "There are always that many fans?"

"Yep. That started after Edward, too. I guess she just didn't like the stillness or quiet of the big old house with him gone."

"That makes sense, I guess." She gazed out her window to watch the sun disappearing into the distant marshland.

"Sorry I didn't give you a better warning about the hand fan, though." He squeezed her thigh again and gave her a guilty smile.

Kay muffled her laugh so as not to wake Danny. "That's alright. I kind of consider it a badge of honor. I think she is the most intoxicating intoxicated person I've ever met."

Wes's eyes grew a size. "Really?" He looked at her and gave a surprised chuckle. "I thought you would hate her."

"Why on earth would you say that? I think she is absolutely spectacular in this weird, eccentric, beautiful kind of way." Kay waved her hands, feebly trying to describe the intriguing Juniper.

"Really? Huh. She doesn't remind you at all of someone you know?"

"No. Who could compare to that?" Kay gushed with blind admiration.

"Someone you don't particularly like?" Wes asked as if he were trying to leave a trail of breadcrumbs. "Blonde, attractive, pretentious, dramatic, kind of evil, manipulative of Matthew?" He held up his marked hand and nodded at Kay's to evidence their matching hand fan welts.

"What are you talking—" The realization hit her like a train. "My God," Kay gasped with recognition and threw her injured hand over her mouth. "Matthew married his mother."

CHAPTER 6

Desperate To Take It Back

"The son of a bitch is cheating." Celeste sipped her mimosa in the courtyard patio of The Greyhound, an upscale eatery located a few blocks away from Jackson Square.

"You're paranoid. I'm sure it's all in your head," Kay said dismissively as she waved to get the waitress's attention. "What even makes you think that?"

In the seven months that followed Matthew and Celeste's nuptials, Kay and her cousin had grown slightly closer. It was almost as if they had decided to call an unspoken truce. They were seeing each other regularly, certainly much more than when they lived together. This was mainly because their significant others were best friends, forcing them to share dinners and social gatherings. They agreed to at least attempt to be friends without either of them actually saying it due to their own pride.

"A real woman knows. I wouldn't expect you to understand." Celeste downed the last bit of her mimosa and swirled her head around the patio. "Where is that damn waitress?"

Kay put on a courteous expression and straightened the napkin in her lap as the overworked waitress scurried up to the table. "Another round?" she asked enthusiastically.

"Yes, please," Kay politely responded. Despite their newfound acceptance of each other's presence, the two women did not normally get together alone. As such, Kay decided mimosas were the best way to endure having Saturday afternoon cocktails at her cousin's request.

"The first year of marriage can be tough." Kay prayed for a quick return of the waitress.

"And how would you know?" Celeste criticized. "You're

forty and have never been married."

Kay raised an eyebrow and curved her neck. "Well, actually, Celeste, I'm twenty-nine. And might I remind you, I'm a year younger than you."

"Hmm." She judgmentally eyed her cousin's left hand. "Those crow's feet and bare ring finger say differently."

Unoffended, mainly because it was par for the course, Kay smirked. *At least she's consistent.* "Well, have you tried talking to him?" She knew Matthew had, in fact, been gone a lot lately. Matthew owned restaurants and bars. Well, owned them at least for a short while. He obviously always had the funding for and the grand idea of some new incredible nightlife venue; however, they never lasted very long. A party boy does not a successful business owner make.

"He left for Cancun again today. He's opening some new bar there. I'm sure he's also opening some Latina's legs while he's down there as well." Celeste stared at the bubbling, tiered fountain in the middle of the courtyard patio.

"Celeste, in all seriousness, do you even—" The waitress arrived with two fresh mimosas, stopping Kay from finishing the question.

"Here we go." The waitress placed down the drinks. "Can I get you ladies anything else?"

"Yes. You can get us whoever has the pathetic role of manager because the service here is appalling." Celeste cocked her head up at the waitress.

"Oh, Celeste." Kay forced an uncomfortable laugh as she took in the poor waitress's scared face. "She's joking. Don't listen to her. She does that everywhere we go." She gave her cousin a play-nice glare. "Right, Celeste?"

"Hmph." Celeste took a sip of her fresh mimosa. "Just go ahead and bring two more."

"Yes, ma'am." The waitress backed away slowly before quickly turning and heading straight into the interior of the restaurant.

"Don't be a bitch," Kay said plainly.

"I'm not a bitch, you're a bitch," Celeste childishly snipped back.

"Fine, I'm a bitch, but let me finish." She took a deep breath and looked her cousin in the eyes. "Do you even really care if he is cheating?"

"Of course not." Celeste looked almost insulted by the question. "I am not naive, Kay. Matthew's infidelity was inevitable. That being said, it is a slippery slope, especially this early in the game. He is very impressionable. I don't need some south of the border señorita stealing my new last name."

Kay rested her chin in her palm, almost saddened that she was not surprised by what she was hearing. "So, what are you going to do?" she asked meekly.

Celeste pushed her drink away. Lacing her fingers together and spiraling her thumbs, she stared back at the fountain. "Unfortunately," she sighed, "I think I know what I have to do."

Kay strolled into the French Quarter condo to find Wes reclining on the couch watching college football on ESPN. Things had been going so well between them that Wes moved in about a month ago. Kay wasn't quite ready to buy yet when Celeste moved out, and her aunt and uncle were more than happy to be receiving rent for a change. It turns out that Celeste had just been pocketing Kay's rent money and not handing it over to her parents.

"How were drinks?" Wes asked, almost not wanting to know as he turned off the TV.

Kay plopped down beside him and gave him a kiss. "Oh, you know. Celeste was Celeste." She leaned down and pretended to adjust the straps of her sandals. Not looking up and attempting to appear mellow, she said, "She thinks Matthew is cheating on her."

Wes tensed slightly. Trying to hide his assuredness that Celeste was probably right, he asked, "Why does she think that?"

Kay tilted her head at Wes and lifted an eyebrow with a gotcha smirk. She could read him like a cheap dime novel. "I don't know, Wes. Why would she think that?"

He gave a transparent shrug of his shoulders. "Uh-huh," Kay responded with a nod and a now knowing small smile. "Ok, I get it. Ask me no questions, and I'll tell you no lies."

"I'm sure they'll be fine." He propped himself upright and

gave her a kiss. "Subject change. The beach."

"Oh my goodness, I can't wait." Kay and Wes had made plans for a week in Florida as a little getaway. Work had been hectic lately for both of them. Sand and waves seemed like the perfect way to relax.

"I have to go into the office for a little bit tomorrow, but after that, we can just pack and have a lazy Sunday." Wes lovingly tucked Kay's hair behind her ear.

"You have to go in on a Sunday?" She didn't really mind, but normally, if Wes had work to do over the weekends, he did it from home.

"Danny and I have to do a call with Fischer." Fischer was their biggest client, so what Fischer wanted, Fischer got.

"F-ing Fischer." Kay dragged her hand down her porcelain face, mimicking Wes's reaction whenever the name was brought up.

He chuckled. "No work at the beach. I promise."

The next morning, Wes climbed into his Tahoe and headed to the office. He waited for his phone to connect and called Matthew as he pulled out of the parking garage. Matthew was his best friend. Wes knew he was probably having an affair but had no intention of telling Kay, or anyone else for that matter.

"Hello," Matthew answered with a relaxed greeting after two rings.

"You're up early." Wes turned onto the main road.

"Early bird catches the worm, brother."

"Where you at?"

"Back in Cancun. Trying to set up this new location down here." Matthew lounged on a beach chair, watching the morning waves.

Wes swallowed his laugh. "Alright, well, I'll let you get back to it then, but I…just wanted to give you a heads-up."

"Whatcha got?" Matthew sat up and took his sunglasses off.

"Celeste thinks you're stepping out."

After a short pause, Matthew responded, "Uh-huh, and what makes you say that?"

"Kay mentioned it."

"Well, squash that shit." Matthew's temper kicked in rather quickly. "I mean, I dabble, but nothing serious. Not that it would be my fault. She's turned into a total bitch. She's like evil or something."

Wes decided to let his friend vent for a minute. He could hear the wind coming off the ocean on the other end of the phone. "I get it. I get it. Just don't get yourself into something you can't get out of."

"I already have, Wes!" Matthew jumped up from his beach chair and kicked at the damp sand. Apparently, his friend had struck a chord. "I'm stuck dealing with Celeste for the rest of my fucking life! She's just like fucking Juniper! These bitches, all they care about is themselves. Getting what they want and tricking us into going along with it," he barked into the phone. "And you should be careful too, brother. I know you're all in love and shit right now, but Kay's her cousin. She probably has that evil blood in her, too. Don't end up like me."

Back at the condo, Kay laid out swimsuits and summer dresses on her bed. She was tapping her finger to her cheek, thinking about which coverup would go best with which swimsuit, when her cell phone rang. It was her boss.

"Hey." She answered the phone, still contemplating her beach attire.

"Hey. What are you doing?" Paul asked in an overly pleasant tone.

"Just packing. What's up?"

"Kilpatrick just quit," Paul informed her flatly through the phone.

"What?" Kay sat on the bed. Kilpatrick was a fellow analyst with Kay. He and Kay both reported up to Paul. Kilpatrick was meant to be taking the lead this week. "When? Why?"

"Just now, and good riddance. I need you to fly to Denver with me tonight."

"Oh, Paul. I can't. You know I'm going to the beach with Wes this week." She nervously bit her thumbnail.

"I know. And I do feel bad, but you know I wouldn't ask if it wasn't completely necessary." The company Kay worked for was acquiring a small but lucrative company, and the deal was set to go through on Tuesday. They really did need an analyst there to help field the last-minute questions.

"Paul...you're killing me." She gripped the sides of her forehead.

"Kay, I need you to come." Her boss had been good to her over the years. She knew if he was asking her to cancel her vacation, he really needed her to go.

Across town, Danny and Wes stared in disbelief at the phone lying on Danny's office desk.

"Are either of you married?" Fischer's voice came through the speaker in a defeated tone.

Danny ran a wretched hand through his hair and piped up, "No, sir."

"Good. Stay that way." Fischer gave one final order before hanging up.

A blindsided Danny and Wes fearfully looked at each other. Mrs. Fischer had unexpectedly filed for divorce. She was going to get half of everything, including the company that her husband had spent decades building. The company was to be liquidated, and operations would be dissolved immediately. Danny and Wes just lost thirty-five percent of their revenue.

"What are we going to do?" Danny threw his glasses on his desk.

"We are...we are going to be okay," Wes tried to convince himself and his partner as he got up and walked to the window. "We'll just have to hit the pavement for new clients."

Danny nodded, trying to force himself to be positive. "You're right. We just hired that new marketing girl. She's pretty sharp."

Slightly sick to his stomach, Wes offered, "I'm leaving for the beach tomorrow with Kay. I'll have plenty of time to do some research and make some calls. I told her no work, but she'll understand."

"Alright. I'm doing that charity run on Saturday. I know

they have a couple big construction company donors there. I can try to get with them." The two men shared a quiet, mournful moment. Danny finally croaked, "Poor Fischer. Worked all his life for that company. Guess his wife was out for blood."

Wes stared out the window and thought back to his conversation with Matthew. "Maybe she just had evil in her blood."

When Wes got back to the condo, his mind was still spinning. He walked straight to the refrigerator and grabbed a beer. He distractedly headed down the hallway and stopped at the open bedroom door to see a worried-looking Kay sitting on the edge of the bed with her roller bag beside her.

"You're packed already?"

"Umm. You could say that." She gave him a nervous look. He stood there at the bedroom entrance, eyes darting between Kay and her luggage.

"I have to fly out to Denver." She shamefully put her head down.

"When?"

"Tonight." She couldn't look up at him.

"What are you talking about? We're leaving in the morning for the beach." Wes was genuinely baffled.

"Paul called. It's an emergency. I need to be in Denver for the acquisition." She began to scramble. "But maybe I could fly back into Florida by the end of the week and meet you there?"

"You're joking?" Wes's blood boiled. All he wanted to do was go to the beach with his girlfriend. After this morning, part of him wanted to go to prove to himself that Kay wasn't just concerned with her own interests like the other women he had heard about that day. He wanted to prove Matthew and Fischer wrong, but in his mind, Kay had just proven them right.

"I'm going then." He stomped back down the hallway.

"Great!" Kay ran after him. "You should, and as soon as I'm done, I'll fly straight out there and meet you.

"No. I mean, *I'm going, going*." Wes didn't turn around.

He felt like he had finally been let in on a bad joke that everyone got but him. Slamming his beer on the kitchen counter, he stormed to the door.

"Wait, what?" Now she was really scared. Kay desperately wanted to explain. "Wes, I can—"

"Have fun in Denver," he called out as he slung the front door open and walked out without looking back.

Kay watched the door slam behind him, begging it to swing back open. Her begging did no use. She hung her head and put both hands over her eyes with regret. *What on earth was I thinking?*

CHAPTER 7

Desperate For A Dog

In the master bedroom of her and Matthew's home, Celeste flipped through one of her social magazines, absolutely enraged that she was not on a single page. She had to do something. She was being honest when she told Kay that she didn't care if Matthew had women on the side. Her major concern was that one of them would find a way to vex him into leaving her. There had been no prenup, so the money wasn't a concern. Celeste didn't need money, though. She wanted to be a Wells and the notoriety that came with it.

She sat up on the edge of the bed and crossed her legs, twirling her foot. *Think Celeste, think.* She knew what she had to do but just didn't quite know how to go about doing it. She tilted her head down and closed her eyes to focus her thoughts. *Of course. If it worked once, it can work again.* Lifting her head and gazing at her perfect reflection in the large mirror hanging above the dresser, it all came together. *I need another dog.* She stood triumphantly and picked up her cell phone from the dresser.

A distraught Kay was parking her Jeep Cherokee in the New Orleans airport parking lot. She laid both hands on the top of the steering wheel and rested her forehead on them. On the verge of tears, she jumped as her cell phone began to ring. She frantically dug through her purse, which was sitting on the passenger seat. *Please be Wes. Please be Wes.* Instead of Wes, the name that flashed across the screen was the last person she felt like talking to right now.

"What do you want, Celeste?"

"My goodness, darling, try using a little phone etiquette." Celeste was taken aback by her cousin's tone.

"I'm busy. What?"

"I need you to send your boyfriend over. I…" She scanned the room for an excuse. "I have a leak in my ceiling and need him to come fix it."

"Well, given that he just broke up with me, you're going to have to call him yourself." Kay choked up just saying it out loud.

"What? Carl broke up with you?" Celeste tried to sound shocked but was now preoccupied, mentally complimenting herself on her own impeccable timing.

"Yes. I mean, I think. I don't know. Look, I have to go. I'm about to fly to Denver."

"Wait, when will you be back?" She needed more information to make this work.

"I don't know, Celeste, probably not till the end of the week. It's not like I have a boyfriend to rush home to anymore." Kay's eyes began to well up, and she didn't want Celeste to hear her cry. "I have to go." She hung up and slung her phone onto the passenger seat. She stared through the windshield, taking several deep breaths before grabbing her purse. Opening the hatch with hardly any energy, she sadly hauled her suitcase out of the Jeep. Kay slumped and started trudging toward the airport entrance, not noticing that her cell phone was still lying on the passenger seat.

Wes sat in a dingy, smoke-filled bar around the corner from the condo, staring down into his flat beer. It was Tuesday afternoon. He had been drunk since Sunday night. Shortly after he stormed out Sunday afternoon, the shock of the massive mistake he had just made sent him spiraling. *Why the hell would I listen to Matthew and Fischer? What is wrong with me?*

Over the last two days, Wes desperately tried to get in touch with Kay. He called her a dozen times, and she never answered. Finally, her phone went straight to voicemail. *I can't blame her for not wanting to talk to me.* He was pretty deep in self-loathing thoughts when his cell phone rang. He scrambled into his pocket and looked at the screen. It was Celeste. Celeste never called him. He answered instantly.

"Wes! I need you to come over right away." She intentionally used his real name and forced a frightened voice.

"What's wrong? Is it Kay? Is she okay?" Her tone was scaring him.

"Just please hurry!" She hung up before he could say another word.

Ten minutes later, Wes screeched his Tahoe into the driveway of Matthew and Celeste's home. He was hammered and shouldn't have been driving, but when he got the call from Celeste, he threw cash on the bar and ran out as fast as he could. Bolting up to the house, he punched in the code to open the front doors. He raced through the center hall and frantically looked around before yelling, "Celeste?"

"Out here." A warm breeze carried a distant voice into the quiet house from the back patio.

Wes rushed to the double glass doors at the rear of the house to find Celeste in a purple bikini, casually floating on a pool raft. "What is it? What's wrong?" He darted to the side of the pool.

Celeste coolly pulled down her sunglasses and pointed a delicate finger to the far corner of the patio. "There was a snake."

"What?" Wes's adrenaline was still coursing through his body.

"A snake." She kept pointing. "Right over there by that palm tree."

"Are you fucking kidding me?" He didn't know whether to be relieved that Kay wasn't in trouble or furious that Celeste made him worry.

"It hissed at me."

Wes slumped his shoulders as he slightly stumbled to the palm tree and scanned the ground. "Well, it's not here now." Sulking as he sat on the closest pool chair, he dropped his elbows on his knees. He was too mentally and physically exhausted to yell at her. "You know, Celeste, you don't have to make things up for attention. It's okay to just say that you're lonely, too."

"Too?" She tilted her head to the side despite already knowing the "too" he was referring to.

"Kay and I broke up…I think." He put his unshaven face in

his hands. Poor Wes looked like something the cat wouldn't even drag in, and he felt even worse than he looked.

"Oh, Wes." Celeste slowly paddled the raft to the edge of the pool and got out. She didn't bother drying off before slinking over and sitting down next to him on the same pool chair.

"I screwed up. She had work. I made a bigger deal of it than I should have. She won't even answer my calls. And…" he looked down and shook his head.

Celeste took off her sunglasses and draped her arm around him. "Please don't be so hard on yourself, darling. Some things just weren't meant to be." She softly lifted his chin and gazed at him with those big blue eyes. Big blue eyes that looked just like Kay's. Somehow, just being next to her cousin made Wes, in some way, feel closer to her. He desperately wanted to be close to Kay again.

Celeste studied the mess of a man staring into her eyes. She could see that the poor guy really was in pain. It almost made her feel bad for what she was about to do. Almost.

Straight out of the shower the next morning, a nauseated Wes quickly dressed. He grabbed his keys and phone and walked purposefully to his car in the condo's parking garage. He was disgusted with himself. *I am so stupid. I have to fix this. I have to make it right.*

Pulling out of the garage, he headed directly for the Causeway, a 24-mile bridge over Lake Pontchartrain that connected New Orleans to the suburban areas located north of the city. He grabbed his phone from the cupholder and called his old friend Ryan, who now lived on the Northshore. Ryan answered on the first ring.

"Wes Allen. What's up, man? Haven't talked to you in forever."

"Hey, I know. It's been a minute." Wes paused. "Are you in the store today?"

"Headed over there right now. Need something?" Ryan asked curiously.

"Yeah. I'm on the Causeway. I need something…today."

"Today, huh? Okay. For you or someone else?"

"I'll explain when I get there. I'm about thirty minutes out."

"Well, alright then." Ryan was more than happy to help his old buddy. "I'll meet you there."

Wes ended the call and shook his head. *How could I have done this? I have to fix this.* The engine revved as he sped up and pounded the steering wheel with his fist. "Stupid!"

On the other side of the country, Kay was doing the same thing. "Stupid!" She banged her palm against the seat in front of her. The passenger sitting in that seat turned around to give her an offended, yet understandable glare.

"Oh, I am so sorry, sir." She came to her senses. "Won't happen again." She looked out the window of the plane and muttered, "Stupid, stupid, stupid." Kay was on her way back to New Orleans.

"Man trouble?" A blue-haired girl in the middle seat pulled down her oversized headphones. Kay turned to see an apathetic-looking girl in her early twenties with a neck tattoo in French cursive that read, "Tout à du sens au final."

"I think it's more of a me problem than a him problem," Kay admitted a bit too openly. "I just did something really—"

"Stupid? Yeah, I got that part." Blue hair looked Kay up and down. "Dump him. They always screw you over in the end," she haphazardly advised before sliding the headphones back in place and returning to her music.

"But—" Kay started to respond as the pilot came over the intercom.

"I apologize, ladies and gentlemen, but there is some bad weather in the area. We are going to wait for it to blow over and hope to have you in the air shortly."

"Really! Are you kidding me?" a frayed Kay yelled at the speaker overhead.

Blue hair sighed at the dramatic reaction and pulled down her headphones. "Look, lady, do you want a Xanax because I'm not doing this the whole flight."

Kay took a moment to consider the offer. Taking drugs from a random stranger on a plane is not the smartest thing for one to do, but she probably did need to relax a little.

"Yes," she caved with a sigh. "Yes, nice stranger. I would like one of your Xanax, please."

Blue hair leaned down and pulled a prescription bottle from her carry-on bag. She opened it and placed a pill into Kay's shaky hand. Returning the bottle to her bag, she caught a glimpse of the elderly woman in the aisle seat next to her licking her wrinkled lips and eyeing the bottle. Blue hair rattled the pill bottle and gave an offering expression to her newly noticed neighbor.

"Would you mind, dear?" the old woman asked hopefully.

"Fine." Blue hair rolled her eyes. "Here you go, granny." She put a pill in the woman's hand as well.

"Oh, thank you so much."

"Don't mention it. And I mean it, don't mention it. I don't want to hear another word out of either of you for the rest of the flight." She returned the bottle to her bag and headphones to her ears.

The old woman and Kay simultaneously leaned forward and gave each other a nod in unspoken agreement. Kay swallowed her pill with her bottled water. The old woman dry swallowed hers like a pro and reclined her seat back with a contented smile.

Kay hustled into the condo that afternoon after landing and immediately put her cell phone on the charger. Her phone was exactly where she thought she had accidentally left it, still sitting on her passenger seat. Heading straight for the bedroom, she quickly stripped her clothes and replaced her suit with a pair of shorts and tank top. She scurried back through the condo, searching for signs of life. She couldn't tell if Wes had been there the past few days or not. Just as Kay reached for her phone to see if it had enough battery to make a call, the front door opened.

"You're back?" a startled Wes said excitedly.

"You're back, too?" Kay said with equal excitement. They had both momentarily forgotten that they may or may not be broken up.

Wes shuffled his feet and slid the bag he was holding behind his back. "I never left."

"You didn't?" Kay gave a sad but encouraged smile.

"I tried to call you." Wes stayed a few feet inside the door. He shifted his weight and attempted to start a sentence quite a few times before eventually breaking down. "Kay, I'm so sorry. I shouldn't have blown up like that. I messed up. I made a huge mistake. Please, please forgive me." He looked absolutely miserable.

Kay ran up to him and threw her arms around him. "No, I'm sorry. I should have talked to you first. That wasn't right of me. I'm the one that messed up." They held each other and kissed in between "I'm sorry" and "No, I'm sorry." It suddenly felt like it had all just been a bad dream. Like the past few days never even happened. That was something they both desperately wanted. Finally releasing one another, Kay's hand snagged on the bag Wes was carrying when he walked in.

"What's this?" she asked, now feeling so happy that everything was going to be alright.

"Well, I…I didn't think you were going to be back so soon." He put his head down, embarrassed. "I hadn't really come up with a plan yet."

"A plan for what?" A small dose of fear returned to Kay as Wes reached into the bag and pulled something out.

"Wait, what is it? You're scaring—"

Wes shyly smiled and slowly knelt down on one knee. His hopeful eyes looked up at Kay as he opened a small ring box. She gasped and put her right hand over her mouth as Wes took her left.

The newly engaged couple lovingly cuddled under the covers together in bed that night. Despite being emotionally drained, they were both too wound up to sleep. Going from breaking up to being engaged within a short seventy-two hours was pretty exhausting.

"I'm so happy." Kay nuzzled into Wes's chest.

"Me, too." He held her tight. "Do you like it?"

"I love it." She raised her hand to admire the beautiful diamond ring.

"You know who else is going to be pretty happy?"

"Everyone. Because this is the best news ever." She bounced under the covers like a giddy teenager.

Wes chuckled. "That is true, but I meant Danny, especially."

"Why Danny?"

"I went to his place when I left here Sunday. He told me I was a complete jackass. When I told him you weren't answering the phone, he said if I didn't get my jackass on a plane to Denver to find you, he would kick it."

"Really? Sweet Danny said that? Awww, he is such a good guy." The thought of gentle Danny squaring up to anything more than overcomplicated spreadsheets made her giggle.

Kay suddenly popped up on her knees with an idea. "We should get everyone together to celebrate. We can make calls tomorrow and meet at the pub or something Friday night."

Wes found his new fiancée's excitement adorable. He pulled her close. "I think that's a great idea."

She affectionately grazed her hand over his chest and then up to his face. "And what is this? A breakup beard?"

"I guess you can call it a betrothed beard now." He squeezed his bride-to-be before scraping his hand along his jawline. "I was kind of a wreck after you left. I haven't shaved in a couple of days."

Kay admired the stubble. "Do you have red in your beard?

"Yeah. It gets like this when I grow it out." He rubbed his stubbly cheek against her soft one.

"Well, I like it. I think you should keep it. Who knew my future husband was secretly a ginger."

CHAPTER 8

Desperate For Another Dog

When Celeste hung up the phone with Kay the next afternoon, she wanted to slam it against the wall. The engagement of Wes and Kay had most certainly thrown a bit of a monkey wrench into her plans. She stood in the center hall and crossed her arms, incensed by the current turn of events. Her blonde bob suddenly ticked to the side as another idea occurred to her. *No matter. New dog, old trick.* She checked the time on the phone that was still in her hand. *Perfect*, she thought. *It's her nap time. She won't be able to tell them no.*

Gauge rushed to the landline phone in the parlor of the Wells estate. This was the time of day that Juniper rested. He didn't want to risk the ringing phone disturbing her.

"Wells residence," Gauge welcomed the caller.

"Gauge or Logan?" Celeste tried to sound pleasant.

"Yes, ma'am, this is Gauge." He recognized the voice but couldn't quite place it.

"Oh, hello, Gauge. This is Celeste Wells. How are you?"

Gauge's head slightly pulled back in surprise. *She never calls here.* "Uh, I'm well, ma'am. Unfortunately, Ms. Juniper is resting right now. Would you like me to leave a message that you called?"

"Actually, I need a favor from either you or Logan." She looked around the center hall of her home for yet another excuse. "I purchased a large piece of art recently, and it was just delivered. I was hoping to have it hung before Matthew returns from his business trip. Could one of you come over and help me? I really would like to surprise Matthew. It would mean a lot to him."

Gauge nervously looked across the room to his brother,

who responded with a curious expression. He knew Juniper would not like this. "Umm, sure, Ms. Celeste. Logan and I are changing out fan blades right now, but one of us can swing by in a bit to help you."

"Oh, wonderful. I really do appreciate it. I'll be home the rest of the afternoon, so feel free to stop by any time."

"Will do, Ms. Celeste. Goodbye." After hanging up the phone, Gauge stared at the receiver, perplexed. *Huh. That's weird.*

Kay and Wes made excited and well-received calls to friends and family over the next two days. An open invitation was extended to anyone who could make it for impromptu celebratory drinks at the Carousel Bar in the Monteleone Hotel Friday night to toast their recent engagement.

A little after eight o'clock Friday night, Celeste admired her reflection in the bathroom mirror as she carefully applied lip gloss. *One more dog should do it. Hopefully.* She blew herself a confident kiss before heading across the empty house and into the garage with her car keys. Opening the driver's door, she slid into her silver Mercedes convertible. Sitting in the driver's seat, she held onto the gear shift and ever so slightly adjusted it out of park. She put the keys into the ignition and attempted to start the engine, which resulted in nothing more than a pathetic clicking sound. Smiling proudly, she closed the door to her Mercedes and returned to the house to call for a car.

Thunder rumbled through the night sky as Celeste's cab pulled up to the Monteleone just before nine that night. She glided through the hotel lobby and into the Carousel Bar. A small group of Kay and Wes's friends were gathered at the bar, chatting and laughing. *Ugh. Dirt people*, she thought before begrudgingly striding up to Kay.

"Hey!" Kay was on cloud nine and beamed at her cousin. "Is Matthew back in town yet?" She looked over Celeste's shoulder for Wes's friend.

"He comes back Monday." Celeste cast a seemingly uninterested glance around. "Where's Carl?"

"Right here," Kay giggled as she turned and extended

her left hand, allowing her new diamond to glitter under the sparkly lights. She placed it on the shoulder of Wes's turned back. "May I steal him for a minute," she politely requested from the gentleman Wes was in conversation with. "Honey, come greet your future in-law." He smiled as he turned to Kay before, unfortunately, realizing who his bride-to-be was referring to, causing the smile to turn into a bit of a sneer. Celeste had no problem snidely squinting back at him.

"Hello, Celeste."

"Carl, you sound much better than the last time we spoke."

He winced and tried to appear unfazed. "It's called not being hammered drunk. Something you might want to try before lunch."

"When did you guys talk?" Kay distractedly asked as she waved her left hand at a friend across the room.

"Well, you sounded so distraught when we spoke, dear cousin, I decided to intervene on your behalf." She flashed a cat-that-ate-the-canary grin to Wes. "You are so obliviously, I mean obviously, in love with and loyal to Carl. I took it upon myself to phone him."

"You did?" Kay looked at Celeste, baffled, and immediately swirled her head to Wes. "She did?" Her new fiancé kept his jaw tight and slowly nodded.

"He was equally as distraught, I must tell you. But don't you worry, I made sure to comfort him."

"You did?" Kay again looked at Celeste, baffled, and again swirled her head to Wes. "She did?" Wes also repeated his response, attempting to contain the escalating urge to sew Celeste's mouth shut with a rusty fishing hook.

"My goodness, Celeste. I…I…" Kay didn't know how to react to an act of kindness from her cousin. "Thank you. That was really…nice of you."

"Oh, he was practically begging for it." She waved a dismissive hand and slid her blue eyes to Wes's stern face. "Comforting, of course."

"I'm going to go get you ladies a drink. I'm sure Celeste is already going into withdrawals from the ride over here."

"Oh, thank you, sweetie. Wow, look at me, surrounded by all these considerate people. How did I get so lucky?" Kay gave her fiancé an adoring peck on the lips. Fuming, Wes walked away, and Kay hushed her voice to her cousin. "He really sounded distraught?"

Celeste smirked. "Like wounded prey."

"And just what foolish men would leave two such beautiful women unattended?" Danny playfully questioned as he strolled up to Kay and Celeste.

"Daniel, so good to see you." Celeste gave him an uncharacteristically warm hug and a kiss on the cheek. "You look terrific."

"You are too kind, Mrs. Wells." A taken aback yet flattered Danny blushed at her greeting. Celeste was surprising everyone this evening.

"Unfortunately, future Mrs. Allen"—he turned his attention to Kay—"I have to go."

"Oh no, so soon. Why?" Kay was a little disappointed.

"I have to run in this charity 5K tomorrow and should probably get as much rest as I can so I don't end up being runner roadkill." He stretched his hamstring as he spoke, already nervous about making a fool of himself.

"Well, good for you. I don't run unless it's from something," Kay joked.

"Daniel?" Celeste saw her opportunity. "If you're leaving now, would you mind giving me a lift? My car wouldn't start this evening, and I had to take a cab here."

A bewildered Kay balked at her cousin. "But you literally just got here."

"I know, but who knows how long you will be entertaining, and I really don't feel comfortable riding in a cab alone at night. Crime has gotten so bad these days."

What are you up to? Kay tried to read her cousin's thoughts. She was beginning to question Celeste's unusual pleasantness.

"It would be my pleasure. It's on the way to my place anyway. I can take a look at your car when I'm there if you'd like. I'm more of a AAA kind of guy, but I can give it a shot."

"That would be perfect," Celeste gushed before turning to Kay, about as fake as zero-calorie bologna. "Please extend my congratulations to your fiancé."

"Bye, Kay. Congrats again." Danny naively smiled as he and Celeste made their way to the front of the hotel.

"Ah-ha," Danny exclaimed, extremely pleased with himself. "I know exactly what the problem is." He was sitting in the driver's seat of Celeste's Mercedes.

"Oh dear. Is it bad?" She leaned into the car, intentionally giving Danny's shoulder a good brush with her chest.

"Not at all. You just didn't have it all the way in park. I did the same thing a while back. See?" Danny put the keys in the ignition, and with a turn, the car started right up.

"Oh, thank goodness." Celeste played the part of rescued damsel in distress quite well as she placed a hand over her heart. "I guess I must have been distracted. So much to do with Matthew being gone for so long. Thank you so much, Daniel."

"Not a problem." Danny got out of the car, happy to have helped, and handed Celeste the keys after closing the door. "Well, guess I better head out now."

"Oh, I can't let you go empty-handed after being so kind. Why don't you come in for a drink?" Celeste fanned him with her long eyelashes. "For old times' sake?" She threw on the last bit to tug at Danny's well-known softer side. It had only been eight short months since she stomped all over his heart in her stilettos and tossed him aside for Matthew.

Danny began to feel a bit uneasy. Sure, he still held a candle for the gorgeous woman standing before him, but that gorgeous woman was now his good friend's gorgeous wife. "I would, but really should get some rest tonight," he stammered as he started shifting toward the open garage door. Suddenly, as if Celeste had planned it herself, the sky appeared to open, cascading down heavy sheets of rain.

"Oh my." Celeste skipped to his side and tugged at his elbow. "Daniel, I simply refuse to let you go out in this. I would die if you got in an accident because you came to my aid. Just come in until it blows over."

Feeling a little torn, Danny pressed his lips together hesitantly. "Okay, I guess you're right. Just until it blows over."

The next morning, Danny was deep in thought as he jogged with the other racers down Decatur Street. He tried to stay focused on his breathing and pace, but his mind was elsewhere. Elsewhere being a place that his mind should never have been. Fellow runners weaved around him, renewing his concentration momentarily, but his thoughts kept returning to last night. His mind was racing faster than he was.

In his haze, Danny didn't notice one of New Orleans' notorious crater-sized potholes directly in his path. The ones that total cars, let alone a distracted runner. Two steps later, Danny's right foot landed squarely in the awaiting pothole, throwing off his balance. He skidded face down on the ground with a crunch as his glasses went flying onto the street.

"Oh my goodness! Are you ok?" Another racer ran to his side and bent down next to him.

Danny stumbled to his feet. "I think so." Disoriented, he tried to take a step but was met with a sharp pain radiating into his ankle.

"Here." A woman propped herself under Danny's shoulder and shuffled him to the curb. "Sit here. Let me find a medic."

"Oh no. I'm okay. Thank you so much. I…I… Do you see my glasses anywhere? I'm practically blind without them." An embarrassed Danny squinted as he scanned the street, which was nothing but a black blur.

"Right here." The woman, who was also just a blur to Danny at this point, ran and grabbed the glasses from the road. She held them up for inspection and wiped the lens off on her tank top. "It doesn't look like they're broken at all." She knelt in front of Danny and gently placed them on his flushed face.

"Thank you. Thank you." Danny blinked a few times and, with clear vision, looked up to see one of the most breathtaking women he had ever laid spectacled eyes on.

"Stay here." The beautiful woman ran to an aide station about twenty feet away and quickly ran back with two cold water bottles. She was tall and tan with a long brown ponytail that swished back and forth with each step. She sat down next to him on the curb. "Here, put these on your ankle until we can get you some ice."

"Thank you so much." Danny rested the two cold bottles on his ankle with a wince.

Feeling the urgency of the situation subside, the woman looked at him with warm, big brown eyes crowned with naturally thick dark lashes and asked sweetly, "So, what's your name, soldier?"

"Danny." He held both bottles with his left hand and extended his right.

"Nice to meet you. I'm Heather. That's quite a spill you took there, Danny." Her arms shimmered with sweat as she took in her handsome patient.

"I'll be alright. I think my pride took the brunt of it." He chuckled at his own roadkill foresight. "Thank you again for stopping. I'd probably still be in the middle of the street crawling on all fours looking for my glasses if you hadn't."

She laughed. "Don't worry. I've fallen plenty of times." She pointed to a scar on her perfectly curved knee.

"Do you run a lot?" Danny saw a chance to keep his lovely rescuer talking.

"All the time. Gotta keep the pounds off." Danny looked at Heather, perplexed by her response after having already viewed her perfect figure. She smirked at his expression. "I own a catering company, and let's just say I love to taste test. Gotta balance it out somehow."

"Oh, that's great." The guilt of derailing Heather's run crept up on him. "You've been so helpful. I guess you should get back to the race. I don't want to keep you."

"Hmm, well, speaking of taste testing, I supply some goodies to this little café around the corner. How about we go over there, and you can give them a try? I'm sure they'll have some ice for that ankle of yours." She smiled at Danny's glasses, which he had already smudged. "Besides, I can't leave you in this condition. No soldier left behind, right?"

Monday night, Matthew parked his Escalade in the garage. He gave a heavy sigh before pulling himself out of the car. Matthew was not looking forward to the icy reception he was about to receive from his wife. He opened the door that led into the house with his luggage in tow.

"I'm home," he called out.

"In the kitchen," Celeste rang back.

Matthew dragged his feet as he walked into the kitchen and then suddenly stopped. "What the hell are you doing?"

He was shocked as he looked around the barely-cooked-in kitchen. White crayons got more use than his stove.

"Cooking!" Celeste sang from the pantry. She jogged over to Matthew and threw her arms around him. He was bewildered not only by the cooking but also by his wife's enthusiasm to see him. "I missed you so much." Celeste pulled back and looked at him lovingly. "You must be exhausted. Have a seat. I'll get you a drink." She scooted off to pour him a whiskey.

Matthew was very confused. Who was this pleasant woman cooking in his kitchen, and where was his wife? He pulled out a barstool from the kitchen island and rested his large, sunburned body, still wondering what exactly was going on.

"Here you go." Celeste handed him a bourbon and followed it with a kiss on the cheek. She circled the island and returned to the lasagna that she strategically planned to be working on when her husband got home.

"So, how was your trip?" she asked brightly.

"Fine." Matthew rubbed the scruff on his face. "Everything's different down there. It takes a lot longer to get things done." He hoped she would buy his story.

"Awww, I'm so sorry. I know how hard you work." She gave him a sympathetic look.

Matthew suddenly felt a little guilty and was eager to change the subject. He looked at the casserole dish. "So, cooking huh? I didn't know I was married to Emeril Lagasse." He gave a teasing smile.

Celeste faked a laugh. "Well, I wouldn't go quite that far, but I assumed you were going to be pretty tired of tacos, so I wanted to make you something special. Remember we had that wonderful lasagna in Vegas?"

Matthew softened a bit at the memory. "I do," he replied with a nod. "I'm sure yours will be even better." He genuinely was appreciative of the gesture and definitely tired of tacos. "So, what have you been up to this week?" He took a swig of his whiskey.

Celeste slid the lasagna into the oven and gave an exaggerated sigh. "Oh dear. Well, it was pretty hectic to tell you the truth." She turned to face Matthew with doe eyes.

"Really, why is that?" He took another swig of his drink.

"Well, first, there was a snake."

Big Matthew jumped a little and scanned the kitchen floor nervously as if the snake might be slithering by his feet.

"Don't worry. Wes scared it off." Celeste waved.

"Wes?" He gave his wife a puzzled look.

"Well, you weren't here, and I didn't know who else to call. I was really scared." More doe eyes ensued.

"Hmmm." He was slightly thrown by this. "I guess I'm glad he could help out then."

"And then I got one of the new pieces of art in and wanted to have it up by the time you got home." She pointed toward the center hall. "But I couldn't lift it, so one of the twins came by and helped me hang it."

"What? How did you—"

"I called over to your mother's to ask. You know how she can be." Celeste gave him a knowing look. "Honestly, I don't know if it was Gauge or Logan. I can never tell them apart. I think the poor boy was happy to take a break from whatever ridiculous to-do list she had for him."

Even though he was thrown by the fact that not one but two men had been in his home to come to the aid of his wife, Matthew did understand the need to take a break from Juniper.

"And then"—throwing her hands up with laughter—"my car wouldn't start. Can you believe it? Daniel came over and fixed it, though. I just didn't have it all the way in park."

"Danny came over and fixed your car?" Matthew was now trying to hide his sense of indignation. *You are my wife. No one should be taking care of you other than me. No one should be petting my tiger.*

Celeste gave herself a mental pat on the back. She knew what she was doing, and she was doing it pretty darn well. "Well, it's all taken care of now, so no need to worry," she said dismissively and glanced back at the oven. "This won't be ready for another thirty minutes. Why don't you go take a warm shower, and we can have a nice cozy dinner." She sauntered up to him and gave him a deep kiss on the lips.

"Sure." Matthew was now distracted by the events of his absence and was feeling a little emasculated. "I won't be long."

"Take your time, darling. We have all night." She gave him a suggestive wink. A very mentally preoccupied Matthew headed for the master bedroom. Once he was out of sight, Celeste coolly strode to the oven and turned the temperature as high as it would go.

Half an hour later, Matthew dressed in the bedroom. His shower had been much longer than usual. Thoughts of jealousy mixed with possessiveness kept churning in his head. He was the man of this house. He didn't need anyone else tending to his manly duties.

As he and his bruised ego exited the bedroom, Matthew was immediately met with the strong smell of something burning. "Celeste!" he yelled out as he ran to the kitchen. Gray smoke was seeping through the edges of the oven. He grabbed a towel from the counter and yanked open the oven door, wafting a cloud of smoke into his face. The casserole dish melted through the dish towel into Matthew's hand as he threw it into the sink, causing it to shatter.

Celeste ran into the kitchen. "Oh my God!" she screeched. Matthew threw the faucet on, and the stream sizzled over the burnt lasagna and shards of porcelain. They both began coughing and waving the smoke away from their faces. Celeste ran to Matthew. "Are you alright? Did you burn yourself? I'm so sorry. I went to the patio. I didn't realize—" She hugged Matthew and immediately burst into tears. Matthew had never seen his wife cry.

"It's okay. It's okay, Celeste." He held her tightly and rubbed her back. She was shaking.

"Thank God you were here. I could have burned the whole house down." She pulled back and looked up at him with tears streaming down her face. "You've been working so hard. I just wanted to do something nice for you."

Matthew pulled her back to his chest.

"I'm so sorry," Celeste wept. "I don't know what I'd do without you."

This pulled at Matthew's heartstrings while simultaneously rejuvenating his ego. He was his wife's protector. He was here when she needed saving. Matthew flexed his arms as he squeezed Celeste even tighter. So tight he couldn't feel her slyly grinning into his chest.

Three weeks later, Juniper sat at the large oak desk in her study, practically spitting fire into the antique rotary phone she used to receive all her calls. She slammed it down onto the receiver, filling the room with a resounding clang.

"Camille!" Juniper's cry echoed throughout the mansion.

Elodie was all too accustomed to constant cries for attention from Juniper, but this one seemed a bit more alarmed. Mid-sentence, she slung down the book she was reading and dashed up the stairs. "Juniper! You alright?" Elodie yelled as she ran down the hall to the study. She halted at the open door to see Juniper sitting in her silk day robe, aggressively drumming her fingers on her desk and glaring at the phone.

"Juniper," Elodie calmly repeated as she eyed her cautiously. "You alright?" The room felt slightly eerie as she took a few hesitant steps toward the desk. Juniper slowly raised her eyes.

"The wench is with child!"

"Noooo." Elodie put a flabbergasted hand over her heart and sat to steady herself. She knew exactly what wench Juniper was referring to.

"Yes," Juniper wailed. "Matthew just phoned to tell me." She threw her head back against her executive chair.

"Here." Elodie jumped up and handed Juniper the hand fan lying on the desk.

"Thank you," Juniper choked as she began feverishly fanning herself. Elodie returned to her seat, still in a state of shock.

"What are we going to do, Camille?" Juniper rose and began pacing the study as the oscillating fans fluttered her robe with each unnerved step.

"Oh, Juniper. I don't think there is much you can do at this point. The deed has been done, dahlin'." Elodie tried to console her honestly. She did feel bad for Juniper at receiving this unforeseen news. Once she had quickly broken her employer of the fan strikes to her wrist, the two had become quite fond of one another. Deep down, she knew that Juniper wasn't as evil as everyone made her out to be, so she felt comfortable posing the question, "Are you…are you perhaps maybe even a little happy about having a grandbaby?"

Juniper stopped dead in her tracks. "Are you mad?" She looked at Elodie seriously, causing the question to be momentarily regretted. "I am absolutely elated," Juniper honestly stated as she went back to pacing and fanning. "I just do not want my grandchild to have some scheming streetwalker for a mother. I don't like it!"

Juniper flopped back onto her executive chair with a dramatic groan. She pensively tapped her finger to her lips as she always did when floating off into thought. "I need a drink," she suddenly concluded.

"It's ten in the morning, Juniper." Elodie raised a disparaging eyebrow at her.

"I am aware of the time!"

Elodie stood to prepare the cocktail with a scolding look. Just as she turned down the hallway, Juniper called yet again, "Camille!" Elodie poked her head back into the study. "Make one for yourself as well. We have a lot of planning to do."

CHAPTER 9

Desperate To Wed

Kay stood on the balcony of her honeymoon suite, breathing in the salty ocean breeze. She desperately needed this. It had been six months since Wes proposed. Much to the couple's dismay upon initiating wedding planning, available wedding dates for most of the local churches were more than a year out. When Saint Joseph's called to say they had an unfortunate cancellation, Kay jumped at the chance. Despite the obvious insanity of planning a wedding in such a short timeframe, she was able to pull together quite the exquisite event.

Wes and Kay arrived in Exuma in the Bahamas late yesterday afternoon for their honeymoon. Unfortunately, only Wes and Kay arrived, not their luggage. Making a mental note that she really needed to start using another airline, Kay knotted the belt of her resort robe and sat on one of the lounge chairs on the balcony. She leaned her head back and exhaled. *It feels so good to finally relax.* Just as she got comfortable, her cell phone began to ring from inside the room.

"Damn it." She left her momentary tranquility to retrieve the phone. It was an incoming call from none other than her cousin. "Double damn it."

"Yes, Celeste," Kay moaned.

"I thought we discussed the issue of your phone etiquette." Celeste was lying in bed with feet propped up, gently rubbing her growing belly. Now six months pregnant, she was not enjoying her swollen ankles and continually expanding waistline.

"My apologies. How are you, dear cousin?" Kay sarcastically corrected and returned to her lounge chair.

"Where are you?"

"Where do you think I am? I'm on my honeymoon. Remember, I got married Saturday." Kay slid on her sunglasses. "Not that you *would* remember. You didn't even come to the reception."

"Excuse me. I am with child. I am nauseous enough as it is. I am quite sure the mere smell of the fried nutria rat that you probably served would have sent me into immediate dry heaves."

"It was Chicken Marsala, and it was delicious." Kay defended her menu choice. "Even your mother-in-law said so." Juniper was, in fact, in attendance at the wedding but did not comment on the food, only that Kay's hair was still the color of bloody fecal matter, and she didn't like it.

"Nice try, trash. You know she doesn't eat in public." A bored Celeste frowned at her puffy feet. "Anyway, what are you doing?"

"Well, I was trying to relax before we go swimming with the pigs."

There was a long pause before Celeste finally questioned, "Excuse me?"

Kay sighed and tried to keep the explanation as short as possible. "We're in Exuma. There is this island with pigs, and they come out into the ocean and swim with you."

Another long pause. "Well, I'm sure the pigs will be pleased to see one of their kind."

Kay pulled down her sunglasses and relented with a smirk. "Alright, well, I guess I kind of walked into that one," she admitted. "Do you want to tell me what you really want now?"

"Who was that…person with Daniel at your wedding?"

"Who? Do you mean Heather? That's his girlfriend. They've been dating for a while now. I think it's pretty serious. I guess you wouldn't know that either because you've been in hiding ever since you've become *with child*."

"Well, I think she's fat," Celeste stated.

"She's not fat. The girl runs marathons, for goodness' sake. She's probably the same size as you…well, the same size you used to be."

"She's fat," Celeste huffed. "She even has the word *eat* in her name."

Kay looked upward as she silently spelled Heather's name,

only to realize Celeste's observation was correct. Not bad for someone who only passed English Lit due to a tawdry affair with the professor. "Anyway, she's not fat. She is very nice. She has her own catering company. She even catered the reception for me, and Danny likes her very much. So, you just leave her alone."

"I can't say that I'm surprised you defend her unfortunate size," Celeste snipped. "You pigs all swim together."

Kay reminded herself that she was on her honeymoon and didn't feel like dealing with a revolving door of insults. "Well, I must be going, dear cousin. Enjoy slathering yourself in cocoa butter." She ended the call without another word and released a deep, relaxing breath.

Just as Kay was attempting to return to her tranquility, she heard the door to the suite open. Wes walked in wearing his shorts and polo from yesterday, carrying two resort gift shop bags. "Alright, so it was pretty slim pickings down there." He laid the bags on the rumpled white comforter of the bed. "But I got toothbrushes and some clothes for us to wear today."

"Perfect. Thank you, husband." Kay kissed him on the cheek before reaching into one of the bags. She giggled as she held up her newly purchased oversized neon pink T-shirt. "I can be ready in ten, and we can—" Kay dropped the shirt onto the bed. "Shit." A panicked look spread across her face.

"What?" Wes became a little alarmed at her sudden change in mood. "Is it the shirt? That was the only size they had. We can pick something else up when we go into town."

She turned to him still with a bit of panic in her eyes. "I was about to get ready."

"Okay," Wes responded carefully, not knowing whether he was in trouble or not.

"I always take my birth control when I get ready." Kay started to pace in front of the bed.

Still confused, Wes watched his new bride chew on her thumbnail as she walked back and forth. "I'm kind of lost here, Kay. You're going to have to help me out."

"My birth control is in my luggage." She stopped to look him in the eyes for a moment and immediately went back to pacing.

"Oh." Now he understood. "Oh well." An unaffected Wes

sat on the bed and began pulling out the rest of the contents from the bags.

"What do you mean, oh well? I could get—" She stopped her nervous mini-parade and cocked her head as she looked at him. "What *do* you mean by, oh well?"

Wes shrugged. "I mean, oh well." He didn't stop pulling the contents out of the bags.

"Sooo, you mean oh well, oh well?" Kay was trying to determine if he meant he didn't care or if he meant this was a blessing in disguise.

Wes cleared his throat and said, "I mean…you know, oh well." He was clearly removing the items from of the bags intentionally slowly so as not to have to make eye contact.

"We…we haven't talked about, oh well. You do know what, oh well, means, right?" She was trying to be as clear as this limited-word conversation would allow.

Wes finally looked up and gave her a small patronizing smile. "Yes, Kay. I know what, oh well, means."

Kay's body straightened as she took a sharp inhale and pursed her lips. After a moment of tossing her head from side to side in thought, she yielded. "Okay, so we're oh welling it then?"

"Yep, we're oh welling it," Wes replied stoically. They both blushed slightly at each other with almost shy eyes for a moment. "Besides, it's not like I'm going to be able to resist you when you're wearing that." Wes pointed at the extra-large neon pink T-shirt with a cartoon pig sporting sunglasses and a big grin printed across the chest.

Three months later, Matthew and Celeste welcomed a healthy baby boy into the world, Charles Edward Wells. A short six months after little Charles's birth, his cousin, Thomas Robert Allen, made his debut as well.

CHAPTER 10

Desperate To Fix It

I am a terrible mother. Kay's old jeep idled as she waited for school to let out in the pick-up line. She pulled forward and an overly enthusiastic teacher yelled, "Allen!" Red-eyed, sniffling little Tommy stood up from the group of waiting children sitting safely against the building and shuffled toward his mother's car.

"Hey, buddy."

"Hi, Mommy." A somber Tommy closed the car door and snapped himself into his car seat. Kay could hear his sniffles.

"You ok?" She looked at her son in the rearview mirror as she pulled away from the school.

"I…" His voice started to quiver. "I got in trouble at school today, Mommy."

"I know, honey. Ms. Wolf called me."

Tommy's kindergarten teacher phoned Kay earlier that day because she needed to discuss an issue that occurred at lunch. Tommy used the *f-word*. "Yes, Mrs. Allen, the f-word." Apparently, when Kay's sweet little boy dropped his lunch tray in the cafeteria, he dropped an f-bomb with it.

Poor Tommy started to cry. "I'm sorry, Mommy."

"Oh, Tommy." Kay frowned. "Where did you hear that word?" Kay knew exactly where he had heard that word: from her. After Tommy was born, Kay's boss agreed to let her work remotely from home and travel just one week out of the month. It limited her growth potential in the company, but traveling constantly with an infant wasn't realistic.

Working from home definitely had its perks, but it did require Kay to be on the phone a lot. Most of her conversations were with the branch managers at her company's various locations. The branch managers were normally good ole boys who thought any word that had more than four letters was high falutin. In an effort to make the managers more comfortable, Kay mirrored their communication style, which unfortunately led to her now having a very colorful vocabulary.

Tommy wiped his nose on his wrist and shrugged. "I don't know."

"You heard it from Mommy, didn't you?" Kay gave him a guilty look in the rearview mirror, and he hung his head. "When Mommy was on one of her work calls?"

"I'm sorry, Mommy."

Kay wanted to start crying right along with him as she pulled into the driveway of their new home. She parked the car and turned around to face her puffy-eyed little boy.

"How old are you, Tommy?"

Tommy looked up at Kay, a little confused by the question. "I'm five years old, Mommy."

"Okay, so that means you'll be eighteen in thirteen years." Tommy nodded, but Kay was pretty sure kindergarten math hadn't gotten him that far yet. "Well, when you're eighteen, you're an adult. You're considered a grown-up." Tommy listened intently to his mother. "The word you used today was a very grown-up word, and you're not a grown-up yet. You still have thirteen more years to go." Kay gave her son a comforting smile. "How about I promise not to use any grown-up words like that at all until *you* are a grown-up, too?"

His little hazel eyes widened. "Ok, Mommy. I promise, too. I won't say those words either."

"Then we have ourselves a deal." Kay stretched her right hand to the backseat. Tommy grabbed it with his little hand, and they shook on it.

"Deal, Mommy."

"So, this looks pretty bad." Danny tapped the end of his pen on his desk. He and Wes were going over projections for the rest of the fiscal year.

"I know." Wes put his elbows on his knees and lowered his head. Business was not good. Wes and Danny's firm never fully got back on its feet after losing the Fischer account seven years ago. The current economy didn't make matters any better. With the recent downturn, people just weren't building. Architects needed people to build to survive.

"We're going to have to make some cuts," Danny mournfully said as he tossed his glasses on the desk and rubbed his eyes.

"I know," Wes repeated. "I don't think that will even be enough, though." The two men sat in quiet despair for a moment.

"The timing couldn't be worse." Danny shook his head. "Heather wants to start fertility treatments. And those do not come cheap." Danny and Heather married three years ago. They truly were happy, but frustration had crept into their blissful union. A year into marriage, they had decided to start a family. Unfortunately, getting pregnant proved harder than expected. After unsuccessfully trying for a year, Heather and Danny met with a fertility doctor. A battery of tests ensued, only to have the doctor assure them they were both perfectly capable of having children. Sadly, though, they were still childless.

Wes gave Danny a weak supportive smile. "That's great, man. I know it works for a lot of people."

"Well, the way these numbers look"—Danny shook his head again as he scrolled through the spreadsheet on his laptop—"that won't be happening anytime soon."

"Yeah. I might have overextended a bit on the new house." Wes rubbed his forehead. "It's been pretty tight lately."

Danny took a deep breath. "So, what are we going to do?"

Wes stood up and walked to the window as he always did. He leaned his palm against the glass and looked down to see the wind carrying a discarded Styrofoam daiquiri cup down the street below. "I might be able to come up with something," he replied almost morbidly.

"Same. I might have an option. Just not sure if it will work." An overwhelmed Danny closed his laptop. "We'll figure it out. We always do." He gave a heavy sigh. "I could use a drink. Want to grab a beer?"

Wes pushed back from the glass. "Yeah. We can deal with this shit on Monday."

Elodie never snooped. Over the past eight years, she and Juniper had become so close it would have felt like a betrayal. She really did care for the "crazy old bitch," not because she had to, but because she wanted to. Elodie was sad that her friend's health was not in the best shape as of late, though. Juniper needed a hip replacement badly. However, she emphatically refused to have the surgery until just after Charlie's birthday. Juniper wouldn't miss her grandson's birthday for the world but also didn't like the idea of missing carnival season either. She knew if she scheduled it just right, she would be able to be there for Charlie on his birthday and have just enough recovery time to still be the most revered attendee at every old money ball Mardi Gras had to offer.

Now, even though Elodie never snooped, as she approached Juniper's study on that Friday afternoon for their usual cocktail hour, she couldn't help but overhear.

"That is correct." Juniper pulled the sleeve of her silk day robe up and rested her elbow on the arm of her executive chair, holding the rotary phone to her ear. Elodie knew better than to interrupt Juniper when she was on the phone, so she waited quietly in the hallway.

"Of course, that is what I want." Juniper felt her annoyance growing as she listened to the person on the other end of the phone rattle on. "Stop." She cut off whoever was talking. "One million for the specified parties, the rest to Charlie, and the physical items to the named persons." Juniper allowed the person on the phone to ask a question. "Fine, an annual three hundred and fifty thousand allotment until he's twenty-one, but then the rest is his."

Elodie did feel a bit guilty for accidentally listening to Juniper's conversation but couldn't help but continue her unintended eavesdropping. "Good." Juniper sounded like she was pleased with the caller's response. "You're picking up the present tomorrow, correct?" Apparently, her question was met with another pleasing response because the ends of Juniper's mouth turned up before saying, "Wonderful. I'll see you and Gauge around one tomorrow afternoon. Tell him I will speak to him about the other matter then." She placed the phone on the receiver and leaned back in her chair with a sense of accomplishment.

Elodie stood in the hallway, trying to piece together what she had just heard. *Did she just change her—* Elodie's thought was cut short by Juniper's voice. "Camille!"

She silently counted to ten and walked into the study with the two drinks. "Don't get your panties in a wad, you old crow. I'm here." She handed Juniper her drink and sat in her usual spot on the chaise lounge adjacent to the oversized desk.

Juniper took a sip and winced. "This is warm." She held up the glass and inspected it.

Elodie felt herself flush but was slightly relieved that she could confess. "Well, I was waiting in the hallway until you finished your call."

Juniper took another sip of her drink and seemed unaffected by Elodie's admittance. "You were, were you? And did you hear anything of importance?"

"Something about a present and…" Elodie took a sip of her drink. "Ugh, these are warm." Juniper gave her a told-you-so look. "Regardless, I heard some of what you were saying. Let me axe you a question."

Juniper straightened in her chair. "We have talked about this! The word is *ask*! It is not a tool used for chopping wood." She rolled her eyes and took another sip of her warm cocktail.

"You are a booshie little thing." Elodie straightened just as high as Juniper and pointed a scolding finger at her friend. "You know an ounce of pretension is worth a pound of manure."

"Don't you quote the Bible to me!" Juniper squinted as she put down her drink to clap at Elodie.

"It's a line from *Steel Magnolias*." Elodie squinted back.

Juniper leaned forward and hissed, "I repeat, don't you quote the Bible to me."

They held each other's gaze for a tense second before Elodie began to roll with laughter, causing Juniper to creak out a small grin. Elodie wiped her tearing eyes, practically crying as she uttered, "Lawd, I do love you." She took a swig of her warm drink. "You crazy old bitch." Juniper snickered, resulting in a small cough. "Anyway"—Elodie composed herself—"now go on and tell me, who were you talking to?"

Juniper plucked a tissue from the box on her desk and

dabbed her mouth. "Not that it is any concern of yours, but that was Logan. You know he handles all my legal affairs now." Upon graduating from law school three years ago, Logan started his own small firm. He had great potential but was still very new to practicing law and needed more experience. Clients were hard to come by. The same might be said for Gauge. After getting his MBA, Gauge became a financial planner. Again, with the current economy, it was not the best time to be ensuring returns on other people's money.

"Then why were you talking to him about a present? Is it for Charlie's party tomorrow?" She released her bun and leaned back onto the chaise.

"Yes, he's picking something up for me to give my Charlie." Juniper seemed nostalgic as she rested her chin on her shoulder and gazed at the framed pictures on her desk, one of Edward (her long-ago departed husband) and one of Edward (her recently departed dog). She was momentarily lost in memory before she sat up and began to fan herself.

"Well, I guess I better get going then. I still need to wrap my present for our little man." Elodie stood and picked up Juniper's now empty glass from the desk. "Want me to roll your hair before I go?" She cast an intentionally noticeable glance at Juniper's hair.

Juniper responded with a slightly offended yet understanding look. "Yes, but get us some fresh drinks first." She raised her eyebrow as much as the Botox would allow. "Cold this time, preferably."

Charlie's strawberry blonde hair bounced with every step he took as he ran as fast as his little legs would carry him. He sprinted to the downstairs guest bathroom with the ringing cell phone. "Ms. Reausaleigh! Ms. Reausaleigh!"

"Yes, baby?" Reausaleigh looked up from the floor she was scrubbing. Reausaleigh (which, coincidentally, to Juniper's credit, was spelled in a ridiculous manner) was Elodie's sister. After Charlie was born, Matthew and Celeste hired her to be a nanny, maid, cook, driver, errand-runner, pool cleaner. You name it, poor Reausaleigh did it.

"Your phone is ringing." Charlie proudly presented the

phone, feeling as though he'd saved the day by delivering it to his beloved Ms. Reausaleigh.

"Oh, thank you, my baby. You are too sweet." Reausaleigh looked at the phone to see that it was her sister calling. She peeled off her rubber gloves and tossed them into the nearby bucket before retrieving the phone from Charlie's little hands. "I'm gonna finish up in here, and then I'll come make you a yummy pre-birthday snack."

"Yay!" An excited Charlie spun around and ran back to his tilting Lego castle in the living area.

Reausaleigh answered the call from her sister. "Hey." She pushed up from the bathroom floor using the sink for support as she lifted her tired body.

"Hey. Whatcha doin'?" Elodie asked as she drove under the dripping moss that led to the exit of Juniper's driveway.

"Tryin' to get everything straight for this party tomorrow." Reausaleigh wiped the beads of sweat from her brow with the back of her hand.

"Need help?" Elodie knew her sister was probably being asked, more likely told than asked, to do entirely too much.

"Naw, I'm good." Reausaleigh tossed her sponge into the bucket, both of which she had purchased herself, along with the rubber gloves.

"Well, you know I'm no gossip…but I did just hear what one might call a very interesting conversation." Elodie cradled her cell phone between her ear and shoulder as she pulled onto the interstate headed toward Chalmette.

"Really? Whatcha got?" An exhausted Reausaleigh perked up. She put the lid of the toilet down and took a seat as she closed the bathroom door, leaving it open a crack to listen for Charlie if he needed her. She didn't mind taking a much-needed break for some girl talk.

Just as poor tired Reausaleigh was getting a chance to rest her aching back, Celeste strolled through the door leading from the garage to the main house. She was careful as she moved in an effort not to knock her newly polished nails on any surface. She entered the living area to see her son diligently working on a tall, multicolored Lego creation. "Where is Reausaleigh?" she asked coldly.

Charlie's dark green eyes lifted to Celeste. "Mommy,

look!" He rose from his knees, pointing at his construction. "I made a castle! Can we keep it out for my party?"

"Well, it will probably just get knocked over." She gave a judgmental scan of her son's work. "It's leaning anyway. You and Reausaleigh can rebuild it after the party." Without giving her commentary a second thought, she looked around the room. "Now, I should not have to ask a question twice, Charles. *Where is Reausaleigh?*"

A disappointed Charlie began to remove the top layers of his castle. "Ms. Reausaleigh is cleaning the bathroom. She is about to make me a snack." Charlie didn't look at his mother as he spoke. He carefully focused on the Lego pieces that he was removing and gently placing into colored piles.

Celeste promptly made her way to the closest bathroom. Her footsteps were muffled by the paper-thin, post-pedicure flip-flops provided at the spa. As she carefully stepped down the hallway, she noticed that the bathroom door was slightly open, and she could hear the echoing of Reausaleigh's voice. Apparently, eavesdropping was the theme of the day, and Celeste stopped just short of the bathroom door to listen to the conversation that was occurring on the other side of it.

"Wait. So, you telling me she leavin' all that money to Charlie? Just him?" Reausaleigh switched the phone to her good ear and held her head up with her fingertips as she listened to her sister explain what she had overheard earlier that day. Recognizing the potential reference, Celeste's heart began to beat quickly, and she crept closer to the door.

"But what about her own damn son?" Reausaleigh threw out a hand, asking her sister as if she was in the bathroom with her. After a moment of description on the other end of the phone, she let out a sigh. "Lawd, guess you can't blame the old bird." At that comment, Celeste slowly pushed the bathroom door open with the palm of her hand to eerily notify Reausaleigh of her presence.

"Ms. Celeste!" Reausaleigh jumped to her feet with a start and dropped the phone to the floor. Hearing this, Elodie knew she might have just gotten her sister into some hot water. She ended the call without officially letting her sister know, though she definitely knew that was probably best.

Celeste leaned her shoulder onto the doorframe and carefully wove her arms across her chest so as not to touch her newly painted nails. Reausaleigh stood in the bathroom, slightly shaking as if an unexpected spotlight had been shown on her. "Who were you talking to, Reausaleigh?" Celeste coolly asked.

"Oh." Reausaleigh lowered her shaking hand to pick up the bucket containing the gloves and sponge. "Just my sister. She was axing about the party details for tomorrow." She felt transparent as she looked up at Celeste's haunting blue eyes locked on her every movement.

"Is that so?" Celeste remained motionless. "It appeared to be a conversation of another sort to me." Reausaleigh lowered her eyes and held both hands tightly around the handle of the bucket. After a long pause, Celeste asked, "Do you like working here, Reausaleigh?"

Scared, Reausaleigh's head jolted up in surprise at the question. "Of course, Ms. Celeste. Working for you is the best thing that ever happened to me. I love lil' Charlie." As the last words slipped from her lips, she knew her mistake as soon as she had made it.

Every vein in Celeste's neck popped out as she screeched, "His name is Charles! If I wanted to name him Charlie, I would have named him Charlie!" She turned from the doorframe and began to stalk down the hallway.

"I'm sorry, Ms. Celeste!" Reausaleigh followed her and watched her blonde bob swing wildly with every angry step.

"I cannot have someone who lies to my face and doesn't even know my own child's name working here," Celeste barked without turning around.

"Please, Ms. Celeste." Reausaleigh was only a few steps behind her. "I lied. I'm sorry. I'll tell you what Elodie said!"

At this plea, Celeste stopped and slowly turned to see the desperate look in Reausaleigh's eyes. She delicately placed her hands on her perfect hips and sucked in her cheeks. "That's better." As if stalking prey, she took two slow steps toward Reausaleigh and pointedly asked, "Now what, exactly, did your sister say?"

CHAPTER 11

Desperate To Speak To Juniper

Logan pulled the black town car into Matthew and Celeste's driveway the next afternoon. The other guests had parked on the street, but Logan knew better than to even suggest that. Gauge was sitting in the passenger seat next to his brother with Elodie and Juniper in the back. Both women had a hand placed on Charlie's present.

"Logan, dear, please escort Camille to the party. I need to speak with Gauge privately for a moment. I'll be up shortly," Juniper politely commanded.

"Yes, ma'am. Would you like me to bring in the present?" Logan nodded at the gift resting on the backseat.

"No, no." Juniper gave a smile of anticipation as she looked up at the house and waved her pale blue hand fan in front of her face. "I want to surprise him."

Juniper adored Charlie. Hearing his little bare feet on the wooden floors of her home made her heart melt. Charlie spent at least one weekend a month with his grandmother. The bedroom next to hers had been redecorated in a baseball theme, complete with custom-made bunk beds and every toy imaginable. However, her sweet Charlie rarely slept in his extravagant bedroom or played with his mountain of equally extravagant toys. He preferred playing with his grandmother and snuggling in bed with her as they giggled through her bedtime stories. Juniper even allowed Charlie's best friend and cousin, Tommy, to occasionally spend the weekend as well. If it made her little Charlie happy, it made Juniper ecstatic.

By comparison, the discussion Juniper was having with Gauge that afternoon in the town car did not make her in the least bit ecstatic but was unfortunately necessary. Juniper slid on her oversized sunglasses, signaling the finality of the conversation. "Then it is settled. I assume you can take care of this quickly?"

Sunlight streaked through the passenger window onto Gauge's light red hair as his sensitive green eyes gave her an apologetic look. He desperately wished the circumstances were different. He never thought it would come to this. "Yes, Ms. Juniper. Consider it done."

"Good." Juniper fanned herself and looked back up at the house in thought. "I want to go see Charlie now. Stay here with the present. I'll send someone for you when it's time."

"Yes, ma'am." Gauge hopped out of his seat and jogged to the other side of the town car to open the door for Juniper. He extended his hand to help her rise from the vehicle. "Would you like me to escort you to the door, Ms. Juniper?" Gauge knew her hip would not enjoy the brick stairs that led to the front doors of the ten-foot-raised home.

Juniper concealed a slight tinge of nerves as she stepped out of the car with Gauge's hand and eyed the obstacle. In her haste to get to the party that day, she forgot to take the anti-inflammatory and pain medication Elodie had laid out for her. She began to fan herself and looked around to see a familiar man walking up the driveway with an oversized gift bag. "You," Juniper called out as she pointed her fan at the man. "What is his name again?" she asked Gauge quietly out of the side of her mouth.

"That's Danny Boutté, Matthew's friend," Gauge whispered into her ear.

"Daniel," Juniper yelled out to Danny as he lifted his hand to block the sun.

"Mrs. Wells!" Danny happily hustled up the drive to greet her.

"Close the door. I don't want him to see the gift," Juniper mumbled to Gauge as Danny approached.

"Mrs. Wells, so good to see you. You look lovely," Danny said cordially. Juniper did look lovely. Thanks to Elodie, her perfectly curled blonde hair was the crown on top of her perfectly fitted pale blue jumpsuit and silver kitten heels.

"Gauge, how are you doing, sir?" Danny extended his

hand to the now not-so-young man.

"Hanging in there." Gauge shook Danny's hand with a friendly grin. Juniper decided that she liked Daniel a bit more after seeing his kindness to Gauge.

"Daniel, escort me to the door. Gauge is attending to another matter for me."

"Well, it would be my pleasure, madame." Danny extended his elbow so that Juniper could wrap her arm through it. As they stepped away from the car, Danny lowered his voice slightly and said, "I'm glad to have run into you, Mrs. Wells. I was hoping you might have a moment to discuss something."

"Is that so?" A mildly curious Juniper slightly turned her head to Danny, attempting to appear uninterested as they took a few more steps together.

"It would only take a few minutes." Danny stopped and looked at Juniper, trying to read her response through her large, dark lenses.

Juniper sighed as she fanned herself and looked at the intimidating stairs. Unfortunately, she would have to allow Daniel this favor to reach her destination of the front doors. "You have one."

Ten minutes later, Danny opened the glass-paned front doors, allowing Juniper and a gust of wind to enter. She stepped out of the sunlight and into the cool interior of the center hall. Bundles of blue and red balloons lined the walls of the hall and continued into the living area leading to the rear of the house. The house was practically empty and surprisingly quiet. The only sounds were echoes of children's laughter and squeals coming from the back patio.

Elodie was just a few paces inside the door, awaiting Juniper's arrival. "He's playing outside," she informed as she kept stride with Juniper, who determinedly marched straight to the rear of the house, leaving Danny still standing in the doorway. The women walked through the back doors to see a pool full of splashing children and adults conversing over cocktails in the shade.

As Elodie helped Juniper down the stairs, Charlie saw his grandmother enter the patio and ran toward her. "JuJu! JuJu!" He threw his arms around her waist, which sent a shock of pain to her hip. The pain was dulled by the excitement she felt wrapping her arms over her beloved grandson's shoulders.

"Happy birthday, my sweet boy." She smoothed his strawberry blonde hair. "Would you like a present?" She gave him a taunting grin.

"Yes! Yes!" Charlie threw his hands in the air as he jumped up and down.

"Alright, come have a seat with your JuJu." She held Charlie's hand as she made her way to the pool chair that Elodie had already reserved for her. She gently sat and crossed her ankles as Charlie plopped down next to her. "Let me see what I have here." Juniper opened her white clutch purse and placed her hand in the bag. "Ah, here it is." She pulled out a gold-wrapped toffee candy. "This is for you, my Charlie. Happy birthday."

A confused Charlie tried to hide his disappointment as his grandmother dropped the candy into his cupped hands. "Thank you, JuJu." He eyed the present, not knowing quite what to do with it.

"Go ahead. Eat it." She elbowed her grandson.

Charlie unwrapped the candy and hesitantly placed it in his mouth. It tasted like dirty carpet. He squeezed his dark green eyes shut as he rolled the candy in his mouth, hoping to disguise his disgust.

"Do you like it?" Juniper raised both well-arched eyebrows as she watched him.

"Uh-huh." Charlie forced a smile.

Juniper immediately burst into laughter. "It's awful, isn't it?" Her eyes watered as she tried to temper her amusement at the look on poor Charlie's face. He nodded his head. "But you were going to let your poor old JuJu think you liked it so you wouldn't hurt her feelings?"

Charlie nodded again. "Here, spit that out. It's probably very old." Juniper put her hand out. "I actually don't even know where I got that." Charlie spit the candy into Juniper's hand, which Elodie immediately retrieved and placed into a napkin.

"JuJu, you played a trick on me," Charlie giggled as he wiped his tongue with the back of his hand.

"Yes, JuJu played a trick on you." Juniper wrapped her

arm around Charlie's shoulder. "Camille, I think my sweet boy here deserves his real present," Juniper called without releasing her embrace of Charlie. "Would you tell Gauge to bring it in?"

"With pleasure, Ms. Juniper." Elodie poked Charlie in the side as she walked past them and lovingly teased, "She got you good."

Heather entered through the front doors and into the party. The energy of the home was much different than when she was there just a few hours prior. She had never been asked to cater a child's birthday party before, but when Celeste requested her services, she was more than happy to oblige. Unbeknownst to Heather, this was due to a prompt and indefinite cancellation of services by her current caterer after Celeste openly compared the taste testing to licking the bottom of a hobo's foot.

Heather and Danny loved Charlie and Tommy. Not having children of their own weighed heavy on Heather's heart, so any chance to be involved in the young boys' lives was considered an honor. When she was prepping the platters earlier in the day, though, her heart became even heavier. Celeste and Matthew seemed so cold to Charlie. The little boy was so excited for his big day, bouncing around Heather as she worked, telling her in detail about each one of his friends that was coming to celebrate. When Celeste entered the kitchen to check on Heather's progress, Charlie grew silent as if he was afraid to speak, and Celeste didn't even acknowledge his presence. She had never observed a more detached mother and son bond.

Heather made her way through the center hall and into the living area. She stopped, and her big brown eyes stared out the large windows that displayed the party outside. Children were running and laughing. Water lapped over the sides of the pool as Charlie's friends cannonballed and splashed into it. She spotted Danny in a water gun battle with Tommy. His gray polo was practically drenched with streaks of spray. She ran her hand through her long, dark hair and sighed sadly. She desperately wished she could have this for her and

Danny. *One day,* she quietly promised herself.

"There you are." An unnoticed Kay walked from the kitchen into the living room to greet Heather with a friendly hug.

"Sorry I'm late. I ended up spending way too long here this morning." She tilted her head toward the kitchen. "I had to scramble to throw myself together."

Kay smirked. "Was she terrible to deal with?"

Heather opened her mouth to respond and then looked back out the window at the party. "Uhhh, she was about how you would expect."

"Understood." Kay knowingly smiled. "Well, everything is delicious. You outdid yourself." She pointed to the long, white linen-covered table outside that was surrounded by parents and children. Heather had prepared everything from gourmet pizzas to mini po' boys to shrimp kabobs. Every bite was delightful. Kay took Heather's overworked, long tan arm. "Well, I definitely think you deserve a drink, missy. Let's go get you one and check on the men folk." Before making it to the back doors, she warned, "Watch out for that chubby kid, though. He nailed me with a water balloon so hard I thought I got hit by a sniper's bullet."

The ladies dodged scampering children as they joined Wes and Matthew reclining against the outdoor bar. Just as they did, a little girl screamed from the pool and pointed at the back doors. "Puppy! Puppy! Puppy!"

Gauge was stepping out onto the patio, holding a tiny bundle of silver fur and floppy ears. Cradled in his arms was a Weimaraner pup with a large red bow tied around its neck. Charlie gasped and swirled his head to lock his big, thrilled eyes with Juniper's. "Well, what are you waiting for?" She pulled down her shades and cracked a smile as she waved her hand toward the puppy. "He's all yours. Happy birthday, my darling."

"Thank you! Thank you, JuJu!" Charlie practically knocked her over with a huge hug and immediately ran up to Gauge. Gauge carefully placed the puppy into Charlie's excited arms as all the children evacuated the pool and gathered around him. Little wet hands reached forward to pet the pup, who looked up at Charlie and presented him with a lick on the nose.

Kay scanned the patio, looking for her cousin, knowing

this definitely would not go over well, but there was no sight of her. Matthew did the same but decided to speak directly with his mother instead. He stormed up to Juniper, who was still resting on the pool chair. In a way, Matthew was jealous of his own son. He had begged his mother for a dog when he was a boy, and each request was always met with an emphatic, "No."

Juniper was fanning herself, relishing in the joy she saw on Charlie's face as Matthew stomped up and blocked her view with his large body.

"No," he commanded sternly to his mother as she looked up at him with annoyance.

"Yes," she unemotionally replied, adjusting her position to watch Charlie with the puppy that was now sniffing the ground surrounded by a swarm of children.

"You always told me no."

Juniper sucked her teeth as she replaced her dark glasses and calmly stood to face Matthew. "Keep it up, son, and I'll cancel your birth certificate."

"Ha, like you would even know where to find it. These lame-ass attempts to overcompensate don't change the fact that you were a shitty mother."

With that, Juniper snapped her fan and attempted to strike Matthew's wrist, but he pulled his large hand away before she could make contact. He let out a heckling chuckle. "Getting slow in your old age, Juniper." The words had hardly left his lips when *FWAPA*. Juniper cracked her fan right across his forehead.

The incident went largely unnoticed by most of the party guests, and those who did notice were unimpressed by yet another Juniper/Matthew altercation. However, Kay noticed and leaned to Wes's ear to advise, "Better get over there before she gives him a fresh one." Wes gave her an acknowledging nod and tried to appear mellow as he walked toward the wounded Matthew and his mother, who had returned to fanning herself. He came to the party knowing he needed to speak with Juniper and already had a plan to get her alone. He was dreading the conversation but knew it was one that needed to take place.

"Hey, man," Wes greeted his friend as he approached.

His hazel eyes widened a few sizes when he noticed the already growing welt stretching across Matthew's forehead. "Umm…" He turned his attention to the unfazed Juniper. "Ms. Juniper, I picked up Tommy and Charlie's Little League pictures the other day. I'm sure Charlie would want you to have some. I have them inside if you'd like to see them." Wes knew she wouldn't turn down the opportunity to have yet another picture of her only grandchild.

"Hmmm." Juniper slightly lowered her sunglasses to see Wes's inviting yet, in her mind, still annoying face. "I would like that, indeed."

"Great." Wes cast a polite directing hand to the house. "They're in the lounge." Juniper began her confident stride toward the back doors as Wes followed. Matthew rubbed his head and snarled one more insult as she passed. "You know you're a bitch, right?"

An unaffected Juniper didn't lose a step or bother to turn around as she flippantly replied over her shoulder, "Dear child, I have heard far worse from far better."

"Where have you been?" Kay cocked her head at a distracted-looking Celeste walking toward her and Heather with a fresh drink. She was absent for the entire unveiling of Juniper's present.

"I'm sure you wouldn't understand the effort involved in hosting a party. The only company you've ever received at that dump of yours is rats." Celeste flicked her blonde hair from her shoulder.

"It was one flipping mouse, and Randy, the exterminator, took care of it," Kay defended.

"I don't know what's worse, the fact that you require an exterminator or that you are on a first-name basis with one." Celeste dabbed beads of sweat from her forehead with her drink napkin.

Heather eyed Celeste curiously. Despite the never-ending heat of Louisiana, she had never actually seen Celeste sweat. However, the normally picture-perfect Celeste stood next to her in a sage green dress with obvious dampening under the arms. She considered the possibility that she might just be a stressed hostess but quickly abandoned the thought, remembering that the only thing Celeste cared about was Celeste.

"Ugh." Celeste turned to see Charlie and the other children petting the new puppy. "Who the hell brings their dog to a birthday party?"

Kay and Heather exchanged a glance in excited anticipation that they would get front-row seats to Celeste's reaction. "Well, dear cousin"—Kay mischievously smiled—"I do believe that's your dog."

"Are you drunk already?" Celeste turned her attention from the dog to Kay with irritation.

The corners of Kay's mouth curled upward even farther. "Well, while you were pretending to entertain your guests, Juniper gave Charlie his birthday present." She lifted her glass in the direction of Charlie and the puppy.

Celeste's mouth gaped open, and her big blue eyes practically turned to flames. She snapped her head back to her son and his new pet, then back to her cousin. "She didn't," Celeste fumed.

Heather's thoughts returned to earlier in the kitchen that day when it felt as though Charlie simply wanted someone to play with him. "Maybe she thought Charlie could use a playmate," she tried to suggest optimistically.

Celeste ignored the comment and kept her attention on Kay. She had now mentally put Heather in "the help" category. Celeste did not socialize with the help and most definitely would not acknowledge some feeble attempt by said help to pacify her. "Did you know about this?"

Kay threw her hand in the air at the absurd question. "You can't be serious. How on earth would I know that she was going to buy him a dog?"

Celeste forced herself to take a deep breath and followed it with a small shrug in a transparent attempt to hide her anger, not wanting anyone to know that Juniper had gotten her roused. She had just spent the past thirty minutes cornering Logan in the garden, attempting to extract information from him. She knew that Logan was now Juniper's legal counsel, and based on the scraps of information provided to her the day prior by Reausaleigh, she was trying to get the scoop on what the old bag of bones was up to. Despite her best attempts, Logan flatly told Celeste that he would not discuss Ms. Juniper's legal affairs.

Logan was especially proud of himself when her first flirtatious, then frustrated, and then finally angry efforts were met with him officially stating, "I do apologize, Celeste. However, that is privileged information. Unfortunately for you, you are not considered privileged." He knew all too well what she was capable of and would rather have a private audience with a hungry gator while wearing a meat suit than the blonde reptile that stood before him.

"And where might I find generous Juniper so that I may thank her properly," Celeste gritted through a fake smile to Kay.

"She went inside a while ago with Wes," Heather answered. Again, Celeste continued to pretend as though Heather was not literally twelve inches from her.

Kay looked at Heather apologetically and then back at her cousin with contempt. She knew what Celeste was doing and why she was doing it. "As *Heather* said, she went inside."

"Thank you, cousin." Celeste twirled around and headed toward the back doors as the sweat dripping down her back absorbed into her dress.

"Sorry." Kay watched Celeste enter the house. "Sometimes she can be a real b-word."

At her apology, Heather turned her attention from Celeste's back sweat to Kay, who was still watching her cousin.

"B-word?"

"Oh yeah," Kay sighed. "I had to quit cursing. Long story." She took the last sip of her Bloody Mary. "But I can still drink. A gal needs at least one vice, right?"

Celeste stormed through the back doors into the house. *Who does this bitch think she is?* She tried to compose herself as her head swung left to right and back again, looking for any sign of her mother-in-law. Her search suddenly stopped when she saw Wes rubbing his hand as he turned out of the front hallway that led from the lounge.

Wes looked and felt defeated after his conversation with Juniper. He wanted to leave but knew there were at least another two hours of cake and balloons. His thoughts were disrupted when he lifted his head to see Celeste standing still in the living area, staring at him. A good forty feet away, they glared at one another for a moment before Celeste asked crisply, "Where is she?"

"Where is who?" He replied, feeling uneasy responding to the silhouette of Celeste as sunlight beamed through the windows behind her.

"You know who."

Wes began making his way toward the back doors behind Celeste. "If you're asking where Reausaleigh is, I don't know," he said coldly as he tried to walk past her. She reached out and snatched his left hand. He jolted to a halt as she pulled his hand to eye level and yet kept her eyes on Wes. The red welt stretching across his wrist was apparent to both of them without either of them directly looking at it.

"Oh, Carl, I am not as dumb as you look." She narrowed her eyes at him with a condescending smile. "Where is Juniper?"

Wes yanked his hand back. "Juniper is in the bathroom, Celeste."

"Thank you." She brushed her hands as if touching Wes left a layer of dirt on her palms. "Your wife and sons," she paused and gave him a wicked smirk, "I mean, son, are outside."

Unaffected by her comment, Wes sternly asked, "How many other guys have you tried to play that card with today, Celeste?"

Celeste stared Wes dead in the eyes, punctuated with several long, slow blinks as she came to the realization that he might just be smarter than she thought.

"You said she was in the bathroom?" she finally croaked.

Wes nodded without breaking eye contact. At this, Celeste turned and made her way to resume her initial goal of confronting Juniper. A confrontation that had nothing to do with the silver puppy that was currently relieving himself all over her patio. She turned down the front hallway to see Juniper coolly stepping out of the bathroom, fanning herself. Juniper took one step down the hallway before seeing Celeste stiffly positioned in her path. "Ugh." She cast her fan over her eyes as if someone had suddenly flipped on the lights in a dark room.

"We need to talk." Celeste laced her fingers behind her back and stepped confidently toward her mother-in-law.

"I would rather have a Bourbon Street hooker spit in my eye." Juniper put her sunglasses on and paused. "However, given the way you splatter when you speak, I assume the two instances would be one and the same." To Juniper's disappointment, Celeste seemed undeterred by the insult. She snapped her fan closed and, with a deep sigh, begrudgingly moaned, "What is it, tart?"

"Perhaps we should return to the lounge for this discussion."

One week later, Juniper and Elodie were relaxing in the study, enjoying their afternoon cocktails. Elodie was lounging on the chaise, explaining the proper way to put on a girdle, when the phone rang.

Juniper's big brown eyes locked on the buzzing receiver. Without letting the phone out of her sight, she ordered, "You answer it."

Elodie popped up in surprise at the unusual request. "You answer it. It's your phone."

"No, you."

"What's wrong with you? Why you want me to answer it?" The phone continued to ring.

"As my assistant, you should answer the phone." Juniper straightened her back.

"I am your caretaker, you old bat. Not your assistant." Elodie dismissively reclined back onto the chaise.

"Assistant!"

"Caretaker!" As Elodie bantered back, she noticed that Juniper was eyeing the phone in such a way that gave her pause to argue any further.

"Call me Elodie, and I'll answer it." She propped up on her elbow as they both looked at the phone. "Better hurry. They gonna hang up."

Juniper pursed her lips and clenched her fists. "Oh, fine! Damn it, Elodie, answer the phone!"

"Hee hee! Yes, ma'am!" Elodie jumped up and clapped her hands together with excitement just before grabbing the receiver. Swallowing her laughter, she politely answered, "Wells residence." After a short request from the caller, Elodie replied, "I'll see if she's available." She put the receiver to her chest and nodded at Juniper.

Juniper mouthed, "Who is it?"

Elodie sucked her teeth and mouthed back, "How the hell should I know?"

Juniper rolled her eyes and put out her hand. Elodie returned to the caller and said, "Just a moment, please." She handed the phone to Juniper with a muffled cackle and mouthed, "You called me Elodie."

Juniper mouthed back, "And it won't happen again. Now out."

Elodie gave her a gloating smile. "Okay," she whispered. "Want me to get us another round?" She picked up Juniper's empty glass.

"Of course I do. Now go," Juniper whispered back and waved her hand toward the door. She waited a few moments to make sure that Elodie was out of earshot with the two empty glasses before placing the phone to her ear.

"This is Juniper." Her face turned to a scowl as the caller identified themself. "I thought it might be you." She drummed her fingers on the desk. "I was wondering if you would actually have the nerve to call."

CHAPTER 12

Desperate To Hide The Truth

Walking toward Charlie's bedroom, Matthew grunted as he struggled to lace his oversized arm into his jacket. A month had passed since Charlie's birthday, and this year's mid-October weather decided to bring a very abrupt yet welcomed cold front with it.

He stopped at the doorway, going unnoticed by Charlie and Reausaleigh. Reausaleigh was sitting cross-legged on the floor with Charlie in her lap. Her left hand was gently wrapped around Charlie's with his index finger tracing the lines on the page of a thin book. In unison, they read, "There once was an old woman who lived—"

"Where's your mother?" Matthew interrupted as he straightened the front of his jacket with both hands.

Reausaleigh and Charlie both jumped at the sound of his voice. Charlie's eyes flashed to his father only for a second before casting them up to Reausaleigh's comforting face. She put a calming hand on Charlie's shoulder and politely responded, "Ms. Celeste brought the puppy to the trainer. Said she had some errands to run and would be back in a bit."

After receiving the new furry family member, Celeste made it her mission to ensure the dog was properly trained and completely obedient. She wanted to make damn sure the pup knew she was his master and would obey her. One of the many things Celeste admired about herself was her dog-handling abilities, even though they had never technically been used on an actual dog.

"Alright. I have some appointments myself." Matthew pulled his phone out of his back pocket and glanced at a text from his party favor provider. “You reading now, Charles?” He looked down at his son.

“Yes, sir.” Charlie slightly lit up at his father’s interest. “It’s really hard though.” His excitement faded a bit as he looked at the book still in Reausaleigh’s hand.

“Well, I…” Matthew didn’t know how to respond and looked at Reausaleigh for parental guidance.

“Oh, he is coming along just fine. Don’t let this boy fool you, Mr. Matthew. He’ll be outreading all of us in no time.” She gave Charlie an encouraging little squeeze.

“Well, if Ms. Reausaleigh says it, then it must be true.” Matthew returned his phone to his pocket. “Keep it up, son. I’ll be back later.” He turned back down the hallway and heard the two giggle before Charlie’s little voice started up again, “There once was an old woman who lived in a shoe.”

Juniper and Elodie were finishing their afternoon cocktails yet again as Elodie reached down to the side of the chaise lounge and picked up a grocery bag. “Well, I got you a little something.” Juniper stopped fanning herself and looked at her friend curiously. “Actually, I got them for myself, but I’m gonna let you borrow ’em.” Knowing Juniper would not be pleased with the gift, Elodie gave her a this-is-for-your-own-good look before presenting it. She reached into the grocery bag and pulled out two pale blue orthopedic shoes.

“Ahhhh!” Juniper yelped as if the mere sight of the shoes seared her eyes.

“Now cut it out with all that. You gonna need these after your surgery.”

“I wouldn’t be caught dead in those!” Juniper pretended to be insulted as she cast her head away in disgust and went back to fanning herself.

“You a lie. I saw you eyeing them on me the other day as that old hip of yours was singing the blues. Sounds like a damn rusty harmonica every time you take a step.”

Not only did Juniper know Elodie was right, but she also knew that Elodie knew she was right. She cast a tempted side-eye to the shoes. “I’ll take them into consideration.”

“That’s my girl. Now give me that glass. I gotta go.” She

replaced the shoes in the grocery bag and rested it next to Juniper's desk. "We got a big day tomorrow."

Juniper handed her the glass. "What are you talking about? We don't have anything planned."

"Oh yes, we do." Elodie took the glass and made her way toward the door. "You gonna be down for a while come Friday. I scheduled you beauty appointments for tomorrow. I ain't looking at those roots and chipped nails the whole time you laid up."

As Elodie left the study, Juniper smiled at her thoughtfulness. Elodie knew that's what her friend was doing, and she also knew acknowledging that fact by turning around would embarrass Juniper. "And don't forget," she called over her shoulder, "those are my shoes. I want 'em back."

Elodie pulled her rusted purple Honda out onto the main road heading toward the interstate. She hummed as she changed the radio station. She was ready to get home. Her feet ached, mainly because she had just given away her best pair of comfortable shoes. Resting both hands on the wheel and staring ahead, she noticed a familiar black Escalade pass her, going in the opposite direction. *Was that Mr. Matthew? Naw, she would have told me if he was coming over. Sho' did look like him, though.*

Meanwhile, Juniper was, in usual fashion, drumming her fingers on the desk in her study and tapping her lips. She was staring at the grocery bag containing the orthopedic shoes. "Oh, fuck it." She reached down for the bag and put it in her lap. Kicking off her feathered house slippers, she picked up one of the pale blue old lady shoes and inspected it with contempt. Begrudgingly, she lowered the shoe, slid one foot into it, and did the same with the other. A sigh escaped her lips as she stood up and immediately arched an eyebrow in pleasant surprise. "Oh my," she whispered as she looked down at her feet with relief. The pain in her hip, although still there, was definitely alleviated.

Juniper took a few steps around the room, enjoying the comforting feeling. Her hip felt so good she walked out of the room and across the upstairs balcony. Just as she was crossing back toward her study, the front doors opened.

"Ugh. Of course, this would be the one instance of your punctuality." She put both hands on the balcony railing and looked down to see Matthew coming through the front doors.

Matthew closed the doors and looked up at his mother in annoyance. "If I were early, you'd bitch. If I were late, you'd bitch. I'm on time, and guess what? You're still bitching."

"Never mind that." Juniper waved her hand. "Come up to the study," she commanded as she walked hastily back to her desk so that Matthew wouldn't see her in the orthopedic shoes. Once back in her office, she sat at her desk and slid a pile of papers out of the top drawer.

Matthew's heavy, moody steps grew closer as she straightened the pile and threw the grocery bag under the desk. "What is it, Juniper?" He plopped down onto one of the leather club chairs opposite her desk.

She straightened the pile of papers once more and cleared her throat. Looking right into Matthew's eyes, she collected her thoughts and sternly said, "I have been approached."

After a bewildered pause, Matthew chuckled hard. "For what, to be the next spokesperson for Depends?" He continued laughing at the mental image of his mother in a diaper.

"It involves Charlie." Juniper's face stayed stern, and Matthew's laughter immediately stopped. He scanned his mother's expression to determine whether what she was about to say was genuinely concerning. His stomach lurched a bit when he realized it was.

"Ultimately…" She straightened the papers yet again and tossed them onto the desk. "Ultimately, your wife is a whore." She took a deep breath. This part was something she desperately wished wasn't true. "Charlie is not your biological son."

Matthew jumped up with such force it knocked his chair on its back. "Out of your mind. You are out of your fucking mind, old lady!"

Juniper sadly stared at him in such a way that he knew she was serious. "Sit," she ordered as she pointed at the chair. Matthew stared back at his mother for a moment before he silently picked up the chair and did as he was told.

"I have been approached by a blackmailer. This blackmailer, who shall remain nameless, has DNA proof that Charlie is not your son. For quite a large sum of money, the party has agreed not to reveal this information."

Matthew sat in the chair, grinding his jaw, not knowing whether to believe his mother, but he knew deep down that she would not make this up. "What kind of DNA proof?"

"A paternity test." She lifted the first piece of paper from the stack and frowned as she viewed it.

"Juniper, people can fake those things. That's just a piece of paper somebody probably edited to make it look legit and get money out of you."

"I wish that were true." She replaced the piece of paper on the stack and looked out the large window next to her desk. The fall wind was stripping the first layer of leaves from her magnolia trees. Holding her gaze on the weaving trees, she sadly stated, "I've known since he was three."

Matthew's voice grew cold. "What are you talking about?" He watched her continue to stare out the window. "Look at me, damn it!"

She left her daze and returned her attention to Matthew. "I didn't know *who* his father was until this blackmailer showed up." She pulled the next page of paper from the stack and viewed it with disappointment before handing it to Matthew, who snatched it from her hand. "That is a DNA test that I had performed when Charlie was three. I was hoping for a different result, but as you can clearly see, the boy is of no blood relation to me."

Matthew's face turned red as his eyes darted left to right, reading each line of the results over and over. "You've known since he was three, and you didn't tell me?" He slammed the paper onto the desk.

"It is not his fault that his mother is a slut," Juniper defended. "Even from a young age, I could tell that he wasn't like us. A blind man could see that!" She smoothed her hair and regained her composure. "I wanted to be certain, so I obtained a sample of his hair and saliva when he was here one weekend. I told no one." She looked intently at him so that he understood that very clearly. "Despite the unfortunate results, I still consider Charlie to be my grandson. I did not see the need to bring shame to the Wells name or that sweet boy. As such, I chose to tell no one, not even you."

Matthew crossed his arms over his chest and shook his head at his mother. "So, why tell me now, Juniper? Just to fuck with me? You could have just paid this person off, and no one would have known."

"I am telling you now to ensure that this information remains private. I have made several installment payments to the blackmailer in the form of cashier's checks to avoid suspicion. I am receiving them this evening to hand over the final payment, and in return, they have agreed to sign a nondisclosure agreement. If broken, this agreement allows for punitive retribution far greater than any sum of money affordable by them."

Matthew couldn't believe what he was hearing. "And what makes you think I won't say anything, Juniper? You expect me to raise a kid that isn't even mine?"

Knowing her son, Juniper assumed this would be his initial response. "Prior to this whole blackmail incident, I made some revisions to my will." Matthew's breath caught in his lungs. He gripped the arms of the chair, fearful of what he was about to hear.

"I could not be certain that you wouldn't somehow come about this information on your own and do exactly what you are suggesting. *That* is why I am telling you now." Juniper pulled a thick stapled document from the stack. "As such, upon my demise, the legal guardians of Charlie will receive a stipend of three hundred and fifty thousand dollars per year until he is twenty-one. At which point the entirety of the remaining estate will be granted to Charlie."

Matthew's face turned pale as he ran a hand through his sandy hair and looked down at his feet. "So, as you can clearly see, if you divulge the identity of Charlie's true father, the stipend would no longer be administered to you." She folded her hands across the desk and leaned forward. "That also means that my grandson is going to be a very rich man someday." Matthew looked up at her in disbelief. "So, I suggest you be very, very nice to him."

Matthew sat up and defeatedly tilted his head back. Silently staring at the ceiling for a long while, he accepted his fate. What else could he do? He knew there would be no changing her mind. Matthew couldn't tell if the empty feeling that had swept over him was because Charlie was not his son or because Juniper had forgotten that he was hers.

Waving a mental white flag, he slowly looked out the window to the swaying magnolia trees. He watched them for a moment before calmly asking, "So who's the father?"

Juniper smirked as she peeled off the last page of the stack and slowly slid it across the desk. "I was hoping you'd ask that."

The tires of Officer Broussard's cruiser splashed through the puddles of last night's rain as he pulled into the entrance of the old, abandoned warehouse. The desolate parking lot on the outskirts of the city was where he always went when he needed to rest his eyes for a bit. Eyes that definitely needed resting after one too many tequila shots to celebrate the Saints' win over the Falcons last night.

He parked his patrol car facing north in the middle of the parking lot just in case the sun decided to peep through the heavy morning clouds. Reclining his seat back, he thought, *Fifteen minutes*. Of course, fifteen minutes turned into fifteen seconds. Just as he was beginning to dose off, his radio buzzed.

"Dispatch to 103," a rattly voice came through.

Broussard groaned and felt for the radio without opening his eyes. Pulling it up to his mouth, he responded, "103, go ahead."

"We got a 29 at 5757 Wells Drive," the dispatcher's voice crackled through the transmitter.

Officer Broussard shot straight up. *Did I hear that right?* "103 to dispatch, comeback."

"Signal 29 at 5757 Wells Drive. Elderly white female at the bottom of the stairs. EMS is en route."

"10-4, en route." Broussard flipped on his sirens and screeched his tires as he sped out of the parking lot toward the Wells estate.

The wet gravel of the driveway sprayed up as Officer Broussard's cruiser came to a grinding stop in front of the Wells residence. "103 to dispatch, on scene," he mouthed into his shoulder radio as he bolted up one side of the stairs to the open front doors.

"NOPD!" he called out as he slowed his pace at the entrance of the home.

"She's in here," a sobbing voice called back.

Broussard's bloodshot eyes took a moment to adjust to the dark coolness of the home's interior. When his vision cleared, he saw a hunched woman sitting on the floor next to what appeared to be a crumpled white sheet. The folds of the sheet fluttered rhythmically from multiple fans blowing throughout the entrance hall.

"Ma'am?" Officer Broussard took a few steps toward the woman but froze when he realized the sheet she sat next to was not a sheet. It was a white silk robe. A white silk robe on the twisted body of a blonde elderly woman lying at the foot of the stairs. It looked like a scene from a movie. A movie with a very sad ending. He had been on the force for two years, but this was his first signal 29.

"Ma'am, I'm gonna need you to come outside with me. Is there anyone else in the house?"

"No, officer." Elodie wiped her eyes and looked back at the body. She placed her friend's lifeless hand in both of hers and softly rubbed it.

"Ma'am," Broussard came closer. "I…I need you not to touch her, okay."

"Okay." Elodie released Juniper's hand and gently rested it on the marble floor. She tried to push herself up, but her knees went weak when she began to stand. Officer Broussard lurched forward and caught her as she stumbled.

"Why don't you come sit outside for me while I secure the scene, ma'am." He steadied Elodie, and they both couldn't help but look down at Juniper. She was clearly dead. A small, winding trail of dried blood curved from the corner of her mouth down her cheek. The dark, dried blood starkly contrasted her now white face and pale blue lips. Pale blue lips that matched the shoes she was wearing. Elodie's shoes.

Broussard put one arm around Elodie's shoulder and the other under her elbow. They slowly shuffled toward the front doors. "What is your name, ma'am?"

"My name is Elodie. I'm Ms. Juniper's caretaker."

"And you found her like this, Elodie?"

"Yes, sir. Just a little bit ago."

"Okay, I want you to sit right here for me, Elodie." He helped her to one of the large rocking chairs on the front porch. She placed a shaking hand on the arm of the rocker to brace herself as she slid into it. "Did you touch anything in the house or…her?"

"I felt for a pulse." Elodie put her face in her hands. "But I knew she was already gone."

"Did you touch anything else?"

She nodded her head and pulled her hands from her face. "Yes, sir. I…" Elodie took a deep breath. "I closed her eyes."

At this, Officer Broussard mournfully put his head down, feeling so sorry for the poor soul weeping before him. "I understand." He laid a sympathetic hand on her shoulder. "Stay here while I take a look around inside." As he turned to reenter the house, dispatch sounded through his shoulder radio.

"103, 82 is en route to assist."

"10-4, 29 confirmed." Broussard shivered as he stepped into the entrance hall to start making any observations he could, desperately hoping his supervisor would arrive soon.

"Daddy," a groggy female voice slurred from her pillow.

"Hmm," Matthew grunted without fully waking up as he rolled onto his side on the leopard print sheets.

"Daddy, answer your phone." The groggy female voice was clearer now. She shoved her petite hand accented with glossy, red polished nails into Matthew's back.

He grumbled as he sat up, exposing the claw marks left on his bare back by the red polished nails from the night before. He reached for his jeans, crumpled on the floor, and pulled the ringing cell phone from the pocket. Resting his elbows on his knees, he answered, "Yeah." He coughed and ran a tired hand over his stubble. "Hello?"

Matthew's hangover disappeared instantly as he listened to the caller on the other end of the phone. "What? When?" He jumped up from the bed and grabbed his pants. Shoving one leg into his jeans and cradling the phone with his shoulder, he frantically asked, "You're sure?" The caller confirmed the certainty of what they were saying. "Jesus, Elodie. I'll be right there."

He threw the phone onto the bed and began gathering the rest of his clothes that were strewn about the room. "I gotta go," he said as he forced his feet into his shoes.

"Fine." The still snoozing brunette covered her face with a pillow. "Leave me a cigarette." Matthew pulled a pack of Marlboro Lights from his wrinkled jacket and tossed it onto the bed before rushing to the door.

Screeching out of the parking garage, the only thing spiraling faster than the wheels of his Escalade were Matthew's emotions. *This is not what I wanted. This is not what I wanted.* "This is not what I fucking wanted!" he screamed at the windshield. Speeding through every light and stop sign had him careening into the long driveway of his mother's home within minutes. His stomach dropped, and his car slowed to a crawl as he saw the word CORONER printed across a white van parked in front of the estate.

Matthew put the car in park and stared at the van. He stared at the word as if he was suddenly unable to read. For some reason, those seven letters were simply incomprehensible. He just sat there, sitting and staring.

A soft knock on the passenger window broke his trance. He turned his attention to the window to see a shaking, tear-stained Elodie looking back at him. Exhaling deeply, he pulled himself out of the car. Matthew trudged around to the front of the vehicle, where Elodie shuffled up to meet him.

"Oh, Mr. Matthew." She shook her head and looked down at the ground.

"So, she's really…" Matthew couldn't finish the question. Elodie sobbed and put her hand over her mouth as she slowly nodded. He grimaced and shoved his hands into his pockets as he looked up at the house. One of the large magnolia trees was leaning against it. It was snapped at the base and tilted against the second story. In that moment, it felt as if the tree was holding the house up and not the other way around.

Matthew paused for a moment, tightly squeezing his fists in his jacket. "What happened?"

Elodie took a deep breath and shook her head again in shame. "I came in this mornin', and there she was. She was at the bottom of the steps. She must of fallen." Her head shook even harder. "And it's all my fault."

Matthew jerked back at this. "What? What are you talking about, Elodie?" He stepped toward her and cupped both of her arms with his hands.

"I gave her my shoes. I gave her those damn shoes to help with her hip. Maybe…" Elodie's lip started to quiver. "Maybe they made her trip. She wasn't used to 'em." She looked up at Matthew, searching for some kind of forgiveness. "Was she wearing them when you came over?"

Matthew suddenly pulled away from Elodie. "What are you talking about? When I came over when?"

"I…I thought I saw you coming down the road when I left yesterday."

A buzzing sound went off in Matthew's head. *She saw me.* The buzzing got louder. *She saw me.* He knew he couldn't let anyone find out that he was there yesterday. No one can know that. The buzzing suddenly stopped as his mind cleared, and he realized how to respond. "Elodie, you're in shock. I wasn't here. You're not thinking right."

The normally strong-willed Elodie felt as if she was coming unraveled. *Did I see him? Oh Lawd, maybe I'm losin' it.* She looked at him with distraught, confused eyes. "But I thought I saw—"

Matthew cut her off. "Elodie…" He looked back at the house and put a large arm around her shoulder as he started guiding her to the passenger side of the car. "I guess I have to ask." He stopped just short of the passenger door and looked down at her. "You didn't"—he frowned—"you know, push her, did you?" If trying to convince Elodie she was confused wouldn't work, he would have to try another approach.

Fearful, bulging eyes shot up to Matthew's, and her mouth went dry. "I-I-I…" Elodie stammered.

"If you did, you can tell me," Matthew said, trying to appear sympathetic.

"No! I would never hurt her. She is my—" Elodie corrected herself as a tear rolled down her cheek. "She was my friend."

Matthew nodded and put his other arm around Elodie to give her a consoling hug. "I believe you. Of course you wouldn't." He opened the car door. "Here, sit. Call your sister. Tell her to come get you." He helped her into the seat and opened the glove compartment. "Take this. Have a sip. It will calm you down." Matthew handed her a silver flask. "I'm going to go talk to the officers now."

"Mr. Matthew?" Elodie held the flask tightly with both hands. He placed a hand on the frame of the car door and looked down at her. "You know I didn't, right?"

"I know."

"Do you…" Her eyes floated through the windshield to the patrol cars. "Do you think they will?"

Matthew intentionally gave an unsure expression followed by a seemingly forced, weak smile. "I'll make sure of it. I'll take care of it. I promise."

Officer Broussard sat in his patrol car with the driver's side door open as he filled out paperwork. He noticed Matthew approaching and stepped out of the vehicle to meet him. He knew who Matthew Wells was; Matthew was a regular.

Broussard worked part-time as a security guard at one of the local high-end gentleman's clubs in the French Quarter. Strip clubs paid well to have an off-duty police officer keeping an eye on things. The nicer clubs never really had much trouble. Just the occasional overserved frat boy that needed to be tossed, but other than that, it was pretty easy side money.

"Mr. Wells, I'm Officer Broussard." He stuck his hand out. Matthew shook it, hoping the officer wouldn't notice that his palms were sweating. "I'm very sorry for your loss."

"Yeah, thank you," Matthew replied distractedly as he looked up at the yellow police tape that was stretched across the open front doors. Broussard noticed Matthew's understandable distress and pointed his pen over his shoulder to the police tape.

"My supervisor is in there with the coroner. They're taking a look at her." He mentally cringed at how his comment might have come across as insensitive; however, it was as if Matthew hadn't even heard him. "I have just a few questions for you for the report, if that's alright."

"Sure. Yeah." Matthew crossed his arms and widened his stance.

Flipping to a clean sheet in his notebook, Broussard asked, "So, Juniper Wells is your mother?"

"Yes, sir."

"Was she on any medications, or did she have any health issues?"

"Umm…" Matthew shuffled his feet. "She had a bad hip. I know she was getting surgery for it. The medications, you'd have to ask Elodie about that." He flicked his head back toward his Escalade.

"Yeah, I spoke with her earlier. She said you might have come over to the house yesterday evening?"

The buzzing sound returned to Matthew's brain as he tried to remain calm. "I know. She mentioned that to me, too." He frowned and shook his head. "Poor old broad, she's really upset. Her mind is all scrambled right now. I didn't come over yesterday. I think she might be in shock or something."

Broussard took in the response with a bit of veiled skepticism. After speaking with Elodie, it was clear that she was upset, but she did seem very certain about the hours that had passed since she left Juniper. Seeing where this would go, he played along. "Yeah, that can happen when someone goes through something traumatic. Wires can get crossed, you know." He nodded agreeably. "So, were you just at home?"

"Uh, no." Matthew rubbed the back of his neck. "I…well, I was with a friend. A…" He looked at the officer sheepishly. "A lady friend. I just left there."

"Alright." Broussard smirked as he jotted down the response in his notebook. "She got a name?"

Matthew ran his palm across his unshaven jaw nervously. "Yeah, it's Natalia. I…" He shrugged. "I don't know her last name."

"Natalia? From the club, Natalia?"

Matthew's head jerked back with surprise as he looked at the officer curiously. "Oh yeah, I thought I recognized you. Sorry, man. Guess I'm kind of off right now. Nick, right?" This recognition now completely changed the tone of the entire conversation. With Matthew now feeling like he had an ally and Officer Broussard feeling a little ego boost that

Matthew Wells knew his name, things got a bit chummier.

"Yeah, don't worry about it, man. I'm sure I'd be the same way." He put the small notepad in his back pocket. "So, Natalia, huh?"

"Yep. Pretty hard to resist." They both chuckled, and then also both quickly recognized they should probably get back to the matter of Matthew's dead mother lying on the floor.

"So, I…I'm not sure if the caretaker lady told you, but it appears she took a tumble down the stairs. When I looked around inside, some of the clocks were blinking. I'm thinking the power went out last night in the storm. She might have tried to come down in the dark and…you know."

Pleased with the officer's impression, Matthew nodded his head with a stern yet appreciative face. "Well, thank you, Nick. Thanks for letting me know."

"Alright. Well, let me see how much longer they're going to be. I'm sure you're ready to get this over with."

"That'd be great. Thanks again, man."

CHAPTER 13

Desperate To Be In The Sunroom

Word of Juniper Wells's death spread quickly. The coroner officially ruled her untimely demise an accidental death. The fall down the stairs broke Juniper's neck. She died instantly. There were the obvious initial responses: *life is so fragile; you never know when your time is up; treat every day as if it's your last*, etc. But then, with any accidental death involving an old rich lady, there is, of course, a hushed tone of suspicion. Nothing that was voiced publicly, that would be ill-mannered and tacky, but the whispers simmered, nonetheless.

"I can't believe it." Kay muted the evening news broadcasting the story of Juniper's death.

"I know." Wes got up from the couch where he was sitting with Kay. "I thought that old lady would live forever." He walked from the living room into the kitchen.

Kay rested her arm on the back of the couch and watched Wes pull a beer from the fridge. "Have you heard back from Matthew yet?"

"No, it's weird. I called, but nothing." Wes shrugged as he opened the bottle. "I'm sure he's got a lot going on right now, though. So, what exactly did Celeste say?"

"Well, it was kind of weird, too. She didn't even call me. She just texted. All it said was *Juniper is dead*." Kay looked at her phone. "I called her as soon as I saw the text. She didn't sound upset or anything. She just said that Juniper must have fallen down the steps last night and that Elodie found her this morning."

Wes sat back down next to Kay on the couch and took a sip of his beer. "I'm sure Matthew is pretty torn up. I mean, obviously they didn't have the best relationship, but she's still his mom." They both sat quietly for a moment before Kay posed the question.

"Where was Matthew last night?"

Wes turned and gave Kay a warning look. He could tell by his wife's tone what she was getting at. "Don't even go there, Kay. She fell."

"I was just asking. I'm allowed to ask a question, aren't I?" she responded defensively.

"You're also allowed to watch less *Dateline*." Wes took another sip of his beer before standing to leave the room. He had no intention of entertaining what he knew his wife was suggesting.

"It's a riveting show, Wes," she called after him.

"She fell, Kay. She fell," he said sternly as he turned down the hallway.

Kay began to mutter to herself, insulted by her husband's dismissiveness. "It was just a question. I can ask a question. Don't tell me I watch too much *Dateline*." She started searching the couch for the remote that she had just been holding. "I'm going to put it on right now." She tossed the couch pillows with frustration before yelling, "Where is the darn remote?"

"Don't know," Wes yelled back from the end of the hall. "I guess it's just a mystery!"

A preoccupied Danny pulled into his driveway. He and Wes received news of Juniper's death when Kay called their office after speaking with Celeste. He tried to call Matthew, but his phone was now going straight to voicemail. Danny pulled himself together and out of his car before walking into his house to find Heather prepping for dinner.

"Hey." She looked up from the cutting board with a sympathetic face.

"Hey." He slumped down at the kitchen table and let his laptop bag drop to the floor.

"Have you gotten in touch with him yet?" Heather wiped her hands on a dishtowel and pulled up the chair next to him.

Danny sighed and rubbed the bridge of his nose. "Nope. It's going straight to voicemail now. I'm sure he's getting bombarded with calls. Might have just shut it off."

"I feel so bad for him. It's terrible." Heather put her chin in her hand. "And poor little Charlie must be devastated. They were so close." Heather thought back to the party when she saw how Charlie charged Juniper with excitement when he saw her. He seemed so happy with her.

"I know. He must be so upset. And I doubt Celeste is being very comforting. She's probably ecstatic that Juniper is gone."

This gave Heather pause. She was so focused on poor little Charlie that she hadn't thought through the whole scenario. A scenario that included a lot of people gaining from the death of a woman that they didn't necessarily like. "So, she fell down the stairs sometime last night?" she asked pensively.

"Apparently so." Danny rolled his sleeves and stood to resume Heather's chopping.

"Was anyone in the house when she fell?" She tried to come across as vague.

"I don't think so. They said Elodie found her this—" Danny stopped slicing and looked up at his wife's suspicious expression. "Heather," he scolded as he laid down the knife and put both palms on the countertop. "I'm sure the police did their job and concluded that she fell."

"I was just curious if there was a possibility that someone else might have been there." Heather raised mock defensive hands as she scooted next to Danny to take over the chopping. "I mean, if I found out that someone, I don't know, say Celeste, threw poor Juniper down the stairs, I just wouldn't be that shocked."

Danny pushed the cutting board away from Heather, and she looked at him with confusion. "Have you been watching *Dateline* with Kay again?"

"It's a riveting show, Danny."

"She fell, Heather."

"Well, how can you be so sure no one was there if she wasn't found until this morning?"

"Juniper fell. End of story." He abruptly turned, leaving Heather bewildered at his unusually aggressive tone. Much like his partner, Danny had no intention of entertaining what he knew his wife was suggesting. "I'm going to shower."

Juniper's funeral was a small service held at the historic Lake Lawn Funeral Home. She was placed in the Wells family mausoleum next to her late husband, Edward Wells. Edward, her treasured silver Weimaraner, had been laid to rest on the very same grounds a few years prior in Lake Lawn's Memorial Gardens, which served as the final resting place for beloved pets. A private reception was to be held at the Wells estate following the mass.

The limited number of guests slowly piled out of their cars and trudged toward the front of the mansion. A thick layer of clouds hung low in the sky making it seem as if the sun no longer existed. Everything felt like it was in black and white. Kay held Tommy's hand as Wes led the way up one of the exterior staircases to the front doors. Everyone was so quiet. There was no small talk to ease the tension, no commentary on the overwhelming amount of flowers that had been sent, no sound of muffled sniffles among the group, not even a peep about how "good she looked." Just the crunching sound of guests stepping on the fallen magnolia leaves Juniper had watched swirl from her trees just a few days ago. The eerie silence felt even more ominous as they entered the front doors. There was no hum.

"Why aren't the fans on, Mommy?" Tommy looked around, still holding Kay's hand as they walked into the entrance hall.

"I don't know, baby. Maybe because it's a little cold outside." She knelt beside her son and gave him a comforting smile. His auburn hair looked brown, and his normally bright hazel eyes appeared dull. She knew, even as young as he was, he was worried about his cousin. "Why don't we find Charlie, and you guys can go play upstairs for a while?"

"Okay." Tommy looked around again. "Look, he's right there." Tommy pointed, and Kay turned to see Charlie sitting alone. His feet dangled from the oversized parlor chair. It was the parlor chair that Juniper always sat in when entertaining social gatherings. She considered mingling and working the room in her own home more an expression of social inadequacy than good manners. As such, guests were always the ones to greet her, in that chair.

"Hey, buddy." Kay walked up with Tommy, trying to seem slightly cheerful. Tommy bounced into the chair next to Charlie, and they shared a contained giggle.

"Hi, Aunt Kay." His sad face seemed to brighten a little at the sight of his best friend and Kay. They hadn't gotten the opportunity to really speak that much at the service.

"Would you two like to go upstairs, and I'll bring you up something to eat in just a bit?"

Charlie looked at Tommy, welcoming the sense of something other than sadness. "Do you want to see my new glove? JuJu bought it for me."

Tommy grinned back at him, exposing the gap where his two front teeth used to be. "Race you there!" He took off toward the staircase with a rejuvenated Charlie hot on his heels. Both boys scampered up each step, not considering these were the very same stairs that Juniper's lifeless body tumbled down just a few days prior.

Kay turned her attention to the rest of the guests in the parlor. There weren't many of them, probably about forty or so. Matthew and Celeste were standing at the bar in the drawing room, speaking to Logan. Logan was doing most of the speaking, though, and the other two appeared to be intently listening. The three made their way through the entrance hall and down the long hallway leading to the rear of the house. Remaining in the entrance hall, with hands shoved in pockets, were Wes and Danny. Their heads hung as they muttered to each other.

"Hi, Danny." Kay gave a weak smile as she approached the two men who looked like scolded schoolchildren.

"Hi, Kay. How are you?" Danny leaned forward and gave her a half hug with a kiss on the cheek.

"Doing okay." She turned to Wes. "I sent the boys up to play in Charlie's room. I was going to bring them up a plate. Want me to make you guys one, too?" She glanced from Wes to Danny.

"I think Heather made something special for them. You know, kid food." Kay's offer broke Danny's mournful cloudiness. His response caused her to look at him curiously. "Oh, Heather called Matthew the other night." He shrugged. "I guess she felt bad for the poor guy. She offered to handle the catering for today so he and Celeste wouldn't have to worry about it."

Wes's head slightly tilted at this. He hadn't even been able to get Matthew on the phone. The thought of him answering Heather's call, and not that of his best friend, somewhat threw him. "Well, that was very sweet of her," Kay honestly admitted. "I was wondering why I saw her cut out of the service a little early."

"Yeah, she said they talked for a long time. That he sounded pretty upset. I haven't even spoken to him, though. I've just been getting all my info from you guys and, well, Heather." The past few days, Celeste relayed the funeral arrangements only to Kay via text, along with, of course, very specific recommendations for her outfit in case the press decided to make an appearance.

"Well…sometimes it's easier to open up to a—" She stopped herself before finishing the sentence. "Someone you don't, you know, know as well." Wes and Danny nodded at this. That notion hadn't crossed their minds; it gave them both some level of solace regarding Matthew's silence, and yet somehow felt unnerving at the same time.

The normally bright and welcoming sunroom in the rear of the Wells mansion felt cold and gray that day. The room was practically wall-to-wall windows providing a relaxing view of an elaborate garden that seemed to protect the home from the dark swampland in the distance. Logan entered the sunroom and proceeded straight to an end table next to a large natural brown wicker sofa. He pulled a thick manila folder from the end table drawer and turned to see Matthew and Celeste already seated in the two matching wicker chairs across from the sofa.

He couldn't help but think the room suddenly felt even colder with their presence. Forcing a considerate smile, he sat across from Matthew and Celeste, laying the manila folder on the glass coffee table separating him from the couple. Neither of them met his glance as he sat and adjusted his tie. Matthew stared out the windows blankly, and Celeste eyed her nails with what felt like agitation as if they were both waiting for their number to be called at the DMV.

Logan cleared his throat to draw their attention. "I am very sorry again for your loss." He swallowed hard and frowned at the thought. "Juniper was definitely one of a kind."

"Ha." Celeste bobbed her head back and uncrossed, then recrossed her legs. "A kind of what?" Her comment drew no response from her husband, who was still staring out the windows.

The normally calm and polite Logan hid his disdain for Celeste even though his restraint was causing the back of his neck to match the color of his light red hair. He then paused and relaxed, reminding himself that he had the privilege of being the bearer of what was sure to be very unwelcomed news. "Well, as I mentioned earlier"—he removed several documents from the folder—"Juniper named me executor of her estate." At this, Matthew and Celeste began paying attention, which was their usual response to anything monetary-related.

Logan handed both of them a copy of Juniper's will. "In short, Juniper has left the majority of her estate to Charlie." Releasing the documents into their hands, he tensed, waiting for some emotional reaction, but to Logan's surprise, the couple did not seem…surprised. Celeste and Matthew haphazardly flipped through the pages as Logan adjusted his posture and continued. "As Charlie's legal guardians, you are provided an annual three hundred and fifty thousand dollar stipend for living expenses and childcare until he reaches the age of twenty-one. You will have full access to all properties, including the family estate. However, once Charlie turns twenty-one, all funds and titles will be transferred to him." Matthew rolled the copy of the will like a scroll and returned to gazing out the windows.

"Once the formal death certificate has been finalized, we can move forward with the annual disbursement." Logan clasped his hands and leaned back on the sofa. "Gauge will be contacting you at that time to provide you with a check for the allotted amount."

Celeste sucked her cheeks and narrowed her eyes before speaking. "I'm sorry. What was that?"

"Juniper retained Gauge as her financial planner about a

month ago. She wanted someone she trusted to handle her personal financial dealings. He will manage all the estate funds and initiate any and all approved monetary transactions. It's all laid out in—"

Celeste cut off Logan by suddenly tossing the copy of the will onto the coffee table and glaring. "What did you mean when you said *the majority of*?"

"Excuse me?" Logan was now confused as to which issue he was supposed to be addressing.

She leaned forward and slowly repeated his words, "Juniper has left *the majority of* her estate to Charles."

"Yes, ma'am." Logan pushed the tossed will back across the coffee table toward her. "There are other heirs. They are noted on page thirteen."

Unwilling to receive the document from Logan a second time, she snatched the scrolled will out of Matthew's hands. She flipped the now curled pages until she reached page thirteen. Her eyes flashed back and forth as she heatedly read the typed lines and then seemed to explode from the inside. "You have got to be kidding me!"

"These were Juniper's wishes, ma'am," Logan stated flatly. Celeste jumped up and threw the will at Logan's chest.

"You will be hearing from our lawyer!"

Logan sighed. "I am your lawyer, Celeste."

"I…" She awkwardly stumbled over her words, realizing her mistake. "I meant our new lawyer. Come on, Matthew. We have guests to attend to." A lethargic Matthew rose to follow his wife.

"Those are Juniper's guests, Celeste, not yours," Logan chided as she made her way with Matthew in tow to the door of the sunroom.

"Not anymore, darling." She flicked her blonde hair and kept walking. "Not any fucking more."

"How are you holding up?" Gauge poured a glass of water from a pitcher and handed it to Elodie. She clasped both hands around the glass and rested it in her lap. Perched on the wicker chair wearing her best black dress, Elodie looked like a very beautiful yet very sad bird sitting on a wire. She knew Juniper would hate it and probably even haunt her if she showed up looking like hell, so she made her best attempt to put herself together. The fifty-year-old Elodie would have definitely made her friend proud that day by looking not a day over forty on the outside. Unfortunately, though, she felt about one hundred on the inside.

"I just keep waiting to hear her holler for me." She gazed up at the ceiling as if hoping to see into heaven. "Knowing her, though, she probably still is." She gave a small, sad laugh. "I just can't hear it now." Elodie released a long sigh and placed the glass of water on the sunroom coffee table next to a pile of papers. She looked up at Gauge and Logan, who were sitting on the sofa across from her. "She loved you two boys very much."

"She loved you, too, Elodie," Gauge said sincerely with a wink. He turned and gave his brother an initiating glance.

"So, Elodie." Logan picked up the pile of papers from the coffee table. "Juniper obviously had a will."

She nodded. "I know. I was pretty sure I heard her making some changes to it a while ago."

"You did?" Logan was taken aback to hear this.

"Overheard her on the phone one day. Sounded like she was giving all her money to Charlie," she absentmindedly admitted. Gauge and Logan gave her such a perplexed look that she suddenly felt the need to clarify. "I mean, I told her I overheard, naturally. Didn't feel right not to tell her."

"So, you know?" Gauge hesitantly asked.

"I don't know, per se, but it sure did sound to me like that was what she was doing." Still feeling guilty about her confession, she continued, "Well, I think Charlie should get all that money. It should go to someone who really loved her. Not one of them vultures."

"Some...*one*?" Logan began to understand that Elodie had not overheard all the details of the phone conversation that day.

"Yes. Charlie." Elodie's eyes darted back and forth between the two men in confusion. "Boys, am I missin' something? Why y'all talking to me about this anyway?"

Logan swallowed his laugh. "Well, Elodie, I agree with you. Juniper wanted her money to go to someone who really loved her." He handed a copy of the will to her. "But there was more than *one* person who did that. Flip to page thirteen."

Elodie furrowed her brow and counted the pages of the document as she turned them. Squinting down at the small type, she tried to make out the text, but her tired eyes wouldn't allow it. "I didn't bring my glasses today." She squinted harder in frustration. "I can't read this. What does it say?"

"It says Juniper left you a little something in her will. Actually, she left each of us a little something. You, me, and Logan."

Elodie's face twisted slightly, not knowing whether the twins were playing a trick on her. "No, she didn't. She woulda told me."

"I guess she wanted to surprise you." Gauge grinned.

Remembering where she kept a spare set of reading glasses for Juniper, Elodie skeptically stood up, eyeing the boys suspiciously. Keeping one eye on the twins, she slowly walked to one of the bookcases behind her. She placed the hidden frames on her face and inspected page thirteen. The papers began vibrating in her hands as she read and reread the small print.

"That crazy, old—" Her shocked eyes shot up at the twins and then back to page thirteen. "Shc didn't really do this, did she?"

"Yes, ma'am, she sure did." Logan stood proudly. "Juniper left each of us one million dollars."

"Oh, and don't forget about the fans," Gauge happily interjected from the sofa.

"Yes, of course. She was also very clear that you should inherit her entire, and one must say, elaborate collection of hand fans. Even the broken ones."

After about two hours of post-funeral formalities, the already small number of guests began to dwindle. This was partly because Logan had returned from the sunroom half an hour ago, signaling that no one else would be receiving good news that day. Charlie peeped his head over the banister to see how many guests remained. He didn't want to see anyone. He desperately wanted everyone to disappear so he could curl up in Juniper's bed and be alone. He crept back to his room before anyone could see him.

"So, we can never share gloves?" Tommy was sitting on the lower bunk, trying to force his right hand into Charlie's new left-handed baseball glove.

"Nope." Charlie climbed to the top bunk and lay flat on his back, staring at the ceiling.

"Maybe I'll be left-handed one day." Tommy stood on the bottom bunk and clasped his hands on the bed rail of the top bunk to see his cousin.

"Maybe. JuJu told me some kids change hands when they get older."

"Do you want to go outside and throw?" Tommy was doing his best to cheer up Charlie.

"Maybe later." Charlie propped up on his elbow, feeling a little bad, noticing his friend was bored.

Tommy's eyes suddenly got big with excitement. "I have an idea! I know what we should do." He flashed his cousin a big grin. "And I know your grandma would really, really like it."

After a brief plan was put into place, Charlie and Tommy marched down the main stairs in their funeral suits like two small soldiers on a mission. Heather and Kay were at the bottom of the stairs talking about how "good she looked" when Heather caught sight of the boys. "Now, what are these two up to?"

Kay turned and couldn't help but laugh at their determined faces. "Honey, can I get you boys something?"

"No, thank you, Mommy. We have to do something for Ms. Juniper." The boys made it to the bottom of the stairs, with Charlie turning right into the parlor and Tommy turning left into the drawing room. They both went directly to the far corner of each room and crouched down practically in unison.

"What on earth are they doing?" Heather laughed as her and Kay's heads swiveled back and forth between the two rooms. And then, they heard it. A very quiet humming sound. Both boys continued to make their way around the perimeter of the rooms as the humming grew louder and louder. The cold, stagnant air suddenly became lighter.

"The fans. They're turning on the fans." Kay's heart swelled as she watched the boys turn on each of the oscillating fans one by one. After that was complete, they both made their way into the entrance hall and turned on every one of those fans as well.

Meeting in the middle of the entrance hall with a prideful sense of accomplishment, Tommy asked Charlie, "Better?"

"Way better. Now let's do upstairs!" The boys dodged Kay and Heather, still standing in awe at the thoughtfulness of the two little men, and scampered up the stairs to the second floor.

"How stinking cute is that?" Heather turned to Kay, misty-eyed. "They are so precious." Heather's warmed heart suddenly saddened when she thought of what would become of Charlie now with Juniper gone. The way Matthew and Celeste completely ignored him was incomprehensible. He needed so much more out of parents. Juniper seemed to fill that void for him, but now that would disappear. The mere thought of it made her ache. *They don't deserve him.*

Her thoughts were interrupted when Logan approached carrying two glasses. A large white envelope was casually tucked under his arm. "You did a wonderful job, Heather," he honestly complemented before handing the bubbly drinks to the two women. "Everything was great."

Kay took a sip. "I must say, I can't blame Juniper for wanting to keep this cocktail all to herself. Never thought I'd actually get to have *a Juniper* without a broken wrist chaser." She sadly looked down at the rising bubbles in her champagne glass. "Quite the beautiful force to be reckoned with. If she were here now, she'd probably have snapped at least fifty fans over our knuckles already."

"Given the circumstances, I think she'll forgive us." Logan tried to conjure some optimism and then mentally admitted that he didn't even believe what he just said.

"Have you seen Celeste? I haven't gotten the chance to talk to her at all today." The only interaction she'd had with her cousin was at the funeral in the form of a disapproving look from across the room after seeing Kay's dress.

"Oh"—Logan cast his eyes upward around the large hall—"I'm sure she's here somewhere. Probably already measuring rooms and taking inventory."

"Sounds about right," Heather unexpectedly piped in. Blushing immediately for fear that she had just been a little too honest, she changed directions. "What about those men folk of ours? Have you seen Matthew and the guys?"

"I think I heard some commotion out back. They're probably out there having something a little stronger than a Juniper to drown their sorrows."

"Also sounds about right." Kay nodded at Heather with a smirk and another sip. "Guess I better grab Wes before they get too rowdy. I'm beat anyway."

"Actually, Kay, could I steal you for a minute before you go?" Logan pulled the white envelope from under his arm. Heather and Kay looked a bit taken aback at the unexpected invitation. Recognizing that this was preferably a private conversation, Heather broke the short, surprised silence.

"I'm going to go tell my guys that they can go ahead and start loading up the van. I'll set some to-go boxes out for y'all with any extras." She left Kay's side and passed Logan, only to quickly crane her neck back to give Kay a pleasantly baffled look. *Maybe he wasn't done with the sunroom discussions after all*, she tried to convey with her eyes.

Once Heather was out of the room, Kay swirled her drink and attempted not to appear anxious. "So, what can I do for you, sir?"

Logan straightened the large white envelope that had been folded in half, causing the outline of an object to become visible. "Well, Juniper did have a long list of specific physical items that she bequeathed to various people."

"Oh, it sure does sound like you have your work cut out for you then." She gave a nervous laugh as Logan placed his hand in the already-opened envelope, not recognizing how uncomfortable Kay had suddenly become.

"She did leave you a little something," he chuckled and then pressed his lips together before continuing. "I'm going to be honest, Kay, I have no idea why she left you this." He pulled a small box out of the envelope. "Sometimes, she could have an odd sense of humor. I…well, I don't even know where she got this. She always went to the salon." Logan almost apologetically handed Kay the contents of the envelope.

Juniper Wells bequeathed Kay Allen one box of L'Oréal Paris hair dye, 9A–Light Ash Blonde.

CHAPTER 14

Desperate For Change

The months that followed Juniper's passing were filled with change. It was almost as if nothing was capable of being the same without her. She wouldn't have allowed that. For starters, the economy decided to make a sudden rebound. Stocks were up, employment was up, and interest rates were down, which gave struggling businesses a well-deserved chance to catch their breath.

Heather's catering business began attracting a new and very wealthy clientele. Apparently, Juniper had put in a few calls to some friends after attending Charlie's birthday party to recommend this "hidden gem" of a caterer that she knew. The fact that she outdid herself on Juniper's post-funeral reception didn't hurt either. Money was so good she decided to convert the detached garage at the back of her and Danny's modest home into a fully functioning kitchen. She could now do a large amount of prep work at home without having to schlep to her downtown location in the catering van—a van which she also recently decided to upgrade.

Truth be told, Heather didn't really mind having to go to her storefront, but she was thinking about the future. After recently starting the long-awaited fertility treatments, she was certain they would soon put her on the path to motherhood. Knowing that with a baby or babies, happily aware that fertility treatments sometimes offered the benefit of multiples, she would need to be home more. The irony of *a bun in the oven* made her beam every time she thought of it.

Danny was feeling optimistic, too. Things seemed more hopeful both at home and at work. His beautiful wife was smiling more and felt more positive these days. The fertility treatments did draw out the occasional emotional outburst, unfortunately. Their doctor warned the couple that was a possible side effect but advised them to welcome it, as it was all a part of the process. Thankfully, the recent uptick in his and Wes's company revenue came just when they needed it to afford the weekly shots. Danny loved Heather very much and desired nothing more than to give her what she so desperately wanted. Her kind nature and determination made him feel blessed whenever he thought of his wife and inspired him to do whatever it took to make her happy.

Wes was also feeling a little lighter lately now that the weight of potential financial ruin had been lifted from his shoulders. Somehow, he and Danny managed to turn the business around in a relatively short period of time. It didn't hurt that their old client, Fischer, reentered the picture after the long and grueling rebuilding of his new post-divorce construction company. Wes hadn't realized how stressed he had been and how that stress was impacting his family. Only after the smoke began to clear did he notice that he had been avoiding Kay for fear of upsetting her with their financial situation. Poor Tommy hadn't been getting much more attention than Kay from his father either. Wes kicked himself for being so mentally absent and immediately volunteered to be not only the corporate sponsor of his son's little league team but the head coach as well.

On some level, Kay did notice that Wes had been a little distant lately but, in all honestly, wasn't that worried about it. Some women might get suspicious if their husbands suddenly started spending way more time at the office and way less quality time with them. But Kay felt that she knew her husband pretty darn well, and if he were up to something, she'd be able to tell. So, willing to give him the benefit of the doubt, she decided to overlook his recent inattentiveness and focus on the new house for now. She figured he was just going through a phase. An opinion that she felt validated in having once Wes seemed to shake off whatever had been distracting him and started making an obvious conscious effort to be more physically and mentally present.

Unfortunately for Celeste, the opposite seemed to be true for her husband. After Juniper died, Matthew became withdrawn. He was never really an active family man pre-Juniper's death, but when he was around, he was normally in a decent mood and always ready to have a good time. Now, he slept in and moped around the house until Charlie got home from school. After a few hours, he would leave and go straight to the gentleman's club where Natalia worked. Matthew would wait until she got off, and then they would return to another night of rolling around on leopard print sheets. This cycle became the new Wells family daily routine.

Matthew was surprised at how hard Juniper's death impacted him. He mistakenly always thought of himself as being mentally tough. Maybe it wasn't Juniper's death that had him depressed. It could be everything he learned that night and came to know soon after. He was sure his fog would clear in time, but for now, he felt he deserved a little drunken, pill-infused debauchery, and his wife deserved to sit back, shut up, and watch him do it. He had not yet told Celeste that he knew Charlie wasn't his son. He didn't know if he ever would.

While Celeste was prepared to shut up and watch him do it, she wasn't on board with the sit-back part. Who did he think he was? He had allowed his mother to leave them with hardly enough to maintain their lifestyle. He hadn't made any attempt to get them moved into the Wells estate. Obviously, they would need to free up some cash given their new "poverty," and selling their home to move into the estate made the most sense. Plus, with Matthew being even more absent lately, she had no one to toy with. She'd have to find a substitute for her easily manipulated husband.

"We need to talk before you head out." Celeste stood at the entrance to the living area with hands on hips, watching Matthew and Charlie play video games. The now six-month-old Weimaraner stood quietly next to her.

Matthew side-eyed her and began to feverishly tap buttons on the controller. "Okay, give me a sec."

"I'm going to beat you, Dad," Charlie taunted as he stood up on the couch with his controller.

"No way, dude," Matthew contended, which was immediately followed by a victory scream from his son.

"I told you! I told you, Dad!"

"Yeah, yeah, you told me." Matthew gave Charlie a playful push on the shoulder before standing. "Alright, I'm gonna talk to your mom and then head out. I'll beat you tomorrow."

"No way, Jose!" Charlie plopped down on the couch and continued playing.

"Not too much longer, Charles," Celeste chided. "You need to do your reading with Reausaleigh." She turned and strutted into the kitchen with the dog beside her and Matthew begrudgingly shuffling as he followed.

"Yes, Celeste?" He leaned his elbows onto the kitchen island and looked up at her. For a moment, he softened, remembering how breathtaking his wife was, and then decided it best to look down instead. It had been a while since he had really looked at her.

"You've been gone a lot lately," she said without looking up from the glass of wine she was pouring.

Matthew shrugged. "Just have a lot going on."

"And when you are here, you've been sleeping in the guest room." Still without looking at her husband, she coolly placed the bottle in the wine fridge.

"Just been needing some alone time."

"Alone, huh?" Celeste flashed her blue eyes at him and raised an eyebrow. "Hmm." She gave a *Let's not be coy* smirk. "Well, I need to talk to you about a few things." Matthew decided to go ahead and sit on one of the island barstools, partly out of gratitude for her obviously letting him off the hook just then. "We need to make some decorating changes to the estate before we can move in. Nothing major, but at some point, we should probably go over there together and discuss what needs to change and what needs to stay."

"Alright." Matthew nodded agreeably.

"Also, a partner at one of my father's firms is going to take over as our legal counsel. Logan is practically still in diapers. We don't need someone who probably still has his graduation tassel hanging from his rearview mirror representing us."

"Done." Matthew waved his hand quickly and sternly.

"Hmph." Celeste popped up from petting the dog still by her side. "I thought you'd put up more of a fight on that one."

"What else?" He pulled his phone from his pocket to check a text from his party favor provider.

"Well, Jackson Bergeron, that's our new lawyer. He suggests we revise our will. We still have the same one we've had since before Charles was born. And given our new"—she paused and licked her lips—"our new financial structure, we should update it."

Realizing this was taking longer than anticipated, Matthew stood to pour himself a whiskey. "Makes sense." He downed the whiskey and poured another before leaning back against the kitchen counter. "Should be simple enough." He looked down at the dog that hadn't moved from Celeste's side as it watched her like a hawk.

"Precisely. We do need to name guardians for Charles in the event of both of our deaths." Matthew knew where this was going and began to watch his wife as intently as the dog. "Obviously, your parents are gone, and my parents are getting a bit up there, so I—"

"Danny and Heather," he abruptly cut her off.

"What?" Celeste's blonde hair swung as she jerked her head back in bewilderment. "Daniel and Heather, what? Should get Charles? Absolutely not. He should go to Kay and Wes. They're family."

Matthew gave a sarcastic chuckle and tried to contain his sudden anger. "Family, huh?" He slugged back his whiskey and slammed the glass onto the counter. "Well, family ain't what it used to be." His brown eyes locked with hers. The expression on his face read very clearly.

"Daniel and Heather it is then," she quickly relented. "I'll speak with Jackson if you would please let Daniel know. I'm sure there will be some papers for them to sign." Matthew clenched his jaw and grunted as he pushed himself from the counter and stalked toward the front doors. "I'll tell him they can have that damn dog, too."

Celeste jumped slightly at the bang of the slamming front doors. She pursed her lips before looking down to confess her newfound fear to her faithful pup. "I think he knows."

"**S**hit! Shit! Shit!" Heather threw the burnt tray of petit fours onto the counter and ran to the sink. She shoved her throbbing hand under the faucet and let the cold water run over her palm. "Shit!"

"Are you alright?" Danny was just coming through the door of their new detached kitchen to see his wife hunched over the sink. Profanity was a rarely used ingredient for her. She didn't raise her head when he entered. Her long dark hair, streaked with flour, covered the profile of her face from his view. She took a deep breath and collected herself before turning off the faucet.

"I'm fine." Quickly pivoting toward the oversized refrigerator, still trying to hide her face and dismay, she attempted to sound pleasantly casual. "Occupational hazard." Opening the top freezer, she let the cold air hit her face to enhance her calm before grabbing a soft ice pack. She wrapped it around her singed hand and sat on a folding chair. Forcing a smile, she finally looked up at Danny, hoping he couldn't see through her cheery disguise. "What's up?"

Danny pretty much only came into the new kitchen to let Heather know that he was heading out for the day, or running an errand, or, of course, for a kiss goodnight if she was working late. On this lazy Saturday afternoon, Danny walked into Heather's workspace wearing an old T-shirt and gym shorts with bare feet, clearly indicating he had no initial plans of going anywhere other than back to the couch to finish watching golf.

"Just coming to check on you. You've been out here all day," he said with a considerate smile, not noticing Heather's forced one. "Matthew just called, though. I might go have a couple beers with the guys in a bit." He rubbed the back of his head sheepishly. "Unless you want to go grab dinner or something."

Heather's stiff smile eased into a natural one. She thought it was endearing that Danny was more so asking permission to have drinks with the boys than telling her he was. Seeing his sensitive nature always made her feel better and more centered. She relaxed and stood to replace the ice pack in the freezer. "Oh, you go have fun." She peeked around the open freezer door and teased her husband with a wink. "Not too much fun, though."

"Now, how could I possibly have any fun without you," he jested back as he came up behind her and wrapped his arms around her. "I was pretty content on the couch, but when Matthew called, I kind of felt obligated." He pecked her neck before pulling his cell phone from the pocket of his gym shorts.

"Oh yeah. And why is that?" She gently pulled away and picked up an oven mitt to handle the still-steaming pan on the counter.

"Well, he called and said that he and Celeste are redoing their will." Danny shrugged at the phone. "He said they want us to be Charlie's guardians, you know, in case anything ever happened to them."

"What?" Heather whizzed around and gave him a crazed look.

"I know. I thought it was kind of odd, but—"

"Why us? That doesn't make any sense!" She slammed the burnt pan into the sink. "What is this, *pity*? Is it because they think we can't have children of our own? Is it because they think I'm barren?"

Danny took two steps back and put two defensive hands up, shocked at Heather's reaction. "Whoa, whoa. What just happened? I thought you would be flattered." His green eyes searched his wife's flushed face, trying to understand why she just exploded. And then he sadly recognized the look in her eyes. It was the look that broke his heart every time he saw it. "Oh honey, I…" he said softly as he stepped toward her.

Heather flung herself around and punched both palms onto the rim of the sink. Letting her hair curtain her face again, she watched her tears fall and sizzle on the pan as she stared down into the sink. "I got my period this morning."

CHAPTER 15

Desperate To Taunt

Wes pulled his green collared shirt over his head. He liked St. Patrick's Day. It was one of those fake holidays. The kind that doesn't require all the stressful overplanning, forced conversations with distant relatives, and constantly checking the time to see how much more "celebrating" you had to do. It was just a chance to drink some green beer and have fun with friends. The timing of St. Patrick's Day was perfect, too. It was an opportunity to get in one last parade, post-Mardi Gras, and the holiday landed just before the summer swelter started creeping in. It was something that he was looking forward to after working so hard lately.

"You ready?" He strolled into the bathroom where Kay was giving her auburn hair a finishing coat of hairspray.

"Yes, sir." She turned from the mirror to her husband. He looked handsome in something as simple as a polo shirt and shorts. "I love you in green." She scooted up to Wes and gave him an adoring peck on the lips. "It brings out the little specks of green in your eyes."

"You do, huh?" He thought it was cute when his wife still tried to flirt with him. "Maybe if you're lucky, I'll show you my green underwear later tonight," he teased with a flash of his dimples.

"Already starting with the lucky jokes, I see." She gave him a scolding slap on the chest. "Come on, let's go. I want to get a good spot. We can talk green underwear, or lack thereof, when we get home." Kay gave him one more flirty peck before they loaded up to head over to Heather's shop.

Heather always closed her storefront on St. Patrick's Day. The parade route passed right in front of her catering company on Magazine Street. The location gave her friends the perfect place to party, watch the parade, and, more importantly, have easy access to a bathroom. Prior to her guest's arrival, Heather laid out guacamole deviled eggs, stuffed green peppers, corned beef and cabbage sliders, and fruit kabobs of kiwi, melon, and grapes.

Danny watched his wife arrange and then rearrange the platters. He stepped away from the makeshift bar he had assembled on the main shop counter. Wrapping two loving arms around her, he honestly complimented, "You've outdone yourself yet again."

"Do you think it's enough?" Heather viewed her spread with concern. "I am still going to make the Shamrock Shakes."

He gave her an adoring squeeze. "It's perfect." Danny tried to nonchalantly gauge her anxiety level. "How are you feeling?"

Recognizing the tone in his voice, Heather's attention shifted from overanalyzing the placement of her trays to her caring husband. "I'm good." She gave him a comforting smile. "Now, how's my bar coming along, mister?" she playfully demanded to change the subject.

"I have us all set up. I—" Just as Danny was beginning to detail his attempt at a proper Irish pub, a breeze and street music swept into the store as Celeste and Matthew walked through the front doors.

"Well, well, well, here come the Wells," Danny cheerfully greeted. "I got your favorite, Matthew." He flicked his head to the Irish Whiskey resting on the makeshift bar.

"Dear God, somehow you can make even my own name sound annoying." Celeste cascaded straight to the bar as she viewed Heather's delightfully charming store with contempt. Matthew met Danny's warm welcome with only a nod as he approached Heather. "Thanks for having us, Heather." He gave her a polite hug with a kiss on the cheek before extending a silent hand for Danny to shake.

"Am I expected to pour my own drink?" Celeste beckoned from Danny's pub setup while using her cell phone as a mirror to freshen her lip gloss.

Matthew huffed and shook his head. "I need to make a

call." Already regretting coming, he abruptly turned around and walked right out of the doors he had just entered.

Not blaming Matthew in the least for wanting to be more than a few Celtic meters away from Celeste, Heather pleasantly offered, "Danny mixes up the most amazing Cucumber Martinis." She politely joined her one unfortunate guest at the bar.

Heather's pleasantness annoyed Celeste greatly. She'd seen cellophane that was less transparent than Heather's goody-two-shoes act. Celeste's spite led to the sudden decision to throw a figurative drink in her hostess's face while commanding her husband to make one for her.

"On it." Danny happily scurried to the back of the counter.

"Aren't we lucky girls to have such a handsome bartender?" Heather tried to play nice with Celeste as Danny assembled the ingredients.

Oh, this is going to be too easy. "Been there, done that." Celeste gave a flick of the wrist before returning her lip gloss to her clutch.

Celeste's response gave Heather a glimmer of hope at some girl-talk comradery. "Oh, do tell, Celeste. Have you broken a few bartender hearts?"

"Ugh, of course not. That is disgusting." Tossing her hair back, she clarified, "I meant this bartender in particular." Celeste gave a misbehaving smirk in Danny's direction. "Remember, I like them strong, Daniel."

Danny popped up from behind the counter with vodka in one hand, cucumbers in the other, and a pair of very startled eyes. Heather's confusion at the comment and her husband's reaction was painfully obvious.

"Didn't you know?" Celeste toyed. Danny took a nervous pull off the vodka bottle as his wife and ex-infatuation focused on one another. "Daniel and I used to be sweet on each other."

Heather remained perfectly still, with the exception of some compulsive blinking that took control of her big brown eyes. "Oh, don't be jealous," Celeste taunted before pouting her freshly glossed lips. "He was the perfect gentleman. He even fixed my car once. Didn't you, Daniel?"

"You fixed her car? You always tell me to call AAA."

Danny swallowed the vodka that was now warming in his mouth and awkwardly adjusted his glasses. "Many moons ago," he managed to croak before giving an uncomfortable laugh. "Mrs. Wells here was good enough to briefly entertain me until I met the love of my life." Overselling it a bit, he affectionately picked up Heather's hand and kissed it. "I was a mere pitstop on Celeste's way to marrying Matthew and going on to have her beautiful family." Danny desperately tried to tame the conversation.

"Yes. Very true, Daniel. I definitely do have you to thank for that." Celeste made sure Heather saw the wink she slid to Danny.

"Who's ready?" Kay excitedly called as she and Wes came through the front doors. A few layers of sparkly green beads already hung around her neck. A thankful Danny almost fainted with relief at the interruption.

"Only my wife *brings* beads to a parade," Wes jested as the doors quickly reopened behind them with Matthew's return.

"Matthew, do you bring beads to a parade?" Kay pointedly asked.

"No." He was slightly confused at her greeting but caught on quickly after seeing Kay's accessories. "But if I looked as pretty as you do in them, I might." He gave her a hug and kiss on the cheek. "Looking good, cuz."

"Hey, brother. How's it going?" Wes extended a welcoming hand to his best friend. Matthew shook it and delivered yet another silent nod. Wes noticed the unusually cold response, and it saddened him. *Still hasn't shaken it off yet.* He hated seeing his friend like this.

"Too early for shots?" Danny eagerly suggested as he lifted the bottle of whiskey to his friends. It was, indeed, a bit early for shots, but Danny was looking for any excuse to distract his wife from the history lesson Celeste had just given her. Heather's compulsive blinking had now turned into a calm yet understandable we'll-talk-about-this-later look.

Matthew let the invitation pull up one corner of his mouth and relax him a bit. "Never."

"I know lots of people that wear beads to parades," Kay continued to defend herself as she walked with Wes and

Matthew to join the others at the bar. "It's inviting to the bead thrower."

"Hush, woman," Wes said dismissively. "Come have a drink before you get yourself worked up." Danny handed him the Irish whiskey as the men gathered behind the bar, and the women commandeered the stools on the other side. Matthew lined up three shot glasses on the counter as Wes cracked the seal of the bottle.

"Ladies first," Celeste reprimanded.

"Right you are, Celeste." Wes casually poured two small shots of the whiskey and placed them directly in front of Kay and Heather, leaving the third shot glass empty. "Here you go, ladies." He didn't bother to receive the death stare that he knew Celeste was currently giving him.

"She's going cut you one of these days, honey." Kay scolded her husband as she slid her shot to Celeste and poured one for herself. Celeste fully intended to cut Wes but decided to throw a dagger of another sort.

"Catch any snakes lately, Carl?" Celeste stared him in the eyes as she downed her shot. Matthew promptly picked up her used glass and filled it to the rim before slugging it back.

Wes jutted his lower jaw and gave an almost unnoticeable shake of his head. "Dang it, Celeste." Assuming the jab was meant for her, Kay obliviously snapped at her cousin, "I told you it was one flipping field mouse, and Randy, the exterminator, took care of it. We don't have any snakes or rats or anything like that. Geez, the things you remember to use as judgmental ammo is bizarre." Matthew gave a snort of agreement before taking another shot.

Hoping for a bit more of a friendlier ambiance to her little gathering, Heather cheerfully stood up to distract the bickering group. "Y'all just have to try the goodies I made for us. Let's start with the deviled eggs." *Mouths full of appetizers were better than mouths full of insults*, she thought. Heather retrieved a tray from the table and placed it on the center of the counter. Matthew instinctively switched places with Danny in the tight area behind the bar. Noticing the position change, Heather offered, "Oh, Matthew, you don't have to move over. Danny already had a few earlier."

"They're both lefties," Matthew knowingly replied. "Can't

have a right-handed person between them, or shit gets spilled."

"Like Charlie." Celeste casually threw in.

"Yep." Matthew sucked his teeth and kicked back another shot. "Just like Charlie."

"Well, I will just have to remember that for our next dinner party seating arrangement." Heather invitingly picked up an egg to encourage the others to eat.

I'm not doing this. Matthew decided party favors and leopard print sheets sounded a lot better than his wife's nails-on-a-chalkboard voice. "I have to go."

"What? No, you just got here. Stay and play with us a little longer," Kay begged genuinely. None of them had seen very much of him lately.

"Yeah, man. Stay. We haven't gotten rowdy in forever." Danny put his hand on Matthew's shoulder.

"How am I supposed to get home?" Celeste looked at him coldly.

Matthew poured another full shot. Keeping his eyes on Celeste, he asked, "One of you boys has no problem giving my wife"—he downed the whiskey—"a ride, do you?"

Celeste's eyes flashed slightly. Danny cleared his throat and sadly released his hand from Matthew's shoulder. "Sure, man. No problem."

CHAPTER 16

Desperate For An Alibi

"He's staring at me again." Kay furrowed her brow at the haunting gray eyes that were locked on her.

"He's probably just trying to figure out how it is possible for him to be better groomed than a human." Celeste looked over her dark sunglasses as she lounged on the pool chair next to her cousin.

"Well, I can't relax with him doing that." Kay put her hand up to block his view of her face.

"Ugh, fine." Celeste snapped her fingers three times and commanded, "Bullet, *bed*!" At which, the now almost full-grown Weimaraner promptly marched away and curled up on his overpriced memory foam dog bed in the corner of the patio. Bullet followed Celeste everywhere and listened to her every instruction, for which he was greatly rewarded with luxuries that should be reserved for the Queen's Welsh Corgis.

"I still don't understand why you named him Bullet." Kay finally leaned back and shifted into a comfortable position on her pool chair. "I mean, he's silver, for goodness' sake."

"So?" An uninterested Celeste sat up to retrieve her sweating glass of champagne from the side table.

"Silver bullet? Celeste, come on, really?" She gave her cousin a dumbfounded look.

"I don't understand you." She flipped her hand. "I'm thinking about breeding him, actually. He has a very good bloodline." Celeste took a long sip before sighing and reclining back contently. "He'll be making some very pretty bitches very happy soon."

Kay muttered, knowing that her joke would fall on deaf ears, "Yeah, silver bullets do have that capability."

Celeste had called her cousin that morning and invited her over for afternoon poolside drinks. She sweetened the pot by offering to have Reausaleigh pick up both Charles and Thomas from day camp so they could have the whole afternoon to relax. It was an offer that Kay was hard-pressed to refuse on an especially hot Friday in late June. Plus, if Celeste was extending an unexpected invitation, it normally meant she had something interesting to discuss that she wouldn't dare divulge to anyone else.

"This heat is unbearable," Celeste complained as she adjusted her swimsuit.

"You're making me hot just looking at you in that." Kay scanned Celeste's perfect body, donning a very bright, multi-colored one-piece swimsuit. "I've never seen you in a one-piece before. Go put on a bikini. It's too hot for all that."

Celeste gave her cousin a condescending side-eye. "I've had Reausaleigh sorting through some old things to prep for the move. She came across it, and I figured I'd see if it still fit." She smoothed her hand over her swimsuit-covered flat stomach. "It's a Luna Mae."

"Well, I think Luna Mae-de a mistake with that one. You look like an eighties aerobics instructor."

"And you look like uncultured trash." Celeste sat up and smoothed her hand over her perfect stomach again. "Now stop obsessing about me, and let's get in the pool."

Updates to the Wells mansion were almost complete. The plan was for Matthew, Celeste, and Charlie to move there at the end of July. After the transition into the estate, arrangements would be made to put their current home on the market. Thankfully, their house was already paid off, so its sale would provide a nice little cash infusion. Of course, Celeste was planning one last party to celebrate getting rid of "the dump," as she now so poetically referred to her own home. The Fourth of July seemed like the perfect opportunity to go out with a bang.

"Reausaleigh!" Celeste unexpectedly screamed, causing Kay to bolt up so fast her sunglasses flew off her face.

"Jesus, Celeste. Warn somebody before you do that. You scared the biscuits out of me."

"Hmm, still not cursing, I see."

"Yep," Kay replied proudly. "I've been swear word sober since September."

"That is surprising. If I looked like you, I'd curse every time I looked in the mirror." Celeste stood and put her hands on her hips, looking up at the house impatiently. "Reausaleigh!"

"Yes, ma'am." A hurried Reausaleigh appeared at the back doors. "I'm sorry. I was going through some of the piles and didn't hear you. Can I get y'all something?"

"Yes, open another bottle of champagne. Put it in an ice bucket and bring it out to the pool."

"Yes, ma'am." Before she could turn to leave, Kay chimed in.

"Hi, Reausaleigh. How have you been?"

"Oh, fine, just fine."

"And how's Elodie?"

Fearing that Celeste would get annoyed at the possibility of a delayed cocktail, she kept it short and repeated, "Oh, fine, just fine."

"Well, send her my best."

"Will do. You'll get to see her next week, though. She's gonna help me with the party."

"Oh, wonderful. Tell her I look forward to seeing her."

Celeste descended the pool steps and was, in fact, starting to get annoyed. "Reausaleigh? The champagne?"

"Yes, ma'am. Right away." With that, Reausaleigh disappeared into the house.

"Geez, Celeste." Kay pushed herself up from the pool chair. "You know, you really should be nicer to her. One of these days, you're going to piss her off and end up floating face-down in this pool." She scurried to follow her cousin into the water as the hot concrete scorched the bottoms of her feet.

Celeste ignored her cousin's comment and propped her torso onto a pool raft. Although deep down she did have some level of admiration for Kay, she never could really understand her. She knew Kay just had to be as maniacal as she was, but chose to hide it for some reason. Maybe Kay, who was definitely attractive but not nearly as beautiful as Celeste, felt more of a need to conceal her true wickedness. Perhaps only the beautiful are allowed to be evil.

Kay wrapped her long auburn hair into a messy bun before leaning her torso onto the other side of the pool raft across from Celeste. "Why are Reausaleigh and Elodie helping you with the party? Heather always has tons of people."

"I'm not using Heather for the party."

"What? Why not? She always does great."

Celeste shrugged. "Someone I know recommended another caterer, so I thought I'd try them."

"Who?"

"No one you know." She smirked. "That's actually something I need to discuss with you."

Just as Kay was preparing herself for a strong dose of gossip, she heard the back doors open. Reausaleigh squinted at the sun and approached the side of the pool with the ice bucket to make her cocktail delivery. "Here you go." She leaned down and handed fresh glasses to Kay, who met her at the pool's edge. "I'm about to go get the boys. Thought I'd stop on the way home to let them get a snowball if that's alright?" Reausaleigh dabbed her forehead. "It's awful hot today."

"That would be fine." Celeste took the glass from Kay and sipped without looking up.

"Thanks, Reausaleigh. They'll love that." Kay smiled up at her. Reausaleigh gave her an appreciative nod and made her way back to the house. Once the doors closed, Kay excitedly turned to Celeste. "Ok, spill it."

"Well," she replied coyly. "I've taken a lover."

Kay's blue eyes bulged as she choked on her champagne. "What?"

"I've taken a lover," Celeste repeated a bit more seriously.

"Oh, no, I heard you," Kay got out between coughs. "It's just…" She cleared her throat and composed herself. "Number one, who the heck talks like that? 'I've taken a lover.'" An insulted Celeste flicked water off her fingertips at her cousin's face. "And number two, who is it?"

"You actually think I'd tell you?" Celeste pushed off the pool raft and into the water.

"Then why *are* you telling me, Celeste?" Kay asked with contained frustration.

Celeste slowly glided across the water to return to her cousin and whispered, "Because I need an alibi."

"Mmm." Kay took a long sip of her champagne to let the odd request linger in the air as she tried not to laugh. "You need an *alibi*."

"Yes. My lov—" Celeste pursed her lips before rephrasing. "My friend and I have an appointment on the seventh, and I need someone to vouch for my whereabouts." Pretending not to seem too desperate for Kay's help, she slid to the edge of the pool and poured herself another glass of champagne. As if simultaneously offering a refill and asking for her cousin's cooperation, she lifted and tilted the bottle in Kay's direction.

Kay gave a surrendering sigh. "Well, you might as well bring the whole bottle over here then." A sinful grin spread across Celeste's face. She contentedly slid through the water to top off Kay's glass.

"So, what do you and your boyfriend have an appointment for? Getting matching tattoos or something?"

"Yes, cousin, you've figured it out. We're getting matching forehead tattoos."

Kay brushed water onto her pink shoulders before asking, "Well, why do you need me anyway? Matthew is never here. He won't know if you're *at an appointment*," she patronizingly air quoted.

Celeste huffed. "Ever since that Medusa died, he lumbers around during the day. Then, of course, he leaves in the evening to spend the night with his whore. The only reason he's not here now is because he's meeting the new landscaper at the estate." She turned her head to look at her own garden and seemed to mentally disappear for a moment. Kay watched her, sympathetically wondering if she cared for Matthew more than she let on. "Anyway, I doubt he *would* notice." Celeste came back to life. "But I just don't know how long it will…" she trailed off and mentally disappeared again, this time staring down at her swimsuit. "You're just going to say that I'm with you if anyone asks, alright."

Kay could see that Celeste was in the unfamiliar situation of being troubled as opposed to being the troublemaker for once. She couldn't help but feel somewhat wistful for her. She was her cousin, after all. In an attempt to be compassionate without wanting Celeste to feel pitied, Kay gently put her hand on her cousin's shoulder. "Ok, I'll do it." She smiled agreeably. She then slid her fingers under the shoulder strap of Celeste's swimsuit, pulled it back, and let it snap like a rubber band on her skin.

"Ouch! That hurt!" Celeste grabbed her shoulder.

"I'll do it if you promise to never wear this ugly f-ing swimsuit ever again. Seriously, Celeste, it looks like a bad acid trip."

Wes tossed his blazer onto the couch as he arrived home that evening. *He really should start having casual Fridays at the office,* he thought. Suit jackets and Louisiana summers do not mix. As he strolled into the kitchen in search of a cold beer, he halted just short of the fridge. A familiar scent stopped him in his tracks. *Fucking Celeste.* He scanned the kitchen, looking for the source of the scent. A lacy white swimsuit coverup was draped on one of the kitchen table chairs. Wes recognized it when he saw it. "Damn it," he mumbled.

"Dad! Dad! You're home!" A flushed-cheeked Tommy bounded through the back door. "Come throw with us!" Kay was right behind him with a welcoming smile.

"They have been waiting for you."

"They, huh?" Wes raised his brow and gave her a knowing look.

She shrugged apologetically. "He wanted a sleepover."

Wes shook his head with a humoring smirk. Part of him was annoyed, but the other part admired his wife putting Tommy's desires before her own; he was sure that yet another sleepover was the last thing Kay felt like doing that night.

"Yeah, Dad. Aunt Celeste said Charlie can spend the night again." Tommy ran toward his father and gave him a big mid-waist hug. "Will you come throw with us?" Tommy begged as he looked up at Wes with big, enthusiastic hazel eyes.

"Of course, buddy." Wes looked down at his little man and gave him a fatherly pat on the back. "Give me about twenty minutes, and I'll get my glove."

"Yay!" Tommy bolted straight back out the door and yelled into the backyard, "Charlie! My dad's gonna come play with us!" The sound of Charlie's distant voice echoed back, "Yay!"

"Hello, husband." Kay slid up to Wes and gave him a kiss.

"Hello, wife." He wrapped his arms around her. It felt good to come home to a warm embrace even if it was a hot day. "What have you guys been up to?"

"Not too much." Kay turned and walked through the back door as Wes followed her. They settled down on the outdoor couch, both seeming a bit tired. "We went swimming at Celeste's." She tossed her book onto the patio table and picked up her glass of wine. "Oh, before I forget, though, my car was making a weird sound on the way home."

"I'll take a look at it." Wes loosened his tie before reaching for Kay's glass of wine and taking a swig. Handing it back to her, he sarcastically asked, "And how is Celeste?"

"Mmm, she's ok. I think she and Matthew are having some…issues."

"Well, that's their business then." Wes really didn't want Kay getting involved with that dumpster fire of a marriage. He looked out into the backyard and watched the boys climb up onto their trampoline, immediately trying to outbounce one another.

"Celeste says he's been pretty distant." She tried to be vague as she didn't want to divulge too much of what she was told that day.

Wes reclined on the couch and put his feet up on the patio table. "I'm not surprised." When he leaned back, the outdoor lighting reflected on his beard, which was now a mix of brown, red, and a few new specks of gray. "I haven't even really talked to him that much lately. He got like that after his dad died. He'll snap out of it eventually. It's only been, what, like eight or nine months since Juniper passed."

Kay wanted to ask about Matthew's possible extracurricular activities but thought it best not to force Wes into a bro-code situation. "Do you think he would ever leave Celeste?"

"Ha, no way," Wes answered honestly as he rested back even deeper into the couch. "The only way he's leaving her is in a body bag."

Kay let out a surprised laugh at her husband's response and gave him a playful slap on the shoulder. "That's terrible. Why would you say that?"

"It's just..." Wes rubbed the back of his neck, trying to figure out how to explain. "It's a guy thing. Even if Matthew wanted to leave, he wouldn't. It's territorial or something. That's his wife, that's his son, that's his family. If he left, then...it's not his anymore." He knew Celeste had probably filled Kay in on the Natalia situation, so he put a comforting hand on Kay's thigh. "Sometimes guys do crazy shit to jeopardize it but would do even crazier shit to keep it. That's just kind of"—he shrugged—"how it is."

Celeste's dog-and-bone analogy couldn't help but creep into Kay's mind. The thought of this was somehow endearing to her, though. It made her feel slightly offended at the prospect of being considered a possession and yet also protected at the same time. As archaic as it sounded, it made her feel safe and wanted. "You told him twenty minutes, right?" She gave Wes *the look.*

Happily recognizing the look, the little flecks of green in Wes's eyes brightened as he perked up. "I sure did."

Kay stood and called out to the boys in the backyard, "Dad will be out in just a bit to play with you guys."

"Ok, Mom," Tommy yelled back as the boys continued giggling and jumping on the trampoline.

"Better make it quick then." She winked. Wes stood and happily adjusted his belt before ushering his pretty little wife into the house.

CHAPTER 17

Desperate For Something

It's always nice when a holiday falls on a weekend, Kay thought as she drove her rental car down Tchoupitoulas Street. Fourth of July landed on a Saturday this year, which conveniently allowed for a relaxing Sunday should any post-party recovery time be needed. She was in an extra good mood this early evening. She looked lovely in her new mint green cocktail dress, and her long auburn locks didn't have a hint of frizz. When Kay pulled onto Esplanade Avenue around six o'clock, the sun was still doing its best to broil the city until its late summer evening departure.

Her dear cousin always made Kay show up an hour early to her parties so that she wouldn't have the uncomfortable situation of entertaining the first guest solo. Celeste was once forced to listen, in entirely too much detail, about an early party guest's episiotomy for a solid ten minutes before the next guest arrived to save her.

Kay parked her car on the street in front of Matthew and Celeste's home. Getting out of the car, she looked up at the front porch to see Matthew leaning on the black iron railing with a cigar and glass of whiskey in hand. As she walked up the drive, she raised her arms victoriously and called up to him, "It looks like the weather gods have smiled upon us!" A warm breeze slid through the waves of her hair.

"Oh, I didn't realize it was you," Matthew thankfully called down, relieved to see Kay and not the episiotomy lady. "Yeah, they said the rain pushed back to later tonight." He gave a confused look at the very small KIA compact that was now parked in front of his house. "Did you get a new car?"

Kay carefully climbed the steps to the front porch in her

nude stilettos. "Oh, no, my Jeep is acting up. That's a rental. She is going to kill me for parking it there, but F it."

An agreeing chuckle and cigar smoke escaped Matthew's lips before he welcomed Kay with a hug and a kiss on the cheek.

"You look very handsome this evening." Kay took in Matthew's party attire of linen shirt, khakis, and boat shoes.

"Thanks, cuz. Not too bad yourself there." He gave a complimentary nod and took another pull on his cigar as he sat down on one of the rocking chairs.

"What are you doing out here anyway? Waiting for the second coming?"

"Might as well be," Matthew snorted. "Waiting for that damn dog to pee." He leaned his head toward the front doors.

"Ah!" Kay turned and flinched as she saw an unnoticed Bullet sitting at the front doors, staring through the glass into the house. Taking a few steps back, she admitted, "I hate that dog." She uneasily sat in the other rocking chair, keeping one eye on Bullet, who continued to eerily stare into the house. "He creeps me out."

"I know," Matthew groaned and sipped his whiskey. "He's not going to go until she tells him to. He follows her everywhere. If she stops short, he runs right into her."

Fearing that starting the evening with an agitated Matthew was not in anyone's best interest, Kay took the conversation elsewhere. "Tommy and Charlie are pretty excited about this week."

Her tactic seemed to work as Matthew began to lightly rock in the chair and looked out to the street with an almost prideful expression. "Yep. It was all he could talk about. Hope he gives 'em hell out there." Wes was taking the little league team for a week-long baseball camp in Lafayette the next morning. This was, in part, the reason for Kay's good mood this evening. As much as she wanted to see Tommy play, she didn't argue when he told his mother that it was a "boys only" week. The thought of a few days with the house all to herself, she had to admit, did sound pretty appealing.

"I'm probably going to make my way over there later in the week to check it out," Matthew said genuinely. This made Kay smile. She spent a lot of time with Charlie, and he recently mentioned that he and his dad were hanging out a lot more lately. She figured that after Juniper died, it changed Matthew's perspective on being a parent, which was a good thing, given his previous level of fatherly involvement. Despite whatever he and Celeste were going through, at least Charlie was getting a little extra attention from his dad.

"Well, I'm sure Wes would love that. They have some other dads going, but I bet they'll need as many as they can get to tame those little hellions." She quickly paused and thought aloud, "Wait, is hellions a curse word?"

Their polite conversation was interrupted by the sound of Bullet's sudden excited whimpering. "He must see her," Matthew grumbled as he got up and walked to the front doors. Pushing one of them open, he yelled into the center hall, "Celeste, tell this damn dog to pee!"

Kay heard three quick snaps followed by, "Bullet! Business!" The dog took off into the front yard and began to sniff the ground for a perfect spot.

With an almost apologetic look, Matthew leaned on the doorframe and held it open to let Kay come in. She hurried inside with the hope that Bullet would be busy for a while. "She's all yours." He extended his hand into the entryway. Standing in the center hall were Reausaleigh, Elodie, and a robe-wearing Celeste with hot rollers still in her hair.

"Close the door," she snapped at Kay and returned to her tirade directed at Reausaleigh and Elodie. "Remember, circle the room clockwise. None of this zig-zagging between guests."

Kay shook her head as she listened before sarcastically interjecting, "Glad to see that you're in a good mood, cousin." Softening to greet the others with a smile, she said, "Hi, Reausaleigh. Hi, Elodie. Good to see you."

"Hello, Ms. Kay." Elodie, who was in no way intimidated by Celeste, had no problem responding.

"Sweet Jesus, I do not have time for this." Celeste began to pull the rollers from her hair as she stormed back to her room. "Clockwise!" she yelled as she disappeared down the hallway.

After hearing the master bedroom door slam shut, Elodie scoffed, "Clockwise. That dumb bitch don't even know how to read a clock unless it says five."

Reausaleigh added, "Well, she must get her fives confused with her ones, twos, threes, and every other number for that matter, because it's always five o'clock up in here."

Per Celeste's request, the sisters were in matching black dresses with matching tight dark buns. They looked so much alike and yet so different somehow. Poor Reausaleigh appeared tired and a bit rundown in comparison to Elodie. They had both worked for Wells women for a very long time. Unfortunately for Reausaleigh, only one of them was treated well by a Wells woman.

"How's it going at the estate, Elodie?" Kay asked.

"Ha, 'bout as fun as folding a fitted sheet."

Juniper stipulated in her will that Elodie remain employed in the event of her death if she so chose. Her role would essentially be to manage the property and handle day-to-day affairs. Of course, Elodie could have simply said *no, thank you* and been on her merry way. She didn't need the money anymore. There was a problem, though. She cared too much for her old friend Juniper to let her belongings be pecked at like a carcass. So, she agreed to stay on until Matthew and Celeste moved into the estate. It was important to her to keep an eye on the modifications to Juniper's home. Anything Celeste wanted discarded or sold, Elodie promptly had it removed and put into storage for safekeeping.

Elodie was obviously not a fan of Celeste, and there was no way that she could ever work for her, but at least she could protect Juniper's personal possessions until the move. She knew Reausaleigh would be there to watch over things in her absence. The only reason she was even at the party tonight was to help Reausaleigh. The way that she-witch treated her sister made her blood boil. Elodie had offered Reausaleigh the money to quit and find a new job, but just as Elodie was loyal to Juniper, Reausaleigh was equally loyal to Charlie. She wouldn't dare leave him voluntarily.

Within an hour, well-dressed guests were beginning to arrive, immediately making their way to one of the several bars being manned by Celeste's new catering staff. Cocktails, hors d'oeuvres, and gossip were passed around the party as guests pretended not to brag about their summer getaway vacations. Kay stood on the tiptoes of her heels to wave from across the room at Danny and Heather when they came through the front doors around seven-thirty.

Heather's pale yellow silk dress made her limbs look even longer and tanner than usual. It was hard to tell whether Danny was prouder of his gorgeous wife or the large bag of fireworks he purchased for the occasion. After a few repeated pleasantries with path-obstructing party guests, they finally made their way to Kay, who was trying to hide the fact that she was spitting something into a napkin.

"Oh my, are you ok?" Heather asked with hushed concern.

"Mmm, fine." Kay took a big swig of her cocktail. "The food is just...well, it's just not...yours." She crumpled the napkin and tossed it into a nearby vase.

"Not surprising." Danny gave his wife's side an adoring squeeze. "Where's Matthew?" He scanned the room as he lifted the bag of fireworks, grinning like an excited little boy. "I brought entertainment for later."

"I just saw him. He was—" Kay turned to point out Matthew's location across the room but halted her response and the sudden urge to spit an expletive when she saw him. Matthew was standing with a group of people, laughing a bit too loudly at his own joke with his wife by his side. Celeste looked absolutely stunning in a flowy white minidress and a pair of ocean blue stilettos. Kay's stilettos.

"That whore has on my shoes." Kay stared in disbelief at Celeste's feet.

"Matthew's wearing your shoes?" Danny and Heather tried to get a better view of his feet.

"No, Celeste. Those are my heels. She stole them from me, like, I don't know, practically a decade ago. That little hussy."

"Well, I guess she really liked them if she kept them that long." Heather leaned to the side to get a better look. "They are really cute, though."

"What are we talking about?" Wes came up behind the three, who were now overly focused on a pair of high heels.

"Oh, Wes, you startled me," Heather said with a little

jump.

"Thank God you're here, man." Danny gave Wes a friendly pat on the back. "I almost just got roped into a conversation about shoes."

"*My shoes*," Kay defended before turning to Wes. "Remember, at Matthew and Celeste's wedding reception, Celeste had on my shoes."

"No," Wes answered honestly.

"Well, she did, and she's wearing them again tonight."

"Uh-huh." He patronizingly nodded at his wife. "I see what you mean, Danny. Let's get a drink."

The party took the usual twists and turns, with everyone mingling, laughing, and drinking. It was a decent turnout. Celeste had even invited Gauge and Logan. This was, of course, more to rub in the fact that she and Matthew would soon be moving into the estate than an actual act of hospitality. When Matthew saw Gauge across the room, though, his resentment got the better of him. He cornered his wife in the kitchen and made his agitation very well known. "Did you invite them?"

"Who?" Celeste gave him a bored look as she sipped her wine.

"The dumb-and-dumber twins."

"Yes, and the problem with that would be?"

"Oh, I think you know the problem with that." He came close to her face. "I don't want them here."

"Well, I guess you'll just have to get over it."

It felt like she was intentionally trying to screw with him. Matthew clenched his fists at his sides in anger. "One of these days, you are going to make me do something stupid."

"Oh, darling," she mocked, "That's every day for you." Celeste patted her husband on the chest and coolly strutted back to the guests.

Around ten o'clock, the crowd started to thin out. The weather was supposed to get nasty later in the evening, causing party guests to call it an early night as opposed to getting stuck. Rumbling thunder scared off the last few guests by ten-thirty, and all that remained were Danny, Heather, Wes, and Kay.

"Reausaleigh." Celeste strolled into the kitchen to find Reausaleigh and Elodie washing glasses. "I'm sending the caterers home. You and Elodie may leave as well. Just make sure to finish cleaning up first thing tomorrow."

"Yes, ma'am," Reausaleigh said with a nod as she dried her hands. Elodie, of course, just responded with a scowl.

The two ladies and the catering staff packed up quickly and were out the door before Celeste could make a random, last-minute request. The group of five was relaxing on the living room couches when Celeste joined them. "Well, I've sent everyone home." She settled down on the couch next to Matthew. Pleased, she complimented herself, "I thought it went very well."

Despite Heather's sweet nature, she just couldn't resist. "Celeste, I've been meaning to ask you"—she leaned forward from one of the other couches—"I just love those shoes. Where did you get them?" She flashed a quick, playful glance at Kay.

"Oh, these?" Celeste loved a compliment, even more so when it came from someone she didn't particularly care for. "I've had them for years. They're vintage, really. Reausaleigh has been going through some old things to prep for the move and came across them. I forgot how much I liked them."

"Well, I think we still have time to blow stuff up before the rain." Danny lifted off the couch to dodge another shoe conversation.

"Damn straight," Matthew heartily agreed with a slur and a slap on the armrest of the couch.

"I'm going to go get us set up." Danny retrieved the bag of fireworks sitting next to the couch and made his way to the backyard.

"I'll join you. I need to let Bullet out." Celeste rose and sashayed down the nearby hallway to her bedroom. Opening the door, she found her faithful pooch patiently waiting for her.

Outside, Bullet sniffed around in the garden as Danny inspected each of his explosive purchases with care. Celeste watched him concentrate on the small writing on each label with only the distant pool lighting to mildly illuminate the darkness of the backyard. For some odd reason, she found herself strangely attracted to him in that moment. "That was really kind of you to bring fireworks." Her usual frigid tone turned more siren-like. "The thought hadn't even crossed my mind."

"My pleasure. I love fireworks. Just wish the boys were here to see them. I can put on quite the show."

"Yes." She moved closer. "Charles loves fireworks as well. So, I guess that would make sense."

"Why is that?" he asked to be polite but was really focusing on the first rocket he was unwrapping.

"Well, because he's yours, of course."

Danny's head shot up, and his big green eyes locked on Celeste's face. He stood frozen, staring at her for a moment, before he fearfully whispered, "What did you say?"

Celeste stepped toward him and took the rocket out of his hand with a coy smile. "I said it makes sense that both you and Charles like fireworks because he's yours."

Danny went pale as if all the blood had suddenly drained from his body. Practically stonelike, he watched Celeste toy with the firework before he finally found the ability to speak. "He is my what?"

"Your son, silly," she replied with a flirtatious curl of her lips.

"What are you talking about?" He could feel himself beginning to panic. "You said the test was negative. You told me it said he wasn't mine."

"Oh, I say lots of things." She tried to hand the rocket back to Danny, but he was still frozen. She carelessly tossed it on the ground. "I have my reasons."

"But, you—" Before Danny could say another word, someone cleared their throat behind them. The startled pair turned to see Wes walking around the edge of the pool toward them.

"How's it coming?'

"What? Oh, yeah." Danny nervously picked up the firework Celeste had discarded. His hands were visibly shaking, and his brain was doing the same. "Ha, you know what?" He patted the pockets of his pants. "I don't have a lighter. I need a lighter. I'm…I'm going to go find one." With that, he scurried back up to the house. He had to get out of there. He desperately needed a minute to process what Celeste had just unleashed on him.

"Come on, Bullet," Celeste snapped three times and called into the garden. As she turned back toward the house, Wes grabbed her by the arm.

"Just what the fuck do you think you're doing?" His voice was hushed but dead serious.

"What are you talking about, lunatic?" She yanked her arm away from his grasp.

"I heard you, Celeste. I heard what you said to him."

"Well, that was a private conversation, and it is of no concern of yours," she hissed.

"The fuck it isn't." Wes stood in her way as she tried to leave with the dog now by her side.

"And just what, pray tell, are you going to do about it?" Celeste cocked her head to the side as Wes ground his teeth in angry silence. He just stared at her. It was all he could do.

"That's what I thought." She gave him an evil blue wink before sliding around him and smoothly making her way back to the house.

Inside, a well-lubricated Matthew had already kicked off his shoes and was providing Kay and Heather with a very animated reenactment of his latest offshore fishing trip. "Where did Danny go," Celeste interrupted as she and the dog came through the back doors.

"Garage," Matthew directed without looking at her and getting right back to his story. "So, I had been fighting this monster fish for like an hour, and then, out of nowhere, my pole *swung*!" Unfortunately, Matthew was a little too animated with the last bit of the story, and he *swung* his entire glass of whiskey all over the front of Heather's dress. She let out a yelp as the bourbon splashed all over her. Celeste, of course, was very happy that she came in when she did.

"Shit! I am so sorry." Matthew ran to the kitchen and grabbed a roll of paper towels. He stumbled back to Heather with the towels, pretty quickly for someone in his state, but the damage was already done. Poor Heather's dress was now saturated with Kentucky's finest bourbon.

"It's okay. It's okay." Heather's voice shook a little as she tried to be polite.

"I really am so sorry. I got carried away." Matthew tried to wipe the whiskey off Heather's dress. "Celeste, give her something to change into." He continued wiping a now uncomfortable Heather. The look on Celeste's face at her husband's command was one that could kill.

Noticing that her cousin was on the verge of impolitely and aggressively protesting, Kay echoed Matthew's request. "I'm sure you have something she can borrow for tonight, right Celeste?" She gave her a scolding look.

"Fine," Celeste huffed. "Come with me." She marched toward her bedroom with Bullet by her side and an appreciative, whiskey-soaked Heather behind her.

"Damn, I feel bad," Matthew admitted as he slumped onto the couch after the two women were behind Celeste's closed bedroom door.

"Oh, don't worry about it." Kay perched on the armrest next to him. "I know a great dry cleaner. Plus, Heather is about as nice as they come, so it would take a lot more than that to get her riled up."

Wes suddenly popped his head in through the back doors. "Are we doing this or what? I gotta get up early." He looked around the living area, confused. "Where is everybody?"

Kay sighed and stood. "Long story." She patted Matthew on the shoulder. "You go outside with Wes. I'll get Danny."

A guilty-feeling Matthew pushed off the couch to join Wes outside as Kay walked through the house and down the hallway that led to the garage. She opened the door to the dark garage, and found Danny sitting in the golf cart parked next to Matthew's Escalade, blankly staring at the wall. He was thinking. He was thinking about the last time he was in that garage. The night he helped Celeste with her car.

"Hey, mister." She clapped her hands together as Danny snapped out of his trance. "What are you doing in here all by your lonesome? The boys want to blow up stuff." Her playful tone changed to one of concern when she saw Danny's face. He was pale, and his hair was disheveled. He looked like he had seen a ghost. In a way, he kind of had. "Are you ok?"

"Yeah, fine," he replied with a forced smile, avoiding making eye contact. "Found a lighter. Just got distracted." He got up and grazed past her in the doorway as he walked directly into the house. Kay quickly considered the possibility that Danny might also be a little too well-lubricated and shouldn't be playing with fireworks. She immediately brushed off the notion, though. Danny, of all the men, was definitely the most responsible.

Outside, Danny began almost compulsively lining up the fireworks by the garden while Wes, Kay, Celeste, and Matthew relaxed on pool chairs. Relax might be a strong word as the thunder in the distance seemed not so distant anymore, and very ominous clouds were swirling above their heads. It was already eleven o'clock, and the forecast promised rain within the hour.

"Well, I'm back." Heather swung the back doors open, carrying a very tall glass of whiskey. The group looked back at her with stunned eyes.

"Oh…my…God," Kay gasped with a burst of laughter. "Why the heck do you still have that?" Her head swirled to Celeste, who was paying no attention to Heather's arrival. Heather was wearing an oversized pair of pink gym shorts, and the one thing Kay brought back to her cousin as a gag from her honeymoon almost eight years prior—an extra-large neon pink T-shirt with a cartoon pig sporting sunglasses and a big grin printed across the chest. The shirt Wes purchased in the gift shop when their luggage was lost.

"I really don't know," Celeste smirked devilishly. "I told you Reausaleigh was going through some old things before the move. She came across it." Celeste leaned up to scan Heather from top to bottom. "Thankfully, she hasn't made the drop-off run to Goodwill yet."

Heather laughed at herself as she joined the group on the pool chairs. "Well, I'm sure I've worn worse outfits."

"Undoubtedly," Celeste mumbled under her breath.

"And Matthew, I even made you an extra tall glass of whiskey to show you no harm done." She happily handed Matthew the cocktail.

"Well, aren't you just a doll? Thank you much, Heather."

Bullet, who was obediently sitting by Celeste's side, began to sniff the air. He then rose and walked straight to

Heather. The dog started to smell her bare legs and finally sniffed all the way up to her shorts. At which point, he dutifully sat and stared up at her as if awaiting instruction.

"Awww, hey buddy." She leaned down and petted the pup's head.

"Uh-oh, Celeste. Looks like you got some competition over here," Wes was more than willing to taunt.

"He must smell her scent on you," Kay offered. This did not make Celeste happy in the least bit. She immediately snapped three times and commanded the dog back to her side. To which, of course, Bullet promptly obeyed.

"Everybody ready?" Danny yelled from the garden.

"YES!" they all yelled back in unison. With that, Danny began lighting each of the aligned fireworks in a row, one by one. The first five beautifully seared into the sky and exploded into illuminating bursts of color. By the sixth, however, the wind chose to pick up, causing the flame from the lighter to extinguish. Danny tried repeatedly to keep the flame alive after striking the sparking wheel again and again, but the wind simply refused to allow it. Just as he was changing positions to block the gusts, down came the rain. Unfortunately, only five fireworks would survive the storm that night.

The group immediately scrambled back into the house. Thankfully, it wasn't a torrential downpour, but it was enough to put an end to the rest of the festive show.

"Well, I guess that's my cue." Wes brushed the rain off his sleeves. "Gonna head on home before this gets worse." He gave Kay a peck on the lips and, in a fatherly tone, warned, "Not too late. It's supposed to pick up soon."

"We better head out, too." Thankful that Wes had initiated the departure pleasantries, Heather picked up her stained dress and heels. "I actually still have a little prep work to do in the back kitchen tonight for a brunch tomorrow."

"At least we got to shoot a few off," Danny said quietly.

"Yes, sir, we did." The words slid from Matthew's mouth a little too easily as he slapped Danny on the back. Apparently, that last glass of whiskey really did him in. He wobbled a bit before saying, "I'm hittin' the hay." Without giving formal goodbyes, he stumbled down the back hallway, ping-ponging against the walls toward the guest bedroom without another slurred word.

"Well, drive safe, guys." Kay gave a round of hugs, leaving the last one for Wes. "I won't be too far behind you. Make sure to give the sitter a good tip." With that, Wes, Danny, and Heather made their way through the house to the front doors.

Eagerly waiting to hear the front doors close, Celeste released a frustrated breath before lamenting, "I hate that bitch."

"Celeste, be nice," Kay chided. "Wanna do one more drink before I go?" Knowing the response would be yes, Kay walked to the bar and poured two glasses of wine.

Reaching for the glass, Celeste snipped, "Something is wrong with that girl. I can sense it. That Sally Sunshine act is just a cover for the fact that she's utterly desperate."

Kay shook her head as she sat back on the couch, now wishing she hadn't suggested the one last drink. "Desperate for what, Celeste?" she indulged her cousin with a sigh.

"Well, everyone is desperate for *something*," she preached with a pompous wave.

"Everyone is desperate for something, huh?" Kay vacantly entertained Celeste as she sipped her wine.

"Yes, you heard me. In that cow's case, she's desperate for a child, and it sure does seem as though the stork lost her address a long time ago."

"Oh, you're awful."

"Awful but correct," Celeste sang as she raised her index finger. Kay could only give a little tilt of her head in agreement as a response. "And Daniel." Celeste gave an exaggerated huff. "That poor son of a bitch is desperate to keep her happy, and that's never going to happen with all of the tumbleweeds rolling around that girl's ovaries."

"Well, aren't we in rare form tonight?" She felt bad for being mildly amused by her cousin's rantings. Celeste normally never got this visibly worked up.

"And Wes." Kay was surprised to hear Celeste actually call Wes by his name instead of Carl. "He's desperate to hide the fact that he is a complete slimeball."

"What the heck are you talking about?" Kay sat up straight and wide-eyed Celeste. She could not and did not want to pretend that her cousin hadn't just gone too far. "Wes is not a slimeball. He's amazing."

"Lord, Kay. How can you be so blind? He is a total sleaze."

"That's enough, Celeste." Kay stood and stormed into the kitchen to get her purse, only to have her cousin follow right behind her. Each step Celeste took in Kay's ocean blue heels echoed throughout the quiet house.

"Oh, don't get so offended. Mine isn't any better. Both of them could probably medal in the Scumbag Olympics. Matthew is desperate to hide the fact that he's a complete fuck up."

Kay slung her purse off the kitchen counter and slammed down her wine glass so hard it was a wonder it didn't break. "I'm leaving." She took two angry steps and then stopped. She knew better than to participate in one of Celeste's tantrums but couldn't help herself. She swung back around to face her cousin. "Actually, before I go, let's finish this ridiculous discussion. Everyone's desperate for something, right?"

"That's right." Celeste downed the rest of her wine and unintentionally sidestepped a bit.

"Then what are you desperate for, dear cousin?"

Celeste took a deep breath in and lifted her eyes to the ceiling. Only the sound of the rain filled the long pause that followed. Finally, she exhaled and honestly stated, "To get rid of something."

Her response caught Kay off guard. *What on earth could Celeste possibly need to get rid of?* She searched her face for some kind of emotion, but there was none. It was as if Celeste didn't even know what she, herself, was feeling.

"And as for you, cousin." Celeste's temporary vulnerability vanished. "You are desperate to hide the fact that you are just like me."

"Oh my God. You are delusional." Kay put both hands on the sides of her head as if it would shield her brain from any more of Celeste's absurd sermon. "You really are crazy. You are a crazy, stupid, evil bi—" Kay's attack came to a halt when she realized what she was about to say.

"Aww, little Kay almost said a big girl word," Celeste pouted her lips and taunted. "What am I, Kay? Go ahead. Say it. It's not like your stupid brat kid is here to hear you."

An explosion went off in Kay. She screamed louder than the thunder overhead, "THAT'S IT!" Kay grabbed her wine glass off the counter and propelled it squarely at Celeste's mouth.

A short distance away, Danny pulled his car into the driveway next to Heather's catering van at their home off Claiborne Street. He had been understandably quiet during the drive home, understandable only to him, of course.

He had, in fact, slept with Celeste all those years ago on the night of Wes and Kay's engagement celebration. Why he did it, to this day, he couldn't wrap his mind around. A lonely man and a determined temptress can lead to some pretty inexplicable things. It never occurred to him that he could be Charlie's father until Celeste called him out of the blue six months after giving birth. "Green eyes don't run in my family," she told him flatly. With that one sentence, he suddenly understood what she meant.

Immediately, he offered to take a DNA test, which Celeste arranged for at a private testing center. Within a week, he felt the weight of the world had been lifted off his shoulders when she phoned to tell him he was not Charles's father. Danny never questioned her or asked to see the official results. He had no reason to, or at least so he thought. Perhaps because he wanted to believe her. Things were going so well with Heather, and impregnating your good friend's wife would have definitely been grounds to terminate their budding relationship.

It could also definitely be grounds to terminate their marriage if Heather were to find out now. He needed to talk to Celeste. He needed to know whether she was lying then or if she was lying now. Either way, this had to get resolved.

Heather observed him with a bit of concern. "Are you ok? You seem a little…off."

Danny turned off the engine and forced a weak smile. "I'm fine. Just have work stuff on my mind." Raindrops drummed on the hood of the car as they sat quietly for a moment.

"Can you believe she made me wear this?" Heather broke the silence with a laugh as she looked down at the shirt. When she did, Danny suddenly considered that Celeste had been alone with Heather. A knot formed in his stomach at the thought of what Celeste might have potentially said to his innocent wife in private.

"Yeah," Danny faked a chuckle. "Did she say anything when she gave you the clothes?"

"Just that this was the only thing she had that would fit me. Oh, and that I better close the door behind me when I was done changing."

"Typical." A somewhat relieved Danny reached for her hand. "You sure you have to prep tonight?" He tilted his head at the dashboard clock. "It's almost midnight."

"Yeah," Heather replied with a moan. "I should have done it earlier." She reached into the backseat for her black rain jacket. "It should only take me an hour or two."

"An hour or two?" Danny was surprised at her response and the way it made him feel. He couldn't tell if he welcomed or feared being alone right now. "Well, in that case, I might take one of your sleeping pills. Too much on my mind." He took off his glasses to rub his eyes with the back of his hand.

"Here you go." Heather reached into her purse and pulled out a pill bottle.

After putting his glasses back on, he took the bottle from Heather and asked, "Why are they in your purse?"

"I filled my prescription today when I was running errands. I'd love to take one with you and pass out. I'm exhausted. But you know how it is." She pulled on her rain jacket in the passenger seat and smiled. "No rest for the weary."

CHAPTER 18

Desperate To Make Sense Of It

Wes leaned against the refrigerator in his kitchen early the next morning, watching Tommy and Charlie at the kitchen table. The two boys were excitedly discussing the upcoming trip to Lafayette in between spoonfuls of brightly colored cereal. He opened one of the kitchen cabinets and pulled out a bottle of aspirin. It had been a long night, and now it would be an even longer day.

"Hey," a groggy Kay croaked as she shuffled into the kitchen.

"Hi, Mommy!"

"Hi, Aunt Kay!"

She let out a small, dry cough and tried to sound cheery. "Hi, guys. Are you excited about the big trip?"

"Yeah!" the boys exclaimed in unison.

Kay spotted the bottle in Wes's hand. "Oh, I'm going to need some of those." He poured a couple of pills into his hand and dropped them into hers as she gave him a kiss on the cheek. "I was late last night, so I slept in the guestroom. Didn't want to wake you."

"I figured." Wes popped the pills into his mouth and swallowed them down with a glass of water. He handed the glass to Kay, who did the same.

"Oh no," Charlie let out a sad cry from the table.

"What, baby?" Kay turned to him with a bit of alarm.

"My lucky glove. I left it at my house." He frowned and looked down at his small hands. "It's the one JuJu gave me."

Tommy took in how sad this made his cousin. He turned his eyes to Kay and gave her a look that only a mother could understand without her child saying a word. *Mommy, can you fix it?*

"Oh, don't worry, buddy." She walked over to Charlie and bent down to put a consoling arm around his shoulder. "You guys can just pick it up on your way out of town." At this, Wes cleared his throat and scrunched his eyes at Kay.

"No?" Kay tried to give him a pretty-please smile, but her hangover only allowed a cracked, dehydrated one.

"No," Wes responded firmly yet politely. The last thing he wanted to do was make a stop at Esplanade Avenue that morning.

"Alright." Kay gave a surrendering sigh. "What time are you guys leaving?"

"About an hour," Wes replied over his coffee cup.

"I'll run over to your house and get it. Okay, Charlie?" She smoothed his strawberry blonde mop.

"Yay! Thank you, Aunt Kay!" Both boys gazed up at her with relieved, grateful eyes.

"Now." She pressed her fingertips into her temples. "Do you know where it is? Tell Aunt Kay very quietly, though, because her headache is reaching epic proportions."

Charlie slowly whispered, "In my closet. On the shelf. On the…" He looked down at his hands to double check his left and right. "On the right side."

"Okay," Kay whispered back. His sweet face gave her a little boost of mom energy. She was going to get the whole week off, so it was the least she could do. "I'll be right back." She mentally and physically pulled herself up and grabbed the keys to her rental car and purse off the kitchen counter. Giving Wes a pathetic look, she headed toward the garage. "Dang it." Kay suddenly swung around and headed in the opposite direction to the front door. "Forgot I parked in the front. Left my dang garage door opener in the Jeep."

Fifteen minutes later, Kay's rental car crunched over downed branches as she pulled into the driveway of Celeste and Matthew's home. After putting the car in park, she leaned the side of her pounding head against the driver's window and looked up at the house. Kay did not want to go in there. She was hopeful Reausaleigh and Elodie would have already arrived, but neither of their cars were parked on the street. "Screw it," she mumbled. Getting out of the car felt like walking into a sauna. The remaining moisture from last night's storm mixed with the early morning heat made the humidity feel like trying to breathe in pea soup.

Condensation dripped down the large, fogged glass panes of the front doors. Kay entered the code into the keypad to unlock the door. When she did, the bolt clicked, locking the doors. *I must have forgotten to lock it when I left last night.* As she went to reenter the code, loud barking from inside made her stumble backward. On the other side of the fogged glass, she could see Bullet yelping at the door, standing on hide legs with his front paws pressed against the glass.

"Hush, dog," she hissed through the glass. Bullet continued to bark. Remembering Celeste's tactic, she snapped her fingers three times and firmly commanded, "Bullet, *down*." To her amazement, the dog responded and became silent as he slid his paws down the glass to sit obediently. At this, though, Kay began to shake. *Is that…?* When Bullet's paws slid down the glass, they left smears, very thick red smears. Smudged down the pane of glass were, most definitely, two distinctive bloody paw streaks.

Kay used her shaking hand to type the code into the keypad again. Hearing the bolt retract, she hesitantly took hold of the doorknob and slowly opened the door. She stepped inside the center hall. The still-lit chandelier sparkled on the surfaces of the quiet hall. It also glistened on what was a very clear path of bloody prints leading to the back of the house. Bullet began to bark uncontrollably again. He ran to the living area on the other side of the center hall and then back to Kay, slipping on his saturated paws along the way.

"Hello?" Kay fearfully called out. Bullet continued to bark and took off down the hallway between the center hall and living area that led to the master bedroom. Kay went into an almost trance-like state. She was seeing, but her mind was not allowing her to process what she was seeing. Side-stepping around the track of bloody paw and shoe prints, her transfixed eyes darted from every smear to every streak. The trembling of her body went as still as her breath when she stopped at the entrance to the hallway. Bullet's barks were escaping from the master bedroom. The most alarming thing in that moment was not the barking, not the blood, but from where she was standing, Kay could see that the bedroom door was wide open.

"Celeste?" she called down the hallway. Her hopeful cry was met with no response. Slowly creeping alongside the trail, she stopped at the bedroom doorway. The lights to the entirely white bedroom were on, and the ceiling fan spun overhead. She could hear Bullet but couldn't see him. His barking was coming from the other side of the king-sized bed positioned in the middle of the room. On the floor, barely peeping out from the end of the bed, was a pair of ocean blue heels. Kay's heels.

"Celeste!" Kay sprinted across the room but became immobile when she reached the other side of the bed. Lying face down on the floor in a pool of blood was her cousin. She was most definitely dead. Celeste's tan skin had faded into a ghostly white translucent shell. Her bloodshot, wide-open, bright blue eyes stared lifelessly into nothingness. Celeste's face, her beautiful face, was draped in the blonde blood-splattered waves of her hair. The white dress she wore the night before was now nothing more than a red shroud perforated by gaping wounds covering her entire back.

Kay lost control of her body as she stumbled backward into the wall, knocking Matthew and Celeste's framed wedding photo to the floor. She didn't know what to do. She just stood there staring at her cousin's rigid corpse in disbelief.

"Will somebody shut that damn dog up?" Matthew roared from the other side of the house. The angry stomps of his approaching feet suddenly stopped when he entered the living area. "What the hell?" he said out loud, looking around for some type of explanation.

"Matthew!" Kay screamed out to him. His pounding footsteps made it to the bedroom door. Matthew halted at the doorway as his wide eyes took in Kay's frightened face. The rumbled clothes he wore from the night before stuck to his clammy skin and sucked in with each heavy breath.

"What's going on? Why is there blood everywhere?"

All Kay could do was point to the floor. He followed the path of her finger to see the ocean blue heels peeking out from the other side of the bed. "Oh my God!" He rushed to the other side of the bed and saw his wife lying dead on the floor. "Celeste!" Matthew began to run to her side but spun around instead and fearfully looked at Kay. "Did you do this?"

"No!" she shrieked. After taking a breath, she stared at Celeste and, without returning her eyes to Matthew, solemnly asked, "Did you?"

"No!" he yelled back at her with a shaking voice. Neither knew whether to believe the other, but in the terrifying shock of that moment, questions and answers didn't much matter. "We have to get out of here. We have to call the police." A dazed yet somehow focused Matthew grabbed Kay by the arm.

"We can't just leave her like this." Kay clawed onto the wall that was holding her up.

"Kay, if you didn't do this and I didn't do this, then whoever did could still be in the house." As scared as she was, Kay recognized that Matthew had a decent point there. Her flight-over-fright instincts kicked in pretty quickly as she released her death grip on the wall and allowed him to drag her.

"Maybe, maybe, the dog attacked her. Maybe the dog did it," Kay naively stammered. They both stopped at Celeste's feet and looked down at Bullet, who was obediently sitting next to Celeste's slashed body.

"Trust me, Kay. A dog didn't do that."

"Can I get you a water or a soda or anything?" Detective Austin Desbordes opened the door to the tiny interrogation room at the 1st Police District Station on North Rampart Street.

"No, I'm alright." Matthew felt like he was floating through a dream as he entered the room. He collapsed onto a metal folding chair at the small table in the middle of the room without Desbordes even asking him to.

"Now, I know you talked to my partner for a while at your house, but I just want to make sure I get everything right." Desbordes sat down on the cheap yet cushioned chair across from Matthew and opened a folder containing the initial notes on the Celeste Wells murder scene. He began to flip through a few pages and grimaced. "You know what?" Desbordes looked at Matthew like he was an old friend. "Screw that." He pushed the folder away and said, "Why don't you just tell me? What happened, Mr. Wells?"

"Like I said, I…I don't know." He let his hands fall into his lap, and his broad shoulders bowed inward. "We had a party last night. I went to bed when everybody left. I slept in the guest room. When I woke up this morning, Kay was there. There was blood everywhere." His eyes grew large as he visualized his wife's lifeless body on the floor. "And Celeste was…dead. Really, really dead. That's…that's all I know." Matthew sounded genuinely dumbfounded by the chain of events. It was as if he, himself, was trying to piece together the few things that he knew or could remember at least.

Detective Desbordes closely watched Matthew as he spoke. Normally, when a guy offs his wife, he has a better story than "I don't know." Especially when that guy is literally admitting to being in the house when the actual murder occurred. The man sitting across from him seemed legitimately baffled. Desbordes knew who Matthew Wells was and figured it would only be a matter of time before an overpriced lawyer showed up, so he needed to get more out of him than "I don't know" and quickly.

"So, Kay is your cousin?" Desbordes opened the folder again even though he already knew the answer to the question.

"She's my wife's cousin, but yeah."

"Was she at the party last night?"

"Yeah, she was there."

"Did she spend the night?"

Matthew shook his head confidently. "No." Then he remembered that he couldn't remember. "I mean, I don't think so. It was kind of crazy after we found Celeste, but she said she came over this morning to get my son's glove. He forgot it or something."

"Okay," Desbordes said, scribbling on one of the pages from the folder. "Were Celeste and Kay close?"

"Yeah, I guess. I mean, they're cousins."

"Are you and Kay close?"

Matthew's head clicked to the side at this. He didn't like the way the detective asked the last question. "What do you mean, are we close?"

"I mean—"

A knock at the metal door to the interrogation room interrupted the detective's clarification. "Hold that thought." He held up a finger and pushed back from the table before rising and sticking his head out the door. There was a hushed, brief discussion with whoever was in the hallway and the passing of a document. Desbordes returned to his seat and laid the document facedown on the table. He placed his forearms on the table and laced his fingers over the document. "What were you wearing last night, Matthew?"

"This." Matthew pulled at the chest of his rumpled linen shirt. I crashed hard last night, so I slept in it."

Desbordes pushed his chair back again and looked under the table. "You wore flip-flops to the party?"

"Oh, no." Matthew looked down at his feet. "I guess I just put these on when I woke up or something. I don't remember. I don't remember where my shoes are."

"Could you describe them for me?"

"Uh, yeah," Matthew answered the detective hesitantly. "Gray Sperrys."

"Size?"

"Um, like twelve, twelve and a half."

"Huh, okay." Desbordes quirked his mouth. "Are these your shoes, Matthew?" The detective flipped over the document and slid it across the table to Matthew, closely watching his reaction as he viewed the image. It was a photograph of a pair of shoes.

"Oh my God." Matthew pushed the photograph back toward the detective in horror. They were definitely Matthew's shoes. The ones he was wearing last night. They didn't look very gray anymore, though; they were now almost completely reddish-brown. "Is that blood? Is that Celeste's blood?"

"Are these your shoes, Matthew?" Desbordes repeated the question with a straight face as he continued to observe Matthew's reaction.

"I don't know! How could I know that?" Matthew's voice went up an octave as he began to panic.

"We found them in the bushes in front of your house. Any idea how they—" Another interrupting knock at the metal door cut off the detective's question yet again. Desbordes pushed the picture back toward Matthew as he rose to answer the door.

After opening the door slightly, he cursed under his breath and pushed it all the way open. "Your attorney is here." Standing in the doorway with another officer was Logan.

"What the hell are you doing here? You're not my attorney." Normally, Matthew would have been much more aggressive at the sight of Logan, but at this point, he was too numb to put up any more of a fight. "Where's Jackson?"

"I spoke with him a little while ago. Mr. Bergeron will not be coming," Logan stated in a stern, polite tone.

Matthew slammed a fist on the table. "The fuck are you talking about? Why isn't he coming?" What Matthew didn't know was Jackson Bergeron refused to represent Matthew per his wife's father's request. Apparently, Celeste's parents had already made up their minds as to who murdered their one and only daughter. Matthew's father-in-law made it very clear to Jackson Bergeron and any other elite attorney in the city that they would not be assisting his daughter's husband. The message had even trickled down to Logan's meager firm. He was only there because he knew that's what Juniper would have wanted him to do.

Logan took a few steps into the interrogation room toward his new client. "He's not coming, Matthew. I'll explain in the car." He turned to face Detective Desbordes and again politely yet sternly said, "We're done here, by the way. I will be present for all future interviews should there be a need for any. Here is my card." Logan cordially handed his business card to Desbordes.

"Oh, there will be a need. We'll be seeing a lot more of each other real soon."

Logan didn't blink as he directed, "Let's go, Matthew."

A few doors down the hallway, Kay was getting a little worked up. Desbordes's partner, Detective Sibley, had a much more direct approach when it came to interrogating.

"So, you assaulted her last night." Sibley tossed her hands up as she confirmed what Kay had just said.

"If by assault, you mean threw a wine glass at her face,

then yes, I guess I assaulted her." Kay's response was followed by a knock at the door. Desbordes peeped his head in.

"May I join?" he asked Sibley. She knew that her partner's presence meant the husband had lawyered up.

"Come on in. Mrs. Allen here was just telling me how she assaulted the victim last night."

Desbordes got a twinkle of excitement in his eyes as he entered and pulled up a chair next to Sibley.

"Ok, I think we're getting a little carried away here with the whole *assault* thing." Kay dismissed the detective's word choice with air quotes.

"She hit her in the face with a wine glass."

"You hit her in the face with a wine glass?" Desbordes repeated his partner's last statement and balked at Kay with disbelief. Maybe he was barking up the wrong tree with the Wells guy after all.

"Incorrect. I threw a wine glass at her face." Kay pointed a finger as she clarified.

"And the wine glass hit her?"

"Yes." Kay gave a nod of agreement that the two detectives volleyed back with disparaging ones.

"What did she do when you hit her in the face with the wine glass?"

"Well, after I threw a wine glass that so happened to hit her in the face, she called me an f-ing b, and I left."

"She called you a what?"

"An f-ing b."

"She said f-ing b?"

"No."

"I'm confused, Mrs. Allen. Did Celeste call you an f-ing b or not?"

"No, she called me an f-ing b, but she used the full words."

"So, she called you a fucking bitch?"

"Yes."

"Then why didn't you just say that?"

"It's a long story." Kay waved her hand decliningly. "Look, I know you have to ask me this stuff, but you're wasting your time with me. I didn't kill Celeste. I have no reason to want her dead. We had a love/hate relationship, that's all." Kay decided to leave out that it was more hate than love. "It couldn't have been me. I wouldn't have left the door open."

Both detectives peered at her curiously, wondering if the woman they were interviewing was suffering from some type of post-homicide psychosis. You couldn't really blame them; Kay's adrenaline was leading her demeanor down a strange avenue. "Excuse me?" Desbordes finally broke the confused silence.

"Celeste always, always, closes doors behind her. Especially her bedroom door. If you forget to do it, she gets irate. So, I guess what I'm saying is, as odd as this may sound, if I had killed her, I would have closed the door behind me."

"Ma'am." Sibley squeezed the bridge of her nose in frustration at the bizarre reasoning behind Kay's attempt to prove her innocence. "You expect us to remove you as a suspect because the bedroom door was open?"

"You're really considering me a suspect?" She was a little stunned, even though her *Dateline* reruns told her that made perfect sense. Then suddenly, the idea of another suspect hit her. "Oh, oh, oh! Boyfriend! She has a boyfriend!"

Sibley took the top off her pen and began to scribble. "Alright, what's this boyfriend's name?"

"I don't know."

The detective's mouth turned into a straight, wrinkled line. She was beginning to feel like she was in an Abbot and Costello skit as she replaced the cap of the pen. "So, how do you know Celeste had a boyfriend, Mrs. Allen?"

"She told me. I don't know his name, but I do know he is friends with the caterer from last night. And they are supposed to get together on Tuesday. She wanted me to cover for her if anyone asked where she was." The hysterical deliria of her realization was interrupted by yet another knock at the door. Thankfully for Kay, Logan had put in a call to his partner on the way to the police station that afternoon. After a brief explanation by Logan, his partner rushed over to assist and get Kay out of there before she could say something incriminating. He probably should have gotten there a little sooner, but he was there, nonetheless.

CHAPTER 19

Desperate For Whats Missing

The next few days were quite the circus. Two Wells women had died just nine months apart. Unfortunately, murders in New Orleans weren't exactly considered newsworthy. Still, the brutal death of a young, gorgeous socialite, preceded in death by her also gorgeous socialite mother-in-law less than a year prior, definitely pulled quite a few headlines. As a result, Matthew, Charlie, and Celeste's adoring pooch were all bunkered down at the Wells estate. Reausaleigh was pretty much staying with them around the clock. She didn't want to leave Charlie, and Matthew wasn't exactly in the best frame of mind to play the role of consoling father.

Returning to the house on Esplanade was not an option. The press had it well staked out night and day. Not to mention, the police were still combing through the large home for evidence. So far, all they had found was Matthew's pair of bloody shoes in the bushes. And then, there was the knife. The weapon used to kill Celeste was easily identified. The eight-inch butcher knife had been returned to the knife block in the kitchen after being sloppily wiped down. There were no usable fingerprints, but the streaks of dried blood were undoubtedly identified as belonging to Celeste Wells.

Reausaleigh enlisted the help of her sister to pick up some spare clothes from Kay and Wes. The limited amount kept at the estate was not going to last long, and going out clothes shopping was not realistic. Thankfully, Wes and Tommy were about the same sizes as Matthew and Charlie, give or take a few vertical and horizontal inches.

"How is it over there?" Wes finished placing the last few pairs of shoes into a large canvas bag. He spoke a bit softly in an effort not to wake Kay, who was finally resting after two sleepless nights.

Sugarcoating things wasn't really Elodie's style, so she answered honestly. "It's pretty quiet. Mr. Matthew stays up in the study, drinking…drinking a lot of whiskey." She shook her head with disappointment and straightened the contents of the bag. "But Charlie seems to be doing alright. Reausaleigh been taking good care of him." *He's used to not having his parents around,* she thought. "Come to think of it, what you think about me taking Tommy with me when I drop off these clothes? Reausaleigh will be there to watch 'em." She didn't want Wes thinking that Tommy and Charlie would be left alone with Matthew.

Wes took a moment to think before responding. "That's actually a good idea. She could probably use some quiet." He pointed to the ceiling in reference to the finally sleeping Kay. "Why don't you take Tommy on over? I think I'll go grab Danny, and we'll stop by. Matthew could probably use a little company, too." Even though he and Matthew had been in a strange place since Juniper died, he knew that his friend needed him. Even if he wasn't willing to admit it.

"Fine by me. I'll call Reausaleigh and tell her y'all are coming." She reached into her shoulder bag and pulled out her keys and her phone. Extending the keys to Wes, she instructed, "You be a gentleman now, and go put these bags in my car."

"Yes, ma'am." Wes gave a more than obliging smile and reached to retrieve the keys from her palm. When he did, she curled her fingers, preventing him from taking them from her hand. Confused, he looked at her. In the blink of an eye, her expression had suddenly turned serious, and her dark eyes looked haunted. "What is it, Elodie?"

"Do you think Mr. Matthew killed her?"

Not completely surprised at the question, Wes shook his head with certainty. "Matthew wouldn't have killed Celeste. He may have wanted to at times, but I know he wouldn't."

Elodie took a deep breath, and the haunted look remained. "I wasn't talking about Ms. Celeste."

Heather watched Danny talk on the phone as he nervously walked from one side of their living room to the other. She pretended to relax on the couch. Celeste's murder hit him hard. She was confused by how emotional he had been, how distant he seemed. Ever since the night Celeste died, Danny appeared to be mentally somewhere else. Heather was also a bit unnerved but had already made peace with Celeste's unfortunate early departure. She was only concerned about how this would affect Charlie.

"That was Wes." Danny stopped his pacing but remained standing as he ended the call.

"Everything alright?" The attempt at a supportive tone practically fell on deaf ears.

"Yeah, we're going to head over and check in on Matthew. Sounds like he's not doing too well." The pacing began again.

"Oh, honey. Come sit." Heather patted the couch cushion next to her. Realizing his wife was worried about him, he softened and did as he was told. She lovingly put her hand on his knee as he sat next to her. "It's going to be alright." She gave him an encouraging look.

"I just still can't believe this is happening." He sadly stared down at her hand that was consolingly rubbing his leg.

"So, he's not doing well?"

"Apparently not. I wouldn't be either if I were him."

"Well." Heather's hand left Danny's knee and took his. "If he's not in a good place, maybe we should let Charlie stay here for a while." Danny turned to his wife at a loss for words. This was not what he thought she was going to say. "I just mean…it's just," Heather sensitively clarified, "we are Charlie's guardians in the event of, well…you know…if Matthew…" Danny suddenly understood what his wife was suggesting. The thought hadn't entered his mind until this very moment.

"You mean if Matthew goes to prison for Celeste's murder."

Heather gave him a pained expression. "It is something we need to keep in mind."

"My money is still on the husband." Desbordes tossed a manila folder on top of the large stack of other folders resting on Sibley's cubicle desk. Four days had passed since Celeste's body was found. The district attorney, Marissa Morgan, had been on the detectives like white on rice before Celeste's body even made it to the morgue. It was an election year, and this was just the type of case that could make or break another six-year stint.

The only physical evidence was still limited to Matthew's bloody shoes, which he continued to neither confirm nor deny as actually being his per Logan's advice. And the bloody knife. However, there was one interesting piece of information that came to light during the autopsy. Celeste's blood, what was left of it at least, unsurprisingly tested positive for very high levels of alcohol, but it also unexpectedly tested positive for high levels of hCG, human chorionic gonadotropin. It turns out that Celeste Wells was pregnant. "I'd say about eight weeks," the coroner reported to Sibley and Desbordes, fully understanding the implications of such a revelation.

In those four days, Sibley and Desbordes interviewed all the known people to have been in contact with Celeste in the last hours of her life. The one thing most of them had in common, unfortunately, was not having an alibi. The catering staff was hit or miss. Reausaleigh and Elodie claimed to have been alone yet together. And then, of course, there was the small group that stayed for the fireworks.

"I don't know." Sibley rubbed her chin with the back of her hand. "It's too easy."

"You always get like this, Sibs." Desbordes opened a bag of chips and began crunching away. "Always want it to be harder than it has to be. Sometimes the easiest answer is the right one," he continued with a mouthful. "Sometimes guys just lose it and butcher their wives."

"Why would he change his clothes but not his shoes? Kill her, toss the shoes in the bushes but not the clothes he killed her in, and then put his party clothes back on?" In their interviews, the detectives saw pictures from that night confirming the clothes Matthew was wearing in their first interview were the same ones he was wearing at the party. "And then where did he toss the bloody ones? He wiped the knife off.

Where is whatever he did that with? Why wouldn't he have tossed the shoes, clothes, knife, all of it somewhere a little less obvious than his front yard?"

Desbordes grumbled as he crumpled the chip bag and threw it in the trash. He and Sibley had been partners for five years now. He was used to this. Sibley would go down these rabbit holes, hoping for some grand mystery, and at the end of the day, it led nowhere. They always came back to the first person on the suspect list. Out of respect for his partner, he decided to humor her yet again. "Alright." He pulled a metal folding chair from the corner of the cubicle and straddled it. "Then who you thinking?"

Knowing that Desbordes wasn't really listening, she used the opportunity to think out loud. "The maid and her sister, for one. They were alone together. Could have come back later. Maybe some kind of stick it to the boss move." She rocked in her office chair. "But I didn't get that vibe."

"Yeah, same," Desbordes agreed.

"The cousin." Sibley held up her finger. "She'd be my first guess. They fought, she slashed her and tossed the clothes on the ride. She and the husband both admit that they never saw each other when she got home that night."

Desbordes tried to muffle his laugh. *There's no way that lady killed anyone. She doesn't even curse.* "Well, why not her husband then? She parked the rental in front. Forensics went through it. It's clean," he reminded Sibley. "She wouldn't have known if his car was in the garage or not. Maybe he came home, paid the sitter, put the kids to bed, and left to slice up the Wells lady."

"Forensics checked his car too, remember?" Sibley dismissed her partner's theory. "It was clean. Plus, what's the motive? She was mean to his wife? Doesn't fly."

Even though he considered this conversation pointless, it was entertaining to see Sibley's mental hamster on the wheel. "What about the other couple then? The nerd and the hot one."

"I thought about that. She went to work in the kitchen out back for two hours. He supposedly went upstairs and went to sleep. Maybe he's this boyfriend the cousin was talking about. He killed her in a lover's quarrel type thing, or she killed her out of jealousy?"

Desbordes chose not to muffle his laugh at his partner's last comment. "No way that guy was banging Celeste Wells. You met him. He ain't the kind. Besides, with a wife like that..." He absentmindedly rubbed his hands together at the thought of marital bliss with someone who looked like Heather.

"Don't be a perv, Austin." She kicked the bottom of the metal chair under his crotch and began slowly spinning in her office chair, trying to make it all fit together. "No way the husband did it. We're missing something. There's a piece missing."

A pudgy first-year officer powerwalked up to Sibley's cubicle. A little out of breath, he panted, "Detectives, there's someone here to see y'all about the Wells case."

"Who is it?" Sibley kept slowly spinning.

"They wouldn't say. They just asked for the investigators on the Wells case."

"They?" Sibley stopped spinning.

"Some guy and his lawyer."

"Lawyer, huh." Desbordes gave Sibley an excited grin. People don't come in voluntarily with their lawyers unless it's something good. "Might be that missing piece you wanted. Ask, and you shall receive, Sibs. Ask, and you shall receive."

Derek Flannery and his attorney sat patiently in one of the precinct's interrogation rooms. They didn't speak. The two men had already discussed, in detail, what was to be said and what was better left unsaid. Even though he was voluntarily inserting himself into a murder investigation, Derek wasn't nervous. If anything, he was eager to talk. Waiting this long had been difficult enough.

The metal door opened, and both men stood. "I apologize for keeping you waiting, gentlemen. I am Detective Desbordes, and this is my partner, Detective Sibley." Hands were shaken, and formal introductions were made.

"Nice to meet you, detectives. My name is Derek Flannery. This is my attorney, Joseph Binnings." Mr. Binnings didn't say a word. He simply shook the detectives' hands. The first thing Sibley thought when she laid eyes on Derek

Flannery was that he bore a striking resemblance to Matthew Wells. He was tall and broad, handsome, with sandy hair. The only noticeable differences between the two men were Derek's bright blue eyes compared to Matthew's brown, and Derek looked like he had a few years on Matthew. The distinctive similarities were only physical, though. Derek Flannery had a different presence, one of composure and confidence. He had that calm, cool, and collected air about him. Matthew had more of a barely-hanging-on-by-a-thread feel to him.

"Please, have a seat. We hear that you have some information about the Wells case." Everyone sat as the detectives opened small notebooks.

Derek Flannery got right to the point. He smoothed his pale blue tie and began without hesitation. "I don't see any need to beat around the bush, so I will be very direct. I assumed it would only be a matter of time before you discovered my association with Celeste, so I decided to be upfront and come to you first." He viewed both detectives stoically. "Celeste Wells and I were in a romantic relationship. We have been seeing each other for about five months." He paused to let that sink in. Sibley thought of Celeste Wells's choice in men. The similarities made sense now. *Guess everybody's got a type.*

"Is that a fact?" Desbordes tried to seem unaffected by this admission. "How did you and Mrs. Wells meet?"

"I've known her for years. I am the Wells family physician. I was Juniper Wells's primary before her passing. I met Celeste when she and Matthew married."

"If you've known her for years, why have you only been in a romantic relationship for five months?"

"That is when my divorce was finalized. I've always had feelings for Celeste but was unwilling to act on them when I was married. My ex-wife and I amicably separated earlier this year, and I felt free to pursue Celeste at that time."

"No qualms about *her* still being married, though?" Sibley asked, noting the hypocrisy.

"That is a fair question." His blue eyes focused on the detective. "Celeste and Matthew may be legally married but on paper only. Their union is not a happy one; however, neither desired a divorce for various reasons." This did not come as a shock to the detectives based on the information gathered in their interviews. "I loved her very much, and while I was not pleased with that arrangement, I was willing to accommodate it." He smoothed his tie again in a cool-headed manner. "I assume that the autopsy results revealed that Celeste was pregnant?"

"They did. Is it fair to assume that you were the father?"

"It is." He calmly nodded. "When it came to Celeste, my passion sometimes clouded my better judgment. The pregnancy was not planned. Neither Celeste nor I desired to have any more children. We made arrangements to terminate the pregnancy. Her appointment was scheduled for this past Tuesday. I planned to accompany her."

"Was anyone else aware of your relationship or the pregnancy?"

"Not to my knowledge, but it is possible. If Matthew did find out somehow, it is my opinion that he was very capable of harming Celeste."

"Why do you say that? Was it a physically abusive relationship?"

"Again, not to my knowledge, but it is possible. I do believe it to have been an emotionally abusive one. Celeste told me that Matthew treated her terribly. She said he made her sadness a priority. She was very unhappy. I have no problem saying, I wish it were Matthew who was dead and not Celeste." Derek's lawyer noticeably cringed and shifted in his seat.

Keeping his eyes on the detectives, Derek tilted his head toward his lawyer. "I would feel the same way if I were him," he said with a small chuckle. It was the first emotion he had shown in the entire interview. The laugh served as a breather for everyone in the room and from the almost robotic pace of the interview. Desbordes knew a quick back-and-forth like this meant someone was either very well prepped or being very honest. "I suppose you will need an alibi for me?"

"Do you have one?"

Dr. Flannery was intent on maintaining control of the interview, and the detectives were more than happy to let him talk as much as he wanted. "I was with my ex-wife and children at our river camp all weekend. As I previously stated, we are on good terms. There were also several friends and family members in attendance. I would, however, like to involve them as little as possible."

"Obviously, you know we will have to contact them."

"I was hoping to avoid that. I do not want to soil Celeste's good name. She was an amazing creature. To taint her memory with the scandal of an affair would be a tragedy. As such, I have a proposal." Another cringe jerked the lawyer's face. "Against his advisement, of course. In lieu of corroborating my whereabouts with my family and friends, I would be more than willing to submit to a polygraph test administered by the police department. I have no doubt the results will confirm my whereabouts and lack of involvement of any kind regarding Celeste's death."

You have got to be kidding me, man. Desbordes tried to keep a straight face as he took in Derek Flannery. *This guy can pull any tail he wants, and he's still trying to win points with a dead lady? No ass is worth that. She must've done one hell of a number on him.*

"That can be arranged, Dr. Flannery." Detective Sibley attempted to conceal her disappointment. "However, if the polygraph does result in any inconsistencies, or should any new information come to light, we can't promise that we won't verify your whereabouts or potential involvement." Part of her wanted the inconsistencies or the new information she alluded to in her warning to Derek; however, knowing he was this willing to cooperate, that was unlikely. It meant that she was still missing something. *He didn't do it.*

"Understood and agreed." Derek nodded with self-assurance. "I am available at your earliest convenience."

CHAPTER 20

Desperate For A Child

Kay felt nauseous. Watching Heather crunch her hands into the bowl of dry breadcrumbs made her think of what her cousin was now reduced to. *Nothing more than crumbs*. It had been two weeks since that fateful night of the Fourth of July party, and Celeste was no closer to a grave than her parent's fireplace mantel in Baton Rouge. Even at an oddly young age, Celeste made it very clear that she wanted to be cremated. "No one ever looks pretty, dead and stuffed in a box," Celeste matter-of-factly whispered to Kay at the ripe old age of eleven as they left their grandmother's funeral. So, per Celeste's longstanding wishes, her pretty body had been burned and stuffed in an urn instead of a box. As cryptic as it might seem, after the way Celeste looked the last time Kay saw her, she began to think her cousin might have been on to something.

"Any news with the case?" Heather perkily asked as she tossed peeled shrimp into the breadcrumbs. She was in an upbeat mood today. She and Danny invited Wes, Kay, and Tommy over to cook and have a relaxing Saturday afternoon. The invitation was also extended to Charlie and Matthew, but only Charlie could make it. Matthew was at the police station again, giving another one of his best mime impersonations per Logan's advice.

Things were not looking good for Matthew. The investigation hadn't turned up any new evidence, and Marissa Morgan was antsy for an arrest. If nothing changed soon, she would give the go-ahead to issue a warrant for Matthew's arrest. With the election just a couple of months away, she couldn't risk looking like she was sitting on her hands with such a high-profile case.

"Nope. I'm still a suspect, but the detectives haven't been bothering me too much lately." Kay didn't want to look at the breadcrumbs anymore, so she absentmindedly started folding paper towels in half. "It looks like they have their sights set more on Matthew."

"You know I hate to say it, but he is the most likely suspect. Not to mention, the only real evidence they have leads back to him." An anonymous source had leaked the details of the bloody shoes and knife to the press earlier in the week, causing a rejuvenated interest in the case and questions as to why an arrest had not yet been made. Heather put the top on the Tupperware bowl and shook the breading and shrimp. "I mean, who else could it be?" she asked almost rhetorically.

"I know"—Kay frowned—"but you didn't see him that morning. He was just as freaked out as I was." Her mind flashed back to the look on Matthew's face when he asked Kay if she had done it. His eyes were genuinely scared, either of her or for her. Maybe a little of both.

"Oh no!" Heather tossed down the mixer and started spinning around, scanning the kitchen countertops. "I forgot the dinners at the shop." She clasped her hands to her cheeks with disappointment.

"What dinners?"

"I made some trays yesterday to send home with Charlie. I'm sure Reausaleigh could use a break from cooking. Plus, I want to make sure the little guy is eating healthy."

"Oh, that is so sweet of you." Kay suddenly felt a little guilty. "Guess I should have thought of that, too."

Heather went back to shaking the shrimp. "Kay, your cousin just died, and you're being investigated for her murder. I think it's safe to say you have a lot going on. Thank God they're finally figuring out it was—" She caught herself before saying Matthew's name. "That it was probably someone else."

The afternoon ended up being a nice one. It was a much-needed break for everyone to take their minds off recent events. Tommy and Charlie wore Danny and Wes out with a perpetual game of catch, and the ladies sipped mimosas in the shade as the cicadas hissed in the bushes.

The only one that seemed frazzled that day was Bullet. Charlie begged to bring him along to the cookout. His little brain had convinced itself that having the dog around was like having his JuJu around, too. Today, however, Bullet was acting strangely. He kept circling the detached kitchen and barking randomly. He darted around in the backyard erratically and only stopped to lap up some water to alleviate his panting.

As the sun began its descent and the mosquitos made their debut, Heather peeled herself off the patio chair. "Well, I guess I better head over to the shop and get those dishes to send back with Charlie before it gets too late. Anybody need anything while I'm out?"

"You sure you don't want me to go for you?" Danny politely offered.

"Nope. I got it," she said with a smile and gave him a peck on the lips. "There're praline brownies in the pantry for the boys. Oh, and keep an eye on Bullet. He must smell something he likes in my kitchen, and I don't want him sneaking in there somehow."

"Yes, ma'am." Danny gave her a salute. He was happy his wife didn't take him up on his offer, especially after hearing about dessert. "Now, where did you say the brownies were?"

Heather headed off, and the adults and boys went inside for dessert. After a couple of second servings, the boys went upstairs to play on Danny's computer while Kay, Wes, and Danny decided on one more drink before calling it a night. Just as they were beginning to relax on the couch, Danny jumped up. "Oh shoot. Where's the dog?"

Wes and Kay looked around the room for Bullet. "I bet he's still outside," Wes offered. Danny hustled to the back door. It was now dark out, and he couldn't see the dog anywhere.

"Bullet! Bullet," he hollered into the darkness of the backyard.

"Do the snap thing," Kay called to Danny from the couch.

"What?" He turned back to her with a confused laugh.

She got up and walked to meet Danny at the back door. "Watch." Stepping out into the yard, she snapped her fingers three times and commanded, "Bullet! Come!" Immediately, there was a rustling sound in the distance by the kitchen, and Bullet came barreling toward them. There was something in his mouth.

"Come on, boy. Inside." As the dog marched into the light of the kitchen, it was apparent he had been digging. His paws were filthy, and kicked-up dirt covered his snout.

"Looks like someone's been busy," Kay stated the obvious with a giggle.

"Whatcha got there, boy?" Danny tried to pull a piece of fabric from the dog's mouth. Realizing the human was trying to take his trophy, Bullet darted into the living room, where Wes was still relaxing.

"I got him," Wes chuckled as he pushed off the couch and approached the dog. "Come here, dog. Let me see what you got into." Bullet darted back into the kitchen and ran for the back door. Kay quickly closed it before he could make his escape.

"Must I do everything around here." Kay snapped three times and commanded, "Bullet! Sit!" The dog immediately obliged. She gave a gloating smirk to Danny and Wes. Again, she snapped three times and commanded, "Bullet! Release!" The dog did as ordered, and the large piece of fabric dropped from his mouth onto the kitchen floor.

Danny scooped up the cloth and unmatted it. "What the heck is this?" Holding it up by the corners, Bullet's trophy was revealed to be a T-shirt, a very large, neon pink T-shirt. A very large, neon pink T-shirt with a cartoon pig sporting sunglasses and a big grin printed across the chest.

"That's my shirt," Kay laughed awkwardly, confused at the sight of it.

A jolt of disbelief shot through Wes's body as he slowly stepped into the kitchen. He couldn't believe what he was seeing. Even worse, he couldn't believe what he was seeing meant. "No." Speaking eerily calmly, he came closer. "It's not your shirt because you gave it to Celeste. The dog…the dog smelled Celeste." Wes couldn't look away from it. "The one Heather wore home the night of the party." He looked at Danny, fearful of the conclusion that his friend had still yet to make. "And those…those are blood stains." He rigidly pointed at the dried streaks and splatters of blood covering the entire front of the shirt.

Kay and Danny's minds swirled as they tried to comprehend what Wes had already figured out. It hit Danny first. He blinked hard as if it would erase what he was seeing and thinking. "I'm…I'm sure there's a reasonable explanation for it." He was still holding the shirt up as if immobilized with fear.

"But why would—" Kay's eyes bulged and flashed from Wes to Danny in shock. "Wait!" She finally caught on, and it was just too unimaginable. "Are you saying that's Celeste's blood?"

At that moment, the front door opened, and Heather hummed as she strolled into the house, balancing several casserole dishes. Oblivious to the revelation that was occurring in the kitchen, she perkily announced, "Got the food!" Walking toward the kitchen, she looked up at her friends and husband. And then, she saw it. The shirt. Heather froze mid-step and turned ghostly white. "Oh," she managed to whisper before slowly lowering her head.

No one spoke. They just stared at Heather with incomprehension for what seemed like hours. It couldn't be. It just couldn't be. It didn't make any sense. How on earth could this be possible? Never was a silence so loud. It undeniably confirmed what they had all hopefully misjudged. Finally, Kay broke that silence with an earth-shattering scream. "You were going to let them think it was me!"

Mervin Boutté sat across from Danny and Heather in his office downtown. When his normally well-behaved, straitlaced nephew called, frantically begging to meet him that Saturday night, he had no idea what he was in for. Not to mention, he sadly did not like what he was hearing. He knew no one would buy the story that his nephew's distraught wife was currently trying to sell him.

With weepy brown eyes, Heather confessed that she had killed Celeste Wells in the early morning of July 5th but that it was an act of self-defense. She was working late in her kitchen when she needed a break and decided to return the clothes she borrowed from Celeste earlier that night. She then drove her catering van to Celeste's home to do so. When she arrived, she and Celeste argued. Celeste pulled a knife from the butcher's block and chased Heather into the master bedroom. At which point, they struggled, and Heather got control of the knife. Heather stabbed Celeste in fear for her own life. In a panic, she wiped down the knife with a rag, returned it to the block, and drove home. She buried the borrowed clothes, the rag, and her rain jacket in a shallow hole behind her exterior kitchen, which Celeste's faithful dog had unfortunately sniffed out earlier that evening.

Mervin tapped the end of his pen on his desk and looked up from the notes he was taking. His eyes stayed on Heather, in part because he didn't want to look at Danny. He and his nephew were close, and if he looked at him, he knew Danny would know what he was thinking. "So, where are the clothes now?" he asked.

"Kay took them." Heather's lip began to quiver.

"All of them?"

"All of them. She said she was going to turn them in to the detectives. She's probably there now." Heather grabbed Danny's hand and began to sob.

Kay had understandably lost it when she realized that it was Heather who had murdered her cousin. There had been a lot of screaming, but to Kay's credit though, no cursing. The odd thing about her reaction was that her rage seemed to stem from, not the act, but the deceit. Anyone could snap; she knew that. But her friend, her dear friend, had acted as if she hadn't repeatedly sliced through her cousin's body with a butcher knife. And then simply went on as if nothing had happened, letting either Kay or Matthew potentially take the fall for it. That was what Kay couldn't fathom. Wes had watched, petrified, as his wife grabbed a trash bag from the kitchen cabinet and threw the blood-stained shirt in it before storming into the backyard to find the hole with the remaining clothes Heather wore that night. Wes knew it was the lie that Kay was raging at, and that scared him.

"Alright then." Mervin tossed his glasses on his desk and rubbed his eyes. "They'll need time to issue a warrant. Tomorrow morning, I'll pick you up, and we will go down to the station. You will confess to causing Celeste's death, but that is it. No details, no chain of events, nothing. Just that you caused her death. Do not use the words kill, murder, self-defense, or anything of that sort." Tears streamed down Heather's face as she nodded. "We will need to work through your story a bit, though." Mervin couldn't help but catch Danny's glance when he said this. He knew his nephew understood. "Let me get to work on this now. I'll tell you exactly what to say tomorrow."

"Thank you, Uncle Merv." Danny rose and gently pulled up Heather's elbow to help her stand. He could feel her arm shaking, not to mention her whole body.

"We'll get you through this." Mervin walked around the desk and gave them both a comforting hug. He put his hands on Heather's shoulders and gave her a consoling yet serious look. "I don't want to scare you, Heather, but I know Celeste's father. He's going to be out for blood." Mervin frowned and let out a deep exhale. "If anything else comes to mind, anything that we could use, let me know right away." The look in his eyes told her she better come up with something, and that something better be good.

The ride home was silent. Danny and Heather didn't know what to say to one another, for different reasons obviously. He pulled into the driveway, and it occurred to him that this was probably the last time he would do that with his wife. These were the last few hours of their life together. He knew nothing would ever or could ever be the same, and it made gentle Danny mad, really mad.

"Bullshit!" he screamed, causing Heather to flinch. "Bullshit! Bullshit! Bullshit!" The gearshift practically broke as he forced it into park. "Why?" Danny looked into his wife's scared, bloodshot eyes.

"I told you why," she tried to scream back but was too distraught to get it out without sobbing.

"That's bullshit, and you know it! Uncle Merv knows it, I know it, you know it, and now the police are going to know it! Now tell me, WHY?!"

"I did it for us! I did it for us!" The sobbing was gone, and now Heather was screaming back at him with determination. Danny didn't know how to respond. He took a deep breath and looked at the woman he loved. Knowing that their life as they knew it was now over, he needed to know exactly why.

"Tell me the truth, all of it," he ordered sternly.

Heather didn't want to tell him but knew that if she didn't, he would hate her forever. If she told him the truth, he might find a way to understand, a way to forgive her. She opened her mouth, but the words wouldn't come out.

"All of it," he grimly repeated.

She faced the windshield and stared at the front of their home. "I planned it. I planned to kill her."

Danny's stomach lurched. Did she know he had slept with Celeste? Did she know that Charlie might be his? Is that why she did this? He swallowed hard. "Go on."

"I know the fertility treatments aren't going to work. Nothing was ever going to work. We were never going to be able to have a child of our own." She began tugging on her hair. "Celeste and Matthew didn't deserve Charlie. They treated him like dirt. He needs parents who really love him." At this, Danny began to tremble, but it went unnoticed by Heather. "When we signed the paperwork to be Charlie's guardians, I realized there was a way to give him the parents he deserved."

Heather had indeed planned to kill Celeste and frame Matthew as best she could. She just wasn't sure if she'd be able to go through with it until that night. If Celeste was dead and Matthew went to prison for her murder, Danny and Heather would be Charlie's parents. The parents he deserved. They could live happily ever after, or at least, that's what poor Heather had convinced herself of.

Originally, she had intended to put her newly filled prescription of sleeping pills in Matthew's drink to ensure he was more comatose than usual and return later that night to stab Celeste as she slept in bed. She just needed to figure out a way to make it appear that it was Matthew who slashed into his wife's body with the knife.

When Matthew kicked off his shoes that night while telling his ridiculous fishing story, Heather considered it a sign but still wasn't sure if she'd be able to go through with it. She wasn't sure until she saw it. The positive pregnancy test in Celeste's bathroom. After she had changed into the borrowed clothes that would end up being her undoing, she snooped a bit in Celeste's bathroom. In the bottom drawer of the vanity, not even very well hidden, was an EPT with two distinct pink lines. Two distinct lines that Heather knew she would never see on a pregnancy test of her own. This was not just another sign; it was the sign. Celeste deserved what Heather was going to do to her, not another baby.

When she exited the master bedroom, everyone was outside, and she was all alone to prep. She moved Matthew's discarded shoes into the closet by the front doors. Then, she quickly crushed a handful of her sleeping pills and dissolved them in a large glass of whiskey. *It was all too easy,* she thought. *It wouldn't be this easy if it weren't meant to be.*

When she returned later that night, Heather assumed both Celeste and Matthew would be asleep. Entering the code into the keypad that she knew from catering Charlie's party, she crept into the house. Retrieving Matthew's shoes from the closet, she stepped as quietly as she could in the oversized shoes to the kitchen, grabbed the biggest knife in the block and instinctively held it behind her back. She was met with quite the surprise when she slowly opened the closed door to the master bedroom. Her future victim was still awake.

"What the fuck are you doing here?" Celeste asked without the least bit of interest before dismissively turning her back to Heather. "Forget your hairnet or whatever it is that you cafeteria workers wear?" A lack of response caused Celeste to slightly turn to view her late-night guest's blank stare. "Oh, I see." She rolled her eyes before once again dismissively, and unfortunately for her, turning her back to Heather. "Daniel decided to let you in on our little conversation about Charles. Pathetic, really. Especially because—"

It didn't matter what Celeste was about to say. If Heather did have any remaining doubts about what she intended to do, Celeste's words had foolishly just carried them away in the wind. Danny was her husband. Charlie should be her son. At the mere mention of their names, Heather flew into a blind rage. A rage that propelled her and the very sharp butcher knife toward Celeste.

She knew the very first stab was a fatal one. Celeste didn't even let out a peep. She simply, immediately, crumpled to the floor. Apparently, if you stab someone once, it's pretty hard to stop. And Heather did not stop for quite some time.

When she finally did, Heather calmly stood and intentionally made very distinctive steps to the kitchen in Matthew's blood-saturated shoes. She wiped down the knife with a kitchen towel and replaced it. She touched nothing else and walked straight to the front door. Turning the knob with the towel, she stepped onto the front porch. Deeply inhaling the forceful wind of the storm, she removed Matthew's shoes and dropped them into the bushes below.

Once home, she stripped in the darkness of her backyard as the rain washed the blood from her bare body. She grabbed an apron to cover herself and a large serving spoon from the detached kitchen. The grass and dirt behind the kitchen were soft from the storm, making it easy to create a big enough hole. Wrapping the rag and borrowed clothes into her rain jacket, she stuffed them into the ground and covered them with mud. Apparently not quite enough mud.

"Then I came inside and took a shower. You were sleeping so peacefully." Heather looked at Danny's stunned eyes as he listened. "I laid beside you. I was too excited to sleep but didn't want to wake you. You seemed so stressed earlier that night. I just watched you dream." She desperately searched Danny's face for some level of understanding, but it was blank, stone-like with incomprehension. "I did it for us."

Danny immediately opened the driver's side door and vomited onto the driveway. It was too much. It was all too much. His wife had committed murder so that Charlie could be their son, and yet Charlie may very well be Danny's son. If he had only told her. Maybe she would have left him, maybe she would have accepted it, maybe she wouldn't have slaughtered another human being.

Heather soothingly rubbed his back as he wiped his mouth with the back of his wrist. She was calm now. Calmer than her husband. Admitting it to Danny was a release and also a confirmation that she would do it again if she had the chance. "Why don't you go inside and lie down? I'll be in soon," she consoled. He looked down at his lap and quietly nodded. He couldn't look at her, not because of what she had just told him, but because of what he hadn't told her.

Danny opened the car door to leave. He put his hand on

the keys still in the ignition and then sadly decided to let them go. It was his way of saying if she wanted to make a run for it, he wasn't going to stop her. She watched her husband walk to the front door. He looked back at her through the windshield and stepped inside.

Heather leaned back onto the headrest of the passenger seat. She could fix this. She had to fix this. Heather knew what Danny's uncle meant when he told her Celeste's family would be out for blood. The death penalty was almost as popular as king cake around these parts. She had to figure out a way where Danny could still have a chance at getting Charlie, and she could still have a chance at staying alive, or else it would have all been for nothing. *Think Heather, think.* And then, it hit her. The only thing that could possibly save her life for murdering one Wells woman was the murder of another.

CHAPTER 21

Desperate To Believe

On Sunday afternoon, Derek Flannery sat in the waiting area of the Cyclone Salon for Men. He missed his standing haircut appointment two weeks prior because he was in the middle of a polygraph test. The only opening available relatively soon after was with a stylist he had never used before. He instructed his secretary to book the appointment anyway, out of necessity. No one likes an unkempt doctor, especially not his clientele. He glanced at his watch, noting the time was 2:59, pessimistically foreseeing a punctuality issue with his new stylist and their three o'clock appointment.

"Derek?"

He looked up from his watch to observe a woman in her early thirties dressed in all black topped with bright blue hair. His pessimism shifted from punctuality to aesthetics. "Yes." He rose with a well-mannered smile. She nodded and reciprocated with a forced polite expression. Derek followed the stylist to her chair, watching her blue hair swish as she walked, giving way to a glimpse of a neck tattoo. More pessimism ensued.

"So, what are we doing today?" she asked the mirror image of Derek.

"A two on the sides and back and trim up the top quite a bit, please." At his response, he noticed a tinge of disappointment taint her apathetic face. "You seem displeased." He gave an observant smirk.

"Honestly, sir, you have fine, light-colored hair. If you keep it a little longer, it will make it look fuller." Derek still had a full head of hair, but one should consider these things when progressing toward fifty. Her reply slightly impressed him, though. People tended to simply agree with the good doctor on most matters. The unusual, straightforward rebuttal was noted and surprisingly well received.

"Longer it is, then." She promptly went to work without a hint of appreciation for his concession.

As Derek's head was leaned down in the standard neck trimming position, their conversation ceased, and the resulting quiet allowed the one next to them to be easily overheard. "Did you hear they arrested somebody in the Celeste Wells case?" An older gentleman made small talk with his stylist.

"Really?" The stylist focused on carefully snipping the few last strands of gray hair that her client had left. "It was the husband, wasn't it?"

"That's what I thought, too, but nope. The news said some lady turned herself in this morning."

"You don't say?"

"Yep, probably some gal the Wells guy was catting around with."

"I bet. They say her name?"

"Uhm, what was it?" Afraid to move his head, the old man lifted only his eyes to the ceiling in thought. "Boutté! Harriet Boutté was the lady's name."

"Geez." She finished trimming his lonely strands. "I'd probably lose it and kill somebody, too, if I had a last name like that."

Derek remained still as he listened. He was aware of the arrest, and it disturbed him. He had been certain that Matthew was the one who murdered his beloved Celeste. From a logical standpoint, that made the most sense. Dr. Flannery was a big proponent of logic; however, the news of the arrest was causing him to have some rather illogical thoughts. Even from the urn, Celeste wielded that type of control.

"Should have dumped him," Derek's stylist muttered as she finished cleaning up his neck.

"Excuse me?" Derek asked.

"I said, she should have dumped him." She gave a hardened sigh. "They always screw you over in the end."

"Who?" Derek tried not to respond defensively at the insinuation that Matthew had "screwed over" Celeste's murderer.

"The wife." She perfected his sides without looking up. "With a guy like that, she probably knew her husband was cheating and stayed anyway. Look at where it got her." She shook her head. "What a way to go. Murdered by your husband's side chick. Should have dumped him," she repeated as she lifted Derek's chin and focused on the symmetry of his hairline. "Now she's dead, the girlfriend will probably get the chair, and he'll get off scot-free."

She picked up her hairdryer and began blowing cool air around Derek's chest and back to remove stray clippings. The gusts blew back her own hair, exposing the neck tattoo that read "Tout à du sens au final." Turning off the hairdryer, she looked at her client and sincerely said, "He's the one that deserves to be dead, not them."

Derek looked back at her and replied with equal sincerity, "I couldn't agree more."

Derek had been completely truthful during the entirety of his one interview with investigators. Especially when he told them that when it came to Celeste, his passion sometimes clouded his better judgment. Those clouds were undeniably rolling back into his freshly trimmed head as he returned to his home that afternoon. Sitting on the edge of his perfectly made bed, he scrolled through the contacts on his phone. He didn't traditionally save patient numbers, but members of the Wells family were not, by any means, traditional patients.

"Hello?"

"Hello, Matthew. This is Dr. Flannery."

"Oh, Doc," Matthew stumbled over his words as he sat up in Juniper's executive chair. "Uh, hi. It's been a while."

"It has." Derek instinctively remained calm despite the disgust he felt at hearing Matthew's voice. "I haven't seen you since Juniper's funeral."

"Well, I, uh…" Matthew felt like a scolded child and moved his whiskey from the bare top of the oak desk to a coaster. "It's been…a little hectic lately."

"Yes. I was deeply saddened by the news of Celeste's death.

Have the police made any headway in the case?"

"Yeah. This morning, actually. A friend of ours turned herself in. I have no idea what's going on. It's crazy. I just—"

"I am sure that comes as a tremendous relief. Did you know this friend well?"

Matthew was so caught off guard by the randomness of Dr. Flannery's call that he didn't recognize the strange nature of it. "I, umm, guess you could say that."

Derek tightened his grip on the phone at the vague answer. Subconsciously desperate to have the response align with his firm belief that Matthew caused the death of Celeste, Derek allowed himself to hear what he wanted to hear. Matthew and "this friend" were most definitely connected. His cherished Celeste had senselessly lost her life over a jealous lover's commitment to the pathetic excuse for a man on the other side of the phone.

"Matthew, whether you realize it or not, you are in need of medical attention. As you know, I am well aware of your history of drug and alcohol abuse. The trauma of the past year has, no doubt, sent you spiraling into a place that may be irreversible if not promptly treated."

Matthew did not like Dr. Flannery. He never did. The way he dismissed him, and spoke to him as if he were a child (despite only being five years his senior). He treated him like someone who had to be endured to stay on his mother's good side. A side that the arrogant doctor was more than happy to tend to if Juniper so much as stubbed a toe.

"Doc, thanks for calling but—"

"It's best if I start seeing you on a weekly basis to assess your physical and mental condition. I would be willing to"—Derek gritted his teeth—"visit the estate for our appointments. I am sure venturing out into the public eye is not desirable or advisable at this time."

The offer surprised Matthew. At-home visits were a luxury that was strictly reserved for Juniper, not her begrudgingly tolerated son. Perhaps Dr. Flannery held him in higher esteem than he thought. As simplistic as it was, to be offered a place at Juniper's hierarchal level felt approving.

"Yeah. Yeah, you're right, Doc. I probably should get myself together. I gotta say, I appreciate the offer."

"I'm glad to hear that you have your priorities straight. I can see that these unfortunate events have matured you." Derek continued to stroke Matthew's ego as a means to an end. "I can visit tomorrow."

"Oh, uh, let me get back to you. With everything going on, I might just need a few days."

Disappointed, yet not wanting to seem too eager, Derek yielded. "Understandable, but I will be checking on you soon. This is my private number. Feel free to call day or night."

"Thanks. I'm glad you called, Doc."

"Happy to be of service. Speak to you soon."

Matthew hung up the phone with an odd sense of renewal. It was a comforting feeling to realize that people can sometimes surprise you in a good way, something he had not been accustomed to in quite some time. *Maybe the guy's not such an asshole after all.* He made a mental note to text his party favor provider that he would be taking a break for a while. Feeling flattered and optimistic, he thought, *Nowhere to go but up from here.*

CHAPTER 22

Desperate To Convict

"I'm not asking if it's probable. I'm asking if it's possible," Marissa Morgan said with exasperation.

"Anything is possible, Marissa, but everything we found suggests that she fell." Coroner David Hebert didn't know how many different ways he could tell someone the same thing.

It was two days after Heather turned herself in to the authorities for "causing the death" of Celeste Wells. Yesterday morning, Mervin Boutté chased down Marissa Morgan in the courthouse to tell her that his client had a bit of information that might prove very useful to the district attorney, that is, if they could make a deal.

When Heather sat alone in the car, desperately trying to think of a way that would still allow Danny to have guardianship of Charlie and keep her from a lethal injection needle, her mind drifted back to a very long conversation she'd had with Matthew. Two days after Juniper's death, she called Matthew, and he surprisingly answered. Naturally, she expressed her condolences and she offered to take care of the catering for the post-funeral gathering. Perhaps he was lonely, or upset, or drunk, or all of the above, but Matthew began to talk. A lot. He told Heather how sad he was, and despite his tumultuous relationship with his mother, he couldn't fathom his life without her. All very innocent and what one might expect from a grieving son. However, Heather would have to say the conversation went very differently if she was going to save her skin.

Mervin Boutté informed Marissa Morgan that Matthew Wells confessed to his client that he had intentionally pushed his mother down the stairs in a fit of rage. Cell phone records would show the lengthy conversation between Matthew and Heather just days after Juniper's death. Of course, that, by itself, wouldn't be enough for a deal, but if she could substantiate Heather's claim, the district attorney would consider playing ball. The possibility of getting two murder convictions for tossing one death penalty was too good to pass up.

According to the notes in the case file, Matthew alleged that he was with someone named Natalia at the time of Juniper's death. Natalia was Matthew's girlfriend, or at least she had been. It's not in one's best interest to have a girlfriend when being investigated for the murder of your wife. As such, Matthew promptly broke off the relationship immediately after Celeste's death. Unfortunately for Matthew, Natalia did not take it so well. Hell hath no fury like a stripper scorned. When detectives came knocking that morning to confirm that Matthew had indeed been with Natalia, she was more than happy to tell them that he most certainly had not been. She hadn't seen him until around one a.m. when her shift ended.

Then, of course, there was a second conversation with Elodie. The ink was barely dry on her inheritance check, but she would rip it up in a heartbeat if she could get her friend back. Elodie didn't truly know how much she loved Juniper until she was gone. She had tried to keep a stiff upper lip, but the past ten months had been hard. And in those past ten months, she thought over and over about that last day with Juniper and how sure she was that she had seen Matthew when she left that afternoon. So sure that she had no problem relating that to the detectives when they visited that morning. "It was definitely him, and it was around five-thirty. Now make sure you write that down this time, damn it," she ordered as she fanned herself with one of Juniper's favorites.

Things were beginning to look up for Marissa Morgan, and Heather, for that matter. She had Matthew's witnessed confession; he had lied about where he was, another witness had put him at the scene, and he had more motives than you could shake a stick at. The district attorney just needed the coroner on board, which was now proving more difficult than she thought.

"So, explain to me again how you can be so certain she wasn't pushed." The frustration was growing in her voice as she was beginning to see this conversation as more of an obstacle than a finish line.

All too accustomed to Marissa's loaded questions, David Hebert stood up from his desk and walked to the corner of his small office to retrieve a collapsed tripod. He extended the three legs and stood it next to Marissa's chair.

"Push it over," he directed.

"Excuse me?" Marissa was insulted at being directed.

"You heard me. Push it over."

She huffed with irritation and slapped the tripod, causing it to fall sideways onto the ground. "Ok." David was enjoying this. He grabbed a piece of chalk from his desk and marked where the top of the tripod hit the floor. "Imagine the top of the tripod is her head. You pushed it, right?"

"Chalk, seriously? Are our budgets really that low?" Marissa asked flippantly.

"If pushed, the landing place of the head would have been at least a body length's distance from the standing point." David picked up the tripod and replaced it next to Marissa. "Now, this is the release button." He pointed to an orange button where the three legs met. "Pressing it will cause all the legs to collapse. Push it." She narrowed her eyes at him. "Why do I have to repeat myself with you? Push the button, Marissa."

With another huff, Marissa pushed the release button, causing the tripod to collapse, landing on the floor in almost the exact same spot that it stood just seconds earlier. "Where did the head land?" David asked as if trying to tutor a pupil. She didn't respond but simply pointed down to the tripod's "head."

"Exactly." David marked the spot on the ground with his chalk. "The only way that could have happened is if someone's legs gave out. If they were pushed, their head would have landed a greater distance away." He pointed to the initial chalk mark on the floor.

Despite her annoyance, Marissa was slightly intrigued. "Do we know where her head hit?"

Entertained by the thought that he now had a captive audience, David picked up a folder from his desk. He pulled out a photo and handed it to Marissa. "What is that?" He pointed to the photo.

"It's a picture of stairs, Dave."

"Those are the top three stairs of Juniper Wells's staircase. And that," he pointed to the second step, "is a smear of makeup."

Marissa squinted and pulled the picture close to her face. It certainly did appear to be a smear of foundation across the white marble step. She surrendered to his logic as she tossed the picture onto David's desk. "Which means her face hit on the second step, not a full body length away." She massaged temples in frustration. "If she had been pushed, her face would have landed farther down the staircase."

"Exactly." David returned to his office chair and leaned back, feeling validated.

"What if he pushed her from the landing, and she fell down the steps. Then the standing point of her body would have been a greater distance away."

"Decent question," he admitted. "Possible, but with that landing force, I would have expected more than just a smear of makeup upon contact with the stairs." He put his elbows on his desk and clasped his hands. "Realistically, the best I could say, if she were on the steps at the point of impact, is that he slightly bumped her, causing her to lose her footing. A smaller force wouldn't cause a long-distance trajectory, which would be consistent with the placement of the smear. But even still—" He shook his head, trying to imagine the far-fetched scenario. "The force would have to have been lower on her body to make her give out like that."

"So, either he slightly bumped her low on her body, or he pushed her from farther back on the landing?"

David sighed defeatedly. "Like I said, Marissa, anything is possible."

"That's insane. You would never do that."

"That's what I'm saying." Matthew was relieved to hear his best friend was as irate as he was. He tossed his cigarette butt into the oversized fountain in front of the Wells estate. His relationship with Wes had been a little off since

Juniper's death. However, when your mother dies, then your wife dies, and then they try to put you on trial for murdering your mother, off or not, you call your best friend.

"What does Logan say?" With Heather's confession, the legal blackball Celeste's father put on Matthew had been lifted, but he had no intention of finding different representation. Despite his feelings toward the twins, Logan showed up when he needed him, and Matthew wasn't going to forget that. Especially because he knew that Logan could prove he was innocent if he had to, but Matthew didn't want it to come to that.

"Said he's seen colanders hold more water, whatever that means." Matthew sat on the steps leading up to the estate. "He also said they're going to arrest me. Apparently, they made a deal with Heather, and they gotta make good on it."

"This is bullshit!" Wes kicked the trashcan in his office. He knew Matthew didn't kill Juniper.

"I know. I mean, my life is over. Even if I get found not guilty, it'll never go away." Matthew's big brown eyes started to well up. "It'll never go away."

Wes didn't know what to say. His friend was right. This would follow him for the rest of his life. What can you really say in that moment? You can't say anything. You can't say anything other than a lie. "I know you're gonna get cleared. The only thing people will remember is that you almost got screwed over but showed them all you're innocent." Wes and Matthew both wanted to believe what Wes had just said to his friend. Sadly, neither of them really did, but the alternative was just too much to even consider.

"Fucking right." Matthew rubbed his eyes. "Fucking right, man."

"Did Logan say when?"

"Probably Wednesday. He's going to bring me in so the cops don't drag me out of the house."

"I'll come with you. I can't believe this is happening. You didn't do it."

"I know." Matthew stood and started up the stairs. "Can y'all watch Charlie for a couple of nights? I got the money for bail. Logan says they should grant it, but the way my life is going, you never know."

"Yeah, of course." Wes sat at his desk. "It's going to be alright, Matt."

Depressed, Matthew hung up with Wes. He stopped halfway up to the house and sat back down on the stairs. He stared at the fountain for a long time and then desperately wished his mother was there. She would know what to do. *Tell me what to do. Tell me what to do, Juniper.* He put his face in his hands and fought off the urge to call for party favors shortly before bursting into tears.

CHAPTER 23

Desperate For Revenge

Kay drove down the long oak-lined driveway Tuesday night. Tommy was in the backseat, looking forward to seeing his cousin. He wasn't sure what had happened the last time they were together. His mom got really mad about something when they were at Uncle Danny and Aunt Heather's house. When they dropped off Charlie, she told Ms. Reausaleigh to tell Uncle Matthew to call her as soon as he got home.

"Tomorrow, we can go to the park and go swimming and stay up as late as we want." Kay looked in the rearview mirror at Tommy.

"Can Dad come too?" Tommy asked hopefully.

Kay tried to hide her sadness. "No, baby. Dad has been really busy lately. Uncle Danny had to take a little time off work." She could see the disappointment in his eyes. "But it's only temporary. Next time, I promise."

"Yay!" Tommy was excited at the thought of it. "Look, Mommy, Charlie is already all packed." He pointed out his window as Kay circled the fountain in front of the Wells estate. Standing at the bottom of the stairs were Charlie and Matthew. Charlie was wearing Tommy's clothes, and Matthew was wearing Wes's. Matthew looked awful. Like a scarecrow come to life. Wes's clothes, which would have normally been a little too tight, hung on him.

Oh dear, Kay thought. She put the car in park, and Tommy immediately hopped out. "Hi guys," she tried to sound cheery as she walked around the car to greet them.

"Thanks for watching him."

"Oh, it's our pleasure. Right, Tommy?"

"Yeah, we're going swimming tomorrow!"

"Dad, did we pack my swimsuit? The one Tommy gave me." Charlie looked up at Matthew.

"Uh, I'm not sure, buddy. Why don't you and Tommy go upstairs and double-check." With that, the two boys happily dashed up the steps and into the house.

Kay watched the boys run through the front doors. "Well, I'm sure we won't see them for another hour." She tried to get a laugh out of Matthew, but it didn't take. "Wes said he'll pick you up in the morning and drive you to Logan's office." He still didn't respond. Kay frowned. She wanted to console him but didn't know how. "You okay?"

Matthew walked toward the fountain. The gravel crunched under the pair of Wes's dark blue flip-flops he was wearing. He stared down into the bubbling water. "Kay…" he started. She walked up beside him without saying a word. She put her hand on his back and rubbed it sympathetically.

"If I don't come back. If something happens—"

She cut him off. "You're coming back."

"If I don't come back"—he looked up from the water in the fountain and directly into her eyes, the ones that looked just like Celeste's—"I need you to do something for me." She nodded as she held his gaze. Normally, she would make another joke to try to make him feel better, but now was not the time. She didn't know what to say, so she just listened.

"I need you to…" He ran his hand through his hair. "Damn, I really don't want it to come to this." He took a brave breath and said, "I need you to go get Charlie's glove at the Esplanade house. The left-handed one. The one you came looking for that morning."

*That's it? You want me to get Charlie's glov*e? Kay was relieved at the simplicity of his request but also confused and fearful Matthew might be losing it. "Sure, no problem." She tried to keep a serious face. "I can go get it now if you want?"

"No. No." He slightly jumped in refusal and looked up at the house to see the boys returning. "Only if I get convicted. Only if there's no chance of me coming back," he whispered.

"Mom! We found it," Tommy announced as the boys bounded down the stairs.

"Great," she called back while still keeping her eyes on Matthew. Charlie ran up and hugged his dad. They piled into

Kay's Jeep while Matthew put the duffle bag in the hatch. She rolled down the driver's side window as he walked to the front of the car. "Try to get some rest. Wes will be here in the morning."

Matthew gave a forced smile. "Be good for Aunt Kay, buddy."

"Yes, Dad."

Matthew watched them pull away and stared down the drive until the taillights faded. *Rest. I wish I could get some rest. Hard to sleep when you don't know where you'll be sleeping tomorrow night.* He remembered he had someone that could help with that. *Fuck it.*

Matthew opened the front doors to the Wells estate. "Thanks for coming on such short notice. I know it's kind of late."

"It's no problem at all. I understand. This is strictly between us, correct?"

Matthew was a little sad to admit, "Yeah, just between us. Nobody's here." A gust of wind practically slammed the doors closed behind his guest. "Starting to pick up out there."

"There's a storm in the gulf, but it appears to be heading east. I think we are just getting some of the outer bands."

"Oh, I haven't really been watching the news lately." Matthew rubbed the back of his neck.

"Understandable."

"Can I get you a drink?" Matthew shuffled in his borrowed, undersized flip-flops toward the parlor.

"I'm alright," Derek Flannery replied. "Have you been drinking?" Both men sat on the opposing couches in the parlor.

"Couple of whiskeys," Matthew answered honestly, "but not much. Want to keep it together for tomorrow. I just gotta get some sleep. I don't think I've slept in two days." By the look of Matthew, that was another honest answer.

"Again, understandable, given the circumstances." Dr. Flannery reached into his blazer pocket and pulled out two medical gloves. After securing them on his hands, he pulled out a Ziploc filled with white pills. "Here, take two of these now." He handed the bag to Matthew. Matthew did as instructed and downed two pills with the rest of his bourbon. "You're fine to take two more each hour until you fall asleep."

"Won't that make me groggy tomorrow?" Matthew questioned as he closed the Ziploc bag.

"A big guy like you? You'll be fine." Flannery pulled a syringe out of his other blazer pocket. "I'm going to give you this as well. It will keep you balanced."

Without questioning, Matthew stood and pulled down the waistband of Wes's shorts for the good doctor to inject the contents of the syringe into his back hip. He recapped the needle and put the syringe back into his pocket. "Well, that should do it."

Matthew pulled up his shorts and said, "Thanks so much. How much do I owe you?"

"Don't worry about it. No charge." He extended his still-gloved hand and shook Matthew's with a very firm grip. "I know Celeste would have wanted me to take care of you. It's the least I can do for her."

"Yeah." Matthew awkwardly rubbed his hip at the odd reference to Celeste. "Well, thanks again, Doc. Juniper told me you only made house calls for her."

Dr. Flannery chuckled at Matthew's stupidity. He had made quite a few "house calls" to Celeste at Matthew's own home. "Happy to make an exception. I better head out before it starts getting bad out there. Make sure you take the rest of those pills, though."

CHAPTER 24

Desperate For It Not To Be True

Dead. Matthew was very much dead when Wes found him the next morning. After banging on the front doors and calling Matthew's cell phone for a solid ten minutes, Wes started back toward his car. In anger, he picked up a broken magnolia branch lying in the drive and hurled it into the fountain. The stick landed in the fountain with an obvious smack, not a splash. The odd sound caused Wes to question the landing spot of the branch. To Wes's horror, there was no splash because the limb did not land in the water. It landed on the back of his best friend's floating corpse. Poor Matthew was wearing nothing more than underwear and flip-flops. Wes's flip-flops.

Derek Flannery was disappointed that the official cause of death was ruled an accidental drowning. The good doctor had filled Matthew with enough opioids to take out an elephant with the hopes of an overdose, but apparently, his patient was so high he opted for an ill-fated swim instead. No matter. Matthew was dead. And Derek had the self-granted privilege of giving him what he deserved for the way he treated his sweet, kindhearted, beloved Celeste.

While many people talked about Matthew's death, very few people mourned it. It was assumed by most that he was about to be indicted for the murder of his mother but chose, either intentionally or unintentionally, the cowardly way out. Of the few, probably no one mourned his death more than Heather. No Matthew meant there would be no trial for Juniper's murder, and that meant there would be no deal. No deal to save her from an injection far more lethal than the one Dr. Flannery gave Matthew.

Matthew's death also meant that Charlie's guardianship would now turn over to the parties designated in his parents' will. Given that Heather was now spending her days and nights in St. Gabriel's Penitentiary, Danny was legally the sole guardian of Charlie. You couldn't really blame Danny for having mixed emotions about the situation. His wife brutally murdered the possible mother of his child and then accused his dear friend of murdering his own mother, which ultimately led to his death. Danny had been through a lot; they all had, no one more so than Charlie. That's when Danny knew he had to step up and do right by his son, whether that son was just on paper or possibly by blood as well. He told no one about the blood part. Charlie had been through enough, and Danny didn't see the need to put him through more.

Danny was no fool, though. He knew that it would take time to figure out being a dad. Kay, Wes, and Danny all agreed to make a slow transition from him staying with Kay and Wes to eventually living permanently with Danny. Celeste's parents were reluctant to the idea. Charlie's guardian would be the husband of the woman who killed their only daughter. But what could they do? The law was the law. Kay assured her aunt and uncle that Danny wanted nothing more than to keep them fully involved in Charlie's life. To be honest, it was an involvement that had been limited to birthdays and holidays, by their own choosing, so their reluctance was short-lived.

The arrangement was working out well. Charlie was doing better than most children would in his position. Some might say that's because it's hard to miss something you never really had. Kay thought differently, though; missing the idea of what you could have had can be far more painful. As such, she got Charlie into therapy as soon as possible. Neither Wes, Kay, Danny, his grandparents, or anyone close to them were fully equipped to help Charlie with what he was going through or probably would be going through for the rest of his life.

"Hey," Kay answered the call from Danny. Before he could speak, she continued as if going over her to-do list, "Wes just left with Tommy, and I'm about to go to pick up the balloons now." She looked around the kitchen for her car keys.

It was Charlie's birthday. Pretty hard to fathom how much had changed since his last one. Danny thought it would be a good idea to just invite some of Charlie's friends to Audubon Park. The kids could play catch, chase each other around, and eat too much cake. Everyone wanted and needed a relaxing, non-stressful day.

"Awesome. I was hoping you could do me a favor. Charlie says he really wants his glove today. He said it's the one JuJu gave him. I couldn't find it at the estate." In an effort not to disrupt Charlie's life even more, Danny moved into the Wells estate. Reausaleigh was more than grateful that he asked her to stay on and help him in his new fatherly role. She had gone back to Matthew and Celeste's home to retrieve most of Charlie's clothes but hadn't packed up all of his personal items yet. One of those items being his lucky left-handed glove from Juniper.

Shoot. Even Kay's thoughts lacked profanity now. Danny was clearly oblivious to what she walked into the last time she went looking for that glove. "Uh, yeah. I think I know where it is." She didn't want to make an already overwhelmed Danny feel guilty by mentioning its whereabouts. "I can bring it to the park."

"You are a godsend, Kay. Thanks so much. See you soon." She heard a relieved Danny report to Charlie in the backseat before ending the call, "Aunt Kay said she's going to bring it for you."

I really don't want to go in there. It was the same thing she was thinking the last time she sat in the driveway of Celeste and Matthew's home on Esplanade Avenue. Funny, yet not so funny, how feelings come full circle.

Guilt crept up on her as she remembered seeing Matthew for the last time. She should have stayed; she should have known something bad was going to happen. The way he kept staring into the fountain. The desperate look in his eyes. Then she remembered what he had asked her to do. Make sure to get Charlie's glove if he didn't come back. It was, unfortunately, safe to say he wasn't coming back from Lake Lawn

Cemetery. Kay intentionally procrastinated by watching lovebugs float in the breeze across the now unkempt front lawn as if dragging this out would make it any better. *Screw it.* She opened the car door. *How bad can it be in there?*

Chills trickled down her spine as she typed the code into the keypad and heard the door unlock. She closed her eyes tightly and took a big step into the house as if walking the plank. When her foot touched the floor inside the center hall, she opened her eyes. The air escaped her lungs from the deep breath she hadn't noticed she had been holding ever since she left the car. It was a breath of relief. Everything looked as it should. Nothing was out of place; every surface was pristine. It was as if nothing had ever happened. She decided to let herself believe that for the moment, just to get through this.

Her forced bravery allowed her to walk to the rear of the house, avoiding eye contact with the hallway to her right, which led to the master bedroom. She went down the opposing hallway to the left that led to Charlie's room. *Hard part is over.* She headed straight for Charlie's closet and pulled open the double doors. She couldn't remember if he had told her left or right, but it didn't matter; there it was, plain as day. The lucky left-handed glove was resting on the top shelf, patiently waiting to be played with.

Due to being vertically challenged, Kay had to jump to snag it, but on her second attempt, she finally did. "Got it," she said aloud triumphantly and squeezed the glove between her hands. When she did, though, the glove let out a crunching sound. She didn't know much about baseball, but she knew that didn't sound right. "Oh no, did I crack the leather or something?" Kay looked down with concern as if she had caused the glove pain somehow.

Something was sticking out of the interior of the glove. It was paper. It was a white, crumpled piece of paper. "What the heck is this?" She pulled out what looked like something a dog had gotten hold of. Straightening the paper, she tried to make heads or tails of what it said. It appeared to be some kind of medical report. It was dated almost seven years ago. And then, she wilted to the floor.

```
'DNA Paternity Report: IDG4569257'
'MOTHER (not tested)'
'CHILD (Charles Edward Wells)'
'ALLEGED FATHER (Wes Robert Allen)'
'Probability of Paternity: 99.9999998%'
'The alleged father is not excluded
as the biological father of the test-
ed child. Based on testing results ob-
tained from the analyses of the DNA
loci listed, the probability of pater-
nity is 99.9999998%.'
```

Through tears, she read and re-read, but there it was in black and white. How could this be? This had to be some sick joke. Sadly, it was not a joke. Her husband had slept with her cousin. Her husband was Charlie's father. Her husband had been lying to her for the entirety of their marriage. Her husband was exactly what Celeste had said he was.

When you see your whole life explode on a single piece of paper, there is only one thing to do. Curse and curse loud. "MOTHER FUCKER!!!"

CHAPTER 25

Desperate To Confess

Apparently, it doesn't take long to get an uncontested divorce in Louisiana. This was news to Wes, mainly because he never planned on getting a divorce. He loved his wife, but when your wife finds out that you fathered a child with her cousin and have been lying about it for seven years, you don't have much of a leg to stand on.

Of course, he begged and pleaded for her to forgive him, but he knew she wouldn't. That is what terrified him the most about Kay's reaction the night they discovered that Heather murdered Celeste. It wasn't the act that was unforgiveable; it was the deceit. That is what he knew she wouldn't be able to get past. There was no point in lying to her anymore. He had, in fact, known the whole time that Charlie was his son.

Three men visited Celeste at her home the week she became pregnant (the first time, at least). Wes, in a drunken state of self-pity to kill a nonexistent snake; Gauge, to hang a hideous piece of art that Celeste fully intended on returning; and Danny, to play mechanic to fix a self-induced car issue. They were all invited over with the same intention: to get Celeste pregnant.

Concerned with Matthew's philandering ways, Celeste needed to ensure her position as his wife. Despite her disdain for children, an anchor baby was the best way to secure that her last name would remain Wells and that she wouldn't be cast aside as another one of those "first wives." That proved to be a little difficult, given that Matthew was spending so much time in Mexico that he had practically become an honorary citizen. So, she had to improvise. No one need know who actually dropped the line on the anchor, as long as it kept her ship in the Wells port.

Why she asked her gentleman callers to take DNA tests, even Celeste didn't know. Perhaps to have some level of control over them. Once a dog submits to you, it's hard to let that feeling go. That said, only two of the three submitted to Celeste in Matthew's absence. Surprisingly, it was the pup who refused her advances, Gauge. Being only twenty-two at the time, he seemed the most likely to tempt; however, Gauge was smart enough to know, you don't shit where you eat.

Something else that was news to Wes was the fact that his best friend knew this and said nothing. After Juniper provided Matthew with the DNA results, he assumed Wes was the blackmailer. Matthew knew the blackmailer was going to his mother's house that night with a nondisclosure agreement, which he oddly never found after Juniper's death. If he told anyone, though, he would be left penniless. Before stuffing the DNA results into Charlie's glove just prior to his death, he thought, *Better to be broke and exonerated than in jail.* He didn't want it to come to that but knew he at least needed a backup plan should things go south.

While that was very clever on Matthew's part, the problem was Wes was not the blackmailer, nor did he kill Matthew's mother. Those two people were not one and the same. There was only one living person on the entire planet that knew who those people were. And that person was about to participate in a child custody hearing at the New Orleans Municipal Courthouse.

Kay held Charlie's hand as they walked down the third-floor hallway designated for family court hearings. She knew where to go, given that she had just been there the month prior for her own family matter. "Okay, so it's supposed to be in room 304. They said we should wait outside until they call for you."

She and Charlie sat on an uncomfortable wooden bench near a window that viewed the cars driving down Perdido Street. The hallway was very quiet, except for the clacking knitting needles of an elderly woman seated on the bench across from them.

She put her hand on Charlie's knee as she tried to convince them both she wasn't nervous. "Remember, the judge is just going to ask you a few questions. He'll talk to you in a private room, so you don't have to worry about everybody hearing what you say. And the judge is a very nice man. You can be completely honest with him." She looked at the ominous door as she smoothed her freshly dyed blonde hair.

Juniper had been right all along. Blonde hair did suit Kay quite well. She hated to be cliché, but a post-divorce new do did lift her spirits, if only momentarily. She even threw in some bangs to serve as a little Cajun Botox. The lines in the porcelain skin of her forehead felt as though they had multiplied due to recent events. Somehow, she'd found the time to do it. Between work, trying not to have a mental breakdown, and taking care of two eight-year-olds all by herself, she was pretty busy these days.

Kay was responsible for the two eight-year-olds (Tommy and Charlie) because the people inside room 304 all wanted Charlie. The only thing the group could agree on was that Kay could have temporary guardianship of Charlie until his permanent home could be determined by the courts. In the wake of the news of Charlie's true biological father, things got a little dodgy. Celeste's parents decided it was time to step in, Wes decided that if he was going to lose a wife, at least he could gain a son, and poor Danny was still grasping onto his will-expressed guardianship. Of course, Elodie, Reausaleigh, Logan, and Gauge were all there as well. Not by choice, but the people who see the comings and goings of the potential guardians of a child were people the judge wanted to hear from.

"I wish I could just stay with you and Tommy." Charlie swung his feet that dangled from the bench.

"I know, sweetie." Kay took his hand again. "But Aunt Kay just doesn't have a dog in this fight." Charlie looked up at her confused. She smirked, realizing the analogy was a little over his head. "It just means that there are a lot of people that get dibs on you before me." Kay poked her nephew/ex-stepson/son's half brother in the side. "You can't blame them. You are a pretty cool dude."

"It's all my fault." He looked down at his shoes as his feet continued swinging compulsively.

"Hey." Kay straightened up and put both her hands on his shoulders, pulling his little torso square with hers. "Listen, sweetie. I love you so, so much, and I don't want you thinking that. None of this, none of any of this, is your fault. You understand me?"

His little brow scrunched, and he tried to smile before looking back at his feet. "That's because you don't know, Aunt Kay."

"Know what, honey?" She tried not to sound unnerved as she released his shoulders. But there was something about the way he said "you don't know" that gave her an uneasy feeling.

"Mommy said she had to give something to JuJu."

"Okay. What did Mommy have to give to JuJu?"

Charlie shrugged. "Mommy said that it was so she would hush." Both Charlie and Kay were completely clueless as to what Celeste meant by that. Unbeknownst to them, what it meant was that Celeste was agreeing to be quiet, quiet about the identity of Charlie's real father. The something she was bringing to Juniper that night was the nondisclosure agreement. Celeste was, in fact, the blackmailer. Her mother-in-law may have cut her out of the will, but Celeste was going to make damn sure she got paid one way or another. Wes and Danny had both separately approached Juniper for money as well, but that was to ask her to be a silent investor in their folding company; it had nothing to do with Charlie. Celeste was the only one who had put her own son up for sale.

"When was this, Charlie?"

"The night the tree fell. The big one that hit the house." His swinging feet had now turned into a slight back-and-forth rocking of his little body.

"Okay, can you tell me what else happened the night the big tree fell?"

"Mommy and me went over to JuJu's. It was raining really bad. JuJu told me to go upstairs and play in my room so she and Mommy could talk. They stayed downstairs, but I could hear them yelling. They were yelling loud. Really loud." Kay noticed Charlie's rocking was becoming faster.

"The wind kept going, *woosh woosh*. It was raining a whole lot. It made the big tree hit my window." Charlie swallowed.

"When the big tree hit my window, all the lights went out." He started to sniffle, and his eyes began to well up. "I got really scared."

"It's okay, buddy. It's okay to be scared sometimes." Kay herself was scared about what Charlie was going to say next.

"It was really dark. I heard JuJu calling for me. She said, 'I'm coming, Charlie. I'm coming.' I started running to the stairs. I was running really fast. I…I didn't see her. I didn't mean to. It was really dark." Charlie put his hands over his eyes and shook his head as if trying to erase the memory. "I ran into her on the steps. It's all my fault. She fell down. She fell all the way down. I didn't mean to, I promise," he sobbed. "It's all my fault." Poor little Charlie's rocking slowly stopped. He pulled his hands down from his tortured green eyes to look at Kay. "I killed JuJu."

Kay grabbed Charlie and hugged him tight. She didn't know what else to do. All she could do was hold him. He cried into her shoulder. "Am I going to go to jail?"

"No, baby. It was an accident. Accidents happen. It's going to be okay. It's going to be okay." They both started rocking together as Kay held him even tighter.

"I want to tell the judge," he said quietly.

"Oh, Charlie." Kay gently pulled back to look him in the eyes. "Maybe we should just keep this our little secret."

"I want to tell him, Aunt Kay. I want to tell him what I did."

"I understand, sweetie. But…but…secrets are okay sometimes. We can just keep it between us. No one will ever have to know."

"That's what Mommy said."

Kay had tried not to think about Celeste over the past year. It was just easier that way. She wanted to hate her but somehow couldn't. Something was holding her back from that. She wanted to hate all of them. Celeste, Matthew, Danny, Heather, Wes. Not for what they had done necessarily, but for hiding things, awful things. Awful things that ruined and ended people's lives in the worst way possible. At that moment, though, she recognized she was telling little Charlie to do just that. Hide awful things to protect the people you so desperately love. Maybe that's why Kay couldn't hate all of them despite how hard she tried. It's hard to hate people who you just sadly realized were just like you.

"But Charlie, what if we—" The door to room 304 opened, and a petite little man popped his head out. It was the social worker assigned to Charlie's case.

"Charlie," he said pleasantly with a warm smile, "the judge is ready for you." The brave little boy nodded.

"Could we have one more minute?" Kay begged.

"It's okay, Aunt Kay." Charlie gave her one last hug. Wiping his eyes on the sleeve of his little blue blazer, he stood without another word, only turning to give a small wave to his aunt before following the social worker into the courtroom.

Kay sat there immobile, staring at the now closed door to the courtroom. She felt numb. Her mind was almost refusing to comprehend what she had heard, what she felt. Her attempts to process Charlie's confession were suddenly interrupted when the old woman sitting across from her loudly cleared her throat. A dazed Kay slowly turned her head across the hallway to the woman staring out the window. She was watching the sparse lining of trees that wrapped around the courthouse parking lot whip wildly around in the wind.

"My, my, my." Doris's eyes stayed on the swaying trees as she rested her knitting needles in her lap. She leaned her head back against the cool courthouse wall. "They real desperate today. It sho' is 'bout to pour."

ACKNOWLEDGMENTS

Somehow, it is easier to write an entire book than to tell the people who actually helped you do it, how much you truly appreciate them. This is my feeble attempt, but please know they deserve far more credit than my words could ever describe.

Dr. Linda Tucker of Cup and Quill, your dedication throughout the entire process made it feel like we were in this together. Having a guiding hand leading me through very unchartered territory was greatly needed and definitely appreciated. Kristin Taylor, my very patient proofreader, thank you for enduring my butchering of the English language. Dr. Joe Dornich, my amazing copy editor, every recommendation you gave had me wracking my brain. The encouraging words that followed each of those recommendations gave me the motivation to go from, *how am I going to do that?* to *how did I just do that?*

Thank you to my publisher, Inicio Press. The direction and support you provided made the finish line seem not so far in the distance, and, as it turns out, attainable.

A heartfelt thanks to my absolutely fabulous girlfriends who have been there for me through more stages in life than any of us would like to admit. And, of course, an even bigger heartfelt thanks to my incredible boys. To my husband and two sons, I love you to all the planets and back.

The final acknowledgment is most certainly reserved for my father. David, you were the first person to ever read my book and the last person I would ever want to disappoint. Sorry, but not sorry, you didn't meet the requirements for the dedication. I guess we're just stuck with each other a little while longer, and I'm pretty okay with that.

Made in the USA
Las Vegas, NV
30 June 2024